First murderer: [*Stabbing him*] Take that, and that.
If all this will not do, I'll drown you in the malmsey-butt
within. [*Exit with the body.*]

William Shakespeare: Richard III, Act 1, Scene IV.

IN DEEP

PAUL FERRAR

By the same author
The Coolabah Creek Maggot
All in the Mind
The Affair of the Deviant Bishop

This book was written on Ngunnawal land
and the author acknowledges its people as the
traditional owners of the land

Copyright © 2025 Paul Ferrar
ISBN: 978-1-923078-84-0

Published by Vivid Publishing
A division of Fontaine Publishing Group
P.O. Box 948, Fremantle
Western Australia 6959
www.vividpublishing.com.au

A catalogue record for this
book is available from the
National Library of Australia

DISCLAIMER
AGRICOZ in this story is an entirely fictitious organisation. It is not Australia's CSIRO, which is multi-disciplinary, although – purely for the story – it does share one common project on dung beetles.

For Pammy

With love, and thanks for everything,
including putting up with
the dung for five whole years....

PROLOGUE

He was seriously wondering what he'd got himself into. It had started with innocent-sounding enquiries about the research that he was doing, but the people who were contacting him about it now were certainly not research scientists. And they were making comments about cooperation that had a distinct tone of menace.

He wasn't worried for his personal security in his apartment. His parking area required an electronic key to open it, as did the lift and the door of the corridor leading to the apartment. The apartment door had a sophisticated lock, and he possessed the only two keys. Inside he had locked away all important items, and he'd recently purchased a handgun and some ammunition. Just in case.

He ordered supermarket supplies online and he did all his financial transactions on the internet, so he had little need to go outside. At his laboratory he had dedicated parking close to his building, so there was little chance of an attack there. Overall he felt that he was reasonably safe.

But as the poet John Donne wrote, no man is an island entire of itself. One day he parked at his apartment, having checked – as he always did - that nobody entered behind him. However, he couldn't see the two figures already concealed behind a pillar near his parking space. As he climbed out of his car the two figures moved quickly and silently behind him. One held him in a tight bear-hug, while the other put a cloth soaked in chloroform over his face. He struggled for a moment, then went limp. The two men then dragged him to a nearby car, loaded him into the boot and drove out of the carpark.

They took him to a quiet piece of bushland, and there did various things that eventually left him dead and mutilated. Finally they disposed of the body.

SYMONSTON, CANBERRA

It was a world class facility. In a nation in which agriculture was a huge part of the economy, the AGRICOZ research laboratories were top of the line. They stretched over a wide area that had included the Symonston caravan park in Canberra, and they encompassed every subject related to agriculture in its broadest definition. Some said that the definition was stretched too far, and there were public murmurings of "Frankenscience" going on within its walls, but certain areas were very secure and no hard facts ever emerged.

There were two very long buildings, each with a corridor of offices, and each office opened behind into a laboratory, glasshouse or whatever was appropriate to the subject under study. Some contained powerful microscopes and other expensive equipment; others were closer to field conditions, with plants in pots and trays. There were also some outlying labs and glasshouses, and beyond them facilities for farm animals, and open-air plots for growing assorted crop plants.

One separate office cum laboratory, plus its glasshouse extension, contained mainly cow dung. It housed an AGRICOZ project for bringing exotic dung beetles into Australia to improve the turnover of cow dung in Australian pastures. Native Australian dung beetles prefer the small dry pelleted droppings of kangaroos, and largely ignore the broad, wet droppings of introduced stock like cattle, so the project aimed to bring in the African and European species of beetle that love large, wet cow pads. This was done under rigorous quarantine so that diseases like foot and mouth didn't come in as well. The project had shown very good promise, and already had a public profile.

That facility was separate from the others because of the odour of cow dung, though the area where sheep blowflies were reared for another project was even more offensive. Lots of rotten meat. Very rotten….

Early each morning a small army of cleaners worked their way through the many rooms and laboratories on the site. Because of the odour, the dung area was not high in the popularity stakes for most of the cleaners, but Maria Szymanowski was actually fond of it. She liked to watch the beetles in their breeding boxes scurrying round on the soil. From a large blob of fresh dung, they would cut off a piece, make it into a ball, lay an egg inside the ball, and then roll the ball over the soil and bury it. Very clever and industrious. Several large bins filled with fresh wet cow dung were the only thing that smelled strongly, and one could soon work one's way past them. Besides, she told anyone who would listen that you soon got used to the smell.

One morning, however, the spectacle was not so pleasant. Maria walked down the path from the main building with her cleaning trolley, heading for the door of the dung laboratory. The door was normally locked and she was surprised that this time it was unlocked, but she thought the team had simply forgotten to lock it the night before.

She backed into the laboratory room with her trolley. She cleaned that room, and then backed into the beetle-breeding glasshouse. As she turned she saw the usual large bins of wet manure, but standing up from one bin were what appeared to be two human legs. The rest of the object was submerged in the soft dung.

She thought at first that this must be a very offensive practical joke by a member of the dung beetle team, but on closer investigation she discovered that the legs were those of a real human. There was clearly a dead body in the bin. At which point she rushed out of the glasshouse, screamed loudly several times, and fainted on the grass.

Luckily another cleaner, Anna, happened to be at the end of the adjacent building at the time, and she rushed over to Maria.

'Maria, love, what's the matter?'

Maria was gasping and couldn't say much. She just pointed to the dung building and said: 'In there!'

Anna screwed up her nose and opened the door to the main room. Seeing nothing in there, she went into the back area at which point she saw the legs in the bin.

'Oh shit!' she yelled. Not inappropriately in the circumstances. She rushed back to the main office where she phoned the supervisor, who said she'd come immediately.

The supervisor saw straight away that this was an emergency. She called triple zero, and with a rather garbled account she asked for both police and an ambulance.

AUSTRALIAN FEDERAL POLICE

SERGEANT ANTONIO (TONY) MAZZINI

AGRICOZ, SYMONSTON

Why am I always the mug that gets jobs like this? We had this bizarre call from AGRICOZ at Symonston, about a dead body upside down in a barrel of wet shit. It wasn't April Fool's Day, but it certainly sounded like some sort of practical joke.

Anyway, I rounded up Bill Hansen who was one of my saner colleagues, and we shot off to Symonston with sirens at full blast. We were met at the gate by one of the AGRICOZ staff, who climbed into the car and directed us to the scene of the crime.

We arrived to see two paramedics lifting up a female who'd been lying on the lawn, and putting her on a stretcher. We went over and one of the paramedics said: 'This is the lady who found the body. She'll be okay. The stiff's in the lab over there.'

The AGRICOZ guy led us to the glasshouse at the back of the lab. The sight that greeted us did look like an April Fool's joke, but in the worst possible taste. A bin of wet cow-shit with two stiff legs standing upwards from it. Too much to hope that it was a tailor's dummy or something.

I looked closely at the legs, then felt them enough to determine that they really were human, not a very good dummy. Hairy legs indicated a male, and the legs were completely cold.

'Bill, we're absolutely going to need a forensic team for this one, and we can't disturb anything till they get here. Scene of Crime people and a cadaver expert. They're going to have to document this one really carefully. God help the pathologist who gets this job – the body's going to come out caked in shit. The post mortem boys will love this one.'

'I'll give 'em a call straight away, mate.'

'And we'd better send a constable to the hospital, wherever the ambos have taken the cleaner, to interview her when she's ready. It sounds like she was the first one on the scene. I don't imagine she's a suspect, but we need to hear what she's got to say.'

Bill made the calls, then said: 'What next?'

'We'd better make a start on examining the scene while the others are getting here. I'll go and check to see if there's any signs of a body being dragged around. There's no reason why the victim had to be killed here, though he might have been. I'll also check what CCTV is in the vicinity, then get a plan of all cameras on the site from the management. You could have a poke around the immediate vicinity of the shit bin to see what you can find, but don't touch anything. Make damn sure nobody comes into this room before forensics get here. Repeat, nobody – not even if they're AGRICOZ.'

'Will do, Tony.'

I went back into the glasshouse and felt the legs of the body again. Rigor mortis was clearly well developed, which was why they were standing so straight upright. I'd been an assistant in a forensic pathology lab for a year before I joined the AFP, and I knew it would take a minimum of four hours for rigor to develop. It was pretty unlikely that the victim was killed in the dung laboratory and then the killer waited for four or more hours to stash the corpse in the dung. I reckoned it must have been brought in from somewhere else, in which case there ought to be drag marks somewhere around the building.

There were no such marks inside the glasshouse or the adjacent office, so I went outside and examined the immediate area. No obvious dragging there either. Maybe two people carried the body in? Come to think of it, it might have needed two people to bury it in the dung. It wasn't so liquid that you could just immerse the body – it would take a fair bit of shoving, and one person couldn't really have done it alone. CCTV pictures might help with that.

Another awful thought crossed my mind. AGRICOZ has got a lot of political clout, and there'll be huge publicity and plenty of ruffled feathers. I'll have to alert my bosses about what's likely to be coming, and fast. I'll do the crime part of it, but I'm buggered if I'm going to get involved with the politics and the media. I called headquarters and briefed the desk officer.

* * *

An hour later the Scene of Crime officers and the forensic pathologist had arrived and were busily working. There were the usual complaints about what they were faced with, and bitter comments about being given the shitty jobs.

I left them to it and went to the main office to talk to the management. I found my boss, Inspector Marcus Wiersma, already there.

'G'day, Tony. This is Frank Arbuckle who's the Chief Personnel Officer and this is Remy Marchand who's the Assistant Chief Administrator.'

Christ, the titles. Shows the level of bureaucracy here.

'We've been discussing how to handle the press and publicity side of this event. It's so bizarre it's going to be hugely sensational, and we need to ensure that the minimum harm is done to AGRICOZ's reputation. I don't imagine you have any idea who the corpse was yet?'

'No, sir – forensics are going to have to clean him up first for that, and I reckon it'll take them a while.'

'Okay. We'll have to hope that it wasn't a staff member from here, but we'll have to be prepared for both contingencies. Whichever, it's going to be very tricky.'

That's the understatement of the year, if not the century. I hope my head'll be far enough below the parapet to escape the worst, but probably not.

'Sir, if it's all right with you I'll leave you to discuss that with the management here, and I'll get on with the investigation. Beginning with looking at whatever CCTV there is on the site. I'd be pretty sure that the victim wasn't killed in the lab because rigor mortis was already well developed, and if we can find that he was brought on site from outside that should reduce the involvement of AGRICOZ, shouldn't it?'

Remy Marchand answered. 'I think that's a very sensible idea. You probably know that we've got sensitive projects going on in some parts of this organisation, so we've got a pretty good CCTV network. I'll get the Chief Security Officer to help you with that.'

God, another Chief. Anyway, my boss nodded, and in a few minutes the head of security arrived and led me away to the main security office. He turned out to be a reasonable bloke, thank God.

'Hi, I'm Pete Smith. You want to know about the CCTV network. Here's a plan of the whole site with the location of every camera. For obvious security reasons it's a classified document and I'm not supposed to copy it, but if you'd like to sit here and see which cameras you'd like the footage of, I can call them up here. And ask for as many as you need – we're as keen as you to have this whole bloody thing cleared up.'

I sat at a table with a notepad. Pete pointed out the dung laboratory to me, and I worked outwards from there. They had a pretty good coverage of most of the site, but as Sod's Law would have it there was the least coverage in the area of the dung lab. I commented on this to Pete who just said: 'We didn't think anybody would want to steal shit. A few gardeners, I suppose. We gave that area the lowest priority because we thought it was the lowest risk.'

I noted all the cameras at entrances to the overall site, where a body could have been brought in from outside. Each entrance had a camera. I also made a note of the cameras closest to the dung building. When I'd got it all down I showed the list to Pete. He grimaced a bit, but said: 'I guess that's about what I'd expected. Come and sit at this screen and I'll get them all up.'

Not surprisingly most of the tapes showed nothing, but we scored off two of them. One was from a camera on the outside of the main building closest to the dung lab. It was shadowy because the camera was some way away and it was still dark, but there seemed to be two figures carrying a longish object between them. They went up to the door of the corridor closest to the dung lab, paused as though they were inserting a key, and then went in. The time showed as 1.54 am.

The other camera had rather clearer vision because the light was better. It was at the external gate that led into Narrabundah Lane, which was also the external gate closest to the dung lab. That suggested that the two people had some prior knowledge of the site. The object was carried in from outside, but the perpetrators could still have been employees of AGRICOZ.

This picture showed one figure going up to the gate and using a bolt-cutter to cut the chain that secured the gate. Then the figure moved out of sight again, and soon after two figures returned carrying the object between them, opening the gate and entering. They closed the gate behind them. The object being carried was about body-sized, and was wrapped in some sort of sheet. Both figures wore nondescript loose clothing, and were hooded. They appeared to be wearing gloves and snap-on surgical masks. Almost certainly male, and slightly above average height – not much to go on by way of ID. Also bad news in that it looked like a pretty professional operation.

The figures left through the gate again at 2.41 am. There was no further relevant activity until the camera on the main building picked up Maria going across to the dung lab, then a few minutes later rushing outside and fainting. There was a little light in the sky by then so the picture was clearer, but the intruders had long gone.

The gate off Narrabundah Lane through which they passed had its CCTV over the carpark beside the gate, but interestingly the two people must have parked just outside the camera's field of view. They were out of their vehicle by the time we picked up the figures, so there was no chance of reading the vehicle rego.

I pointed out the relevant images to Pete and said: 'How come nobody picked up these two intruders when they came in?'

'Mate, you've seen how many cameras we've got around the site. We've got two security guards in the office during the night, and they can't watch every camera every minute of the night. They give top priority to the areas where the sensitive projects are going on, and the dung lab would be near the bottom of that list. Sorry, no pun intended.'

'Okay, the first camera. The door to the corridor where the dung lab is located – would that be locked at night?'

'It certainly would be, and we can check that because the night-watchmen go around the whole site between nine thirty and ten o'clock every night and check that all the doors are locked. I'll get last night's detail in and we can check with them.'

'That would be good, because the camera vision showed the door being unlocked quickly and easily, which suggests that the perpetrators had a key. It would have taken longer if they were picking the lock.'

'Good point. The nightwatchmen will be off shift now, but I'll get them in as soon as I can and give you a shout.'

I thanked Pete, and went across to the Narrabundah Lane gate. This was open now and cars were coming into the parking area just inside. I looked closely at the areas of grass on either side of the gate that would have been just outside the field of the gate camera. There was freshly flattened grass on one side, and signs of recent trampling. Nothing else except for one boot-print in a dip where the soil had been wet. However, it was of a type that would be worn by lots of workmen around Canberra, and probably not much use.

The experts had all arrived, so I left them to it and went back to the station. There wasn't much more I could do until I received their reports.

* * *

And when the reports did come in, it became obvious that this was no ordinary case. The most startling report was that of the forensic examiner, who had painstakingly removed all of the sticky, wet cow dung to reveal the whole body. The victim had a broken skull caused by a hard blow to the side of the head, and the throat had been cut and the corpse bled out. After that the victim's penis and testicles had been cut off and stuffed into his mouth, which was then sealed shut with industrial tape. It was professional, systematic and vicious, and clearly designed to send a message.

The final shock came when the victim was identified. It was Dr Mervyn Hardcastle, one of the most senior and distinguished scientists at AGRICOZ....

AGRICOZ HEADQUARTERS

No Assistant Chiefs for the next conference – we had the Director General, Dr Harcourt Johnson, the Assistant DG Ratko Petković, and the Chief Administrator, Frank Portillo, in addition to the other bureaucrats we'd already met.

The DG kicked off the meeting. 'Thank you all for coming. I think you will have heard that the dead body in the dung was Mervyn, and the horrible details of how he was found. I suspect there's no way we'll be able to keep this out of the public domain' – he was certainly right about that – 'and the press will no doubt sensationalise it to the maximum.' Spot on with that too. 'It's going to be extremely embarrassing for AGRICOZ. I'll try to work out a public statement that'll calm things as much as possible, and I'll handle any press interviews as long as I'm around and available.'

My boss spoke up. 'Thank you for that. We're very much in agreement with you on this one, and we'll do our best to keep things cool as well. There's one thing we'd very much like to suppress altogether if possible, and that's the sexual mutilation that occurred. I think it would help our investigation greatly if that wasn't disclosed to the general public.'

'Well, we can most certainly refrain from mentioning that, and we'd be very grateful if you do too.'

'We'll certainly try. You can't always manage it, but any extra time we can get would be most helpful. And in relation to that aspect, are you aware of anything that had happened with Dr Hardcastle in this organisation that could relate to the mutilation? Was he perhaps involved in harassment of any sort, sexual or otherwise? Was he involved in anything else that might have led to a brutal murder?'

The AGRICOZ staff all looked at each other, and there was silence for a bit. We had our answer then, regardless of what the DG was about to say.

'Dr Hardcastle was a very senior and well-respected scientist. He has an international reputation, and he was recently elected a Fellow of the Australian Academy of Science which is a very high honour.' All of which was completely irrelevant to our question, of course. 'I am not aware of any disciplinary proceedings taken against him in relation to sexual or other harassment, or other matters, but I can enquire further.'

"**Can** enquire", not "**will** enquire", I noted.

My boss thanked the DG, and said we'd do all we could to keep a lid on this. He then indicated me and said to the senior management: 'This is Sergeant Tony Mazzini who'll be in day-to-day charge of the investigation.' He turned to me and said: 'Tony, before we go, is there anything that you'd like to know from the management?'

'Yes, sir. I'd be grateful to know in general terms what Dr Hardcastle's area of work was in this organisation.'

Again there was a moment of total silence, and everyone turned to look at the DG. He thought for a moment, obviously considering how little he could say and what the peasants might be able to comprehend. 'His area was plant pathology. That's the study of diseases of plants. Many crop plants in Australia have one or more disease problems, some very serious. Many of the diseases are not susceptible to chemical control, and Dr Hardcastle was investigating alternative means of disease management, including getting the plants to develop their own protective mechanisms. He was also looking at the possible uses of plant diseases to bring noxious weeds under control. I should mention that these areas are confidential research at this stage, and we wouldn't wish to see any public discussion of them.' Another warning.

I thought for a moment more. 'What we need before anything else is to follow up on relatives and a search of his residence. Could your staff please give this to us as quickly as possible?'

They put me on to a very helpful lady called Stella, who dug out all of Mervyn Hardcastle's personnel records. It turned out that he wasn't married, nor did he have a partner as far as AGRICOZ or Stella knew. Their records showed one person as next of kin – a cousin in the UK. The more interesting bit was Hardcastle's residential address – a penthouse at the top of what was probably the most expensive of the blocks of apartments along the Kingston Foreshore. He must have had serious money to have bought or even rented that, and it's going to make for an interesting search.

KINGSTON FORESHORE

Kingston Foreshore was unusual for Canberra. Although Canberra has the large Lake Burley Griffin curling through its centre, there are no waterside mansions or other dwellings along most of the lake's edge. The grounds of Government House do run down to the water, but the House itself is set well back from the lake. However, in the suburb of Kingston there's one section built around a small, quiet bay, with waterside walkways and landing platforms, and filled with apartments, restaurants and offices. It could be a little inlet off Sydney Harbour in appearance, but it is indeed Canberra.

There are plenty of people who want to live in such an atmosphere, so property prices are high, and Mervyn Hardcastle's apartment was in the block that was known to be the most expensive of the lot. Interesting for someone who was just a scientist, even if a senior one. Most such residences are owned by property developers, or by the most successful of real estate agents, or by Mafiosi.

The apartment block itself stood in a prime area, with beautiful views over the lake, and towards the Brindabella Mountains as a backdrop. Dr Hardcastle's penthouse would have had just about the best view of all. The block itself was called Lakeview Mansions – a totally pretentious name, but it hadn't deterred Dr Hardcastle.

By afternoon Bill Hansen and I had secured a warrant to search the premises, and as a precaution we took with us a colleague who could open almost any lock. Many apartment blocks in Canberra have no concierge, but this one did. I guess for the money you get that service as well. We went up to the desk, introduced ourselves and showed the warrant, and then asked the concierge if he had a key to the apartment.

'No, mate. The only people who get keys here are the apartment owners themselves. If there's a fire the firemen have to smash the door down. If the owner loses their key they have to get a locksmith. Nobody else can get in.'

'Well, we've brought our own locksmith, so we'll get on up to the apartment.'

'You won't get very far without one of these.' He opened a wall safe behind him and pulled out an electronic fob. 'You'll need this to get up in the lift. Just wave it over the black gizmo on the wall near the lift buttons, then press 5. At that level there's just the two penthouses. The gizmo will also open the corridor door to the right, which is the one for Dr Hardcastle's penthouse, and then you're on your own with the apartment door. When you come back down you won't need the fob, but make sure you give it back to me. I'll need you to sign this register for it.'

The lift was fast and quiet and the upstairs corridor was pristine, with a gentle and pleasant scent about it. The penthouse door looked pretty solid – I wouldn't have liked to be a fireman who had to smash it in.

Our locksmith cum security expert, Jenny McIlroy, looked at the door lock and groaned. 'I hope you brought something to read with you. This is probably going to take me some time.'

In the event it wasn't too long, and we walked into a light and airy apartment. My first surprise was how relatively plain the furnishings and decorations were – in fact there weren't many decorations at all, and the furniture was functional but plain. It was just that I'd expected such an expensive place to have equally lavish fittings.

It also looked neat and tidy. There were no signs of a struggle from someone breaking in and attacking Dr Hardcastle. Nothing out of place, no blood on the floor or anything.

We'd walked into a spacious living room, with a huge picture window along one wall. The window opened on to a balcony, from which there were superb views across the lake. To one side of the living room was a large kitchen, with marble bench, sink, ovens and a cook top. There were also plenty of cupboards, but the whole area was somewhat sterile. Few loose appliances, and not a great deal of food and other items in the cupboards. It didn't look as though Dr Hardcastle spent much time on catering for himself. Though maybe that wasn't so surprising given that there were all sorts of ethnic and other restaurants along the waterfront promenade.

Beyond the living room were three bedrooms, and a large study cum office which was clearly the room that had been used the most. This would be the area in which we would do most of our searching. However, one should never presume anything, so we started by looking through the living room, kitchen and bedrooms. If he'd had anything that he was keen to hide, the study might be too obvious.

The living room yielded nothing. A long sideboard was largely empty apart from some plates and glasses. There was nothing under the chairs or the sofa. One bookshelf contained a number of novels, and a flip through their pages yielded nothing. Another cupboard was empty. On the patio there was an outdoor table and two chairs, and a barbecue that didn't look as though it had ever been used. I looked under the barbie cover – nothing other than the cooking plate.

The bedroom had nothing hiding in the wardrobes or drawers, and nothing in the bed or under the mattress. The kitchen had saucepans but nothing hidden in them, and the pantry had a few items like breakfast cereals, coffee, biscuits and a half empty bottle of wine. I didn't recall seeing a wine storage anywhere in the apartment on the first look, which reminded me that he probably had a basement storage area and that would need to be searched as well.

The basement storage area would presumably be locked. There was no obvious key rack in the apartment, and a quick search of the office drawers showed no keys either, so I sent Bill and Jenny back to the concierge. If he had no relevant key, Jenny would have to try to open the lock on the storage door.

Meanwhile I started going through the office. There was a large desk in the centre of one wall, with shelves at the back of it and a computer in the middle. The desk had drawers on either side of the sitting area. The top drawer on each side was unlocked, and all the others were locked. The shelves at the back of the desk had piles of paper files on them. There were two other cupboards in the room, both locked.

On one wall hung a large picture, of a scene in what was probably Florence. It was the only ornamentation in the room, and I thought surely it couldn't be that corny a hiding place, but it was. The picture lifted off easily to reveal a wall safe. The safe looked a modern one with a very good lock, but Jenny ought to be able to cope with it.

I tried to start up the computer, but it immediately came up with a requirement for a password. I could guess at several possible ones, but I suspected that it would only give me a very few tries and then lock up altogether, so I didn't even try. Almost everything in the room was locked in some way, and I'd have to wait for Jenny to get back from the basement. To pass the time I thought I'd start with the files on the back shelves. There was a substantial pile of them, and I got out my tablet and started typing in the titles and a rough description of the contents. As I did so I began to wonder just what Dr Hardcastle had been up to. We'd need to do a thorough examination of all of them in due course.

Jenny and Bill returned after a while to report that Jenny had managed the padlock to the storage area quite easily. The cubicle was quite large, and the main item in its open part was a quite large wine storage rack. Along the back wall were three tall and deep metal cupboards, all padlocked. Jenny opened all three, and they found an assortment of laboratory glassware in the first cupboard and various chemicals in the other two, mostly in bottles but some in tins. A number of these had labels indicating toxicity so they left them untouched. Bill noted down the labels of all that were visible, and then they relocked the cupboards.

They also looked into the BMW four-wheel drive in the parking space in front of the storage area. The rego was MH1, would you believe? What a prat. Jenny got the car door open, but the car had nothing of any obvious interest in it.

When they came back upstairs, Jenny opened the locks on the remaining desk drawers and the two cupboards, and then started to work on the wall safe. The drawers were interesting in that they contained a number of files and a large dossier of financial transactions and bank statements. From several different banks, which was also interesting. We decided that we'd take all of those back to HQ and study them at our leisure. We might need a finance expert for some of them.

Also, somewhat surprisingly, the bottom left drawer contained a handgun and several boxes of ammunition. Not the sort of thing the average research scientist has in their house, surely?

After quite some time and a certain amount of swearing, Jenny got the wall safe open. It proved to contain a second computer, and we decided to take both computers back to HQ as well for expert examination. I was getting an ever-deeper feeling that this was going to be a very tricky case, with a lot of ramifications. Bill went back to the basement to pick up some empty cardboard boxes from the storage area, and we packed up as many items as we could and left. The only things remaining were the files on the shelves – we didn't have enough capacity to carry those. I'd come back and get them in the morning – they should be safe enough overnight, given that the apartment would be locked again, since Jenny had found what was Dr Hardcastle's second key among the contents of the safe.

KINGSTON AND AUSTRALIAN FEDERAL POLICE HEADQUARTERS

It was late when we got back with all the stuff we'd brought from Hardcastle's apartment, so we put it in secure storage until the next day.

In the morning I thought I'd go back and collect the files from the apartment shelves, so I took a couple of large carry bags and went back to Kingston. Jenny came with me to help carry stuff, and the concierge gave me the lift fob again.

Upstairs Jenny unlocked the door, and we went in with our bags.

No files on any of the shelves.

Shit.

Merda! Double *merda*. Why didn't I take them back yesterday? We were quite loaded up, but we could just have done it. I didn't think anyone could get in here to take them, nor did I think anyone would be after them so quickly.

I hunted everywhere, but I knew they were gone. I'd definitely left them on the shelves.

We relocked the apartment and went back down to the concierge.

'Mate, we came to collect something from Dr Hardcastle's

apartment that was there yesterday but isn't now, so somebody's been in there. Do you have CCTV here?'

'Of course we do. We're quality apartments here. What do you want to look at? Access to that apartment late yesterday or early today?'

'Well, that would be good, yeah.' Bleedin' obvious, actually, but don't lose your cool.

The concierge called up the CCTV on the entrance hallway near the desk. A number of people had come in, but the concierge was able to identify all as residents or people in the company of residents. Then he looked at vision from the basement garage areas. Four cars came in, and he could identify three as being driven by residents. The fourth came in just after ten at night, and went into one of the two parking bays belonging to Dr Hardcastle's penthouse, but a bit hesitantly as though it wasn't quite sure which space it was looking for. The car was a dark sedan, probably a Toyota Camry, and its number plate was easily readable – YZD24Q. The car parked and a man got out, with a handkerchief held over his face as though he was sneezing. He took a suitcase out of the boot and went towards the lift. The same person came back, again with the suitcase, at ten thirty. His back was to the camera this time.

'It looks as though that's the person who must have taken the files I was after. Do you have a register of keys and fobs for the apartment, and who holds them?'

'Of course we do. I told you these are quality apartments.'

If he told me once more about the quality of the apartments I was likely to throttle him, but not until I'd got my answer.

He opened a file on the computer, and said: 'Every fob gives access to the parking area, and to the lift for the level that the apartment's on. On Dr Hardcastle's level there are only two penthouses, so only two owners have relevant fobs. However, there's also a corridor door before you get to each penthouse, and you need fob access for that. Only Dr Hardcastle's fob would have opened his corridor door.

'There are three fobs with that particular access. One is Dr Hard-castle's, one is held at the desk here, but under lock and key and it's always signed out if it's given to anyone, like you guys yesterday.' He looked in the register, then said: 'You guys were the only ones at all recently who've had it. The third fob's held by the strata agents who manage the complex. I can give you a contact name for them, but I can assure you that they're very careful with theirs at all times.

'And then keys. I think I told you yesterday that there are only two keys for every apartment in the complex, and both are given to the apartment owner. We don't have any here, and neither does the strata agency. In any case of an emergency the fire people or ambos or whoever have to smash the door down, or you get a professional locksmith like you did. But they're pretty hard locks to pick – not just anybody could do them.'

'Yeah, tell me about it.'

He must have seen my glum look because he then said: 'What we do have is a facility at this desk that can tell you whose fob was used last night, because it leaves an electronic record.'

Again he opened something on the computer, and then he said: 'It shows that it was Dr Hardcastle who was in last night.' He had the grace to look a bit puzzled.

For a moment I was as puzzled as he was, and then I realised that whoever had killed Dr Hardcastle must have taken his fob and key from the body at the same time. Our only hope then would be the registration number on the car that came in last night.

Another thought suddenly crossed my mind. The chemicals and glassware in the basement storage area might also be important evidence, and we would need to secure them as well.

Jenny and I went back down to the basement storage area, and she picked the cage padlock and the cupboard locks. We opened the cupboards and peered at the various containers. I'd done enough basic science to know that the markings on a number of the containers indicated hazardous contents – some apparently very hazardous.

'Jenny, could you take the car back to the office and get Bill or someone to come back here with a HAZMAT suit and enough boxes to put all this stuff in? And tell him some of it might be pretty nasty. I'll wait here and keep an eye on the cage till Bill gets here.'

* * *

The shifting of the chemicals went well, and we put them in safe storage at HQ, with warning labels on the cabinet. Then I checked the number of the car that had gone into the apartment car park last night, and any hope of clues from that was soon dashed. The car was of course stolen. We were clearly dealing with a person or people who were careful, clever and well organised.

We returned to the station and told Marcus about the disappearance of the last few files.

He said: 'I'm getting increasingly angry about this whole case, starting with yesterday's effort at AGRICOZ. What did you make of all of that, Tony?'

'Well, they knew plenty about Dr Hardcastle's behaviour but they certainly weren't going to tell us.'

'I couldn't agree more, and I don't know what they're playing at. They must realise that in a case like this any relevant information has to be divulged. I wonder how we can find out a bit more inside information on the place. They're a secretive lot, so it won't be easy.'

'Could I make one suggestion, mate? My wife has a good friend she plays golf with, and I'm pretty sure she's at least a middle-level scientist in AGRICOZ. I also know that she's been there for some years, so she must know some of the scuttlebutt about the place. The way Ella talks about her, she sounds like a sensible contact who wouldn't blab about anything. I'd be prepared to try to talk to her for some background if that's okay with you?'

'If you think you can do it tactfully, go for it. But please don't rock any boats. If management gets to hear what you're doing, we'll all go down. And you'll be first in the bucket of shit.'

'Soul of discretion, mate. I'll talk it over with Ella tonight, and I'll check back with you before I go any further.'

* * *

My wife Ella and I always sit with a glass of wine before dinner, and I used the opportunity to tell her about the new case. And how I as a significant investigator would be as deeply in the doodoo as the victim was if I stuffed up. I didn't put it quite like that, but she got the message. Then I put the key question.

'What we need above all is information from someone who knows AGRICOZ well and can give us the vibes – about the place, and if possible about the victim. I remember you play golf regularly with Susie – can't remember her surname – and I think you said that she's been at AGRICOZ for a number of years. Do you think she might be prepared to talk to me about the place? I'd guarantee complete confidentiality and I wouldn't misuse any information.'

Ella looked a bit doubtful, but she said she'd give Susie a call.

She went into her study for the call, and it lasted for a while. When she came back she said:

'Susie told me she'd be prepared to talk to you about what you're after. If she doesn't like it she'll say no, and if there are specific things she wouldn't be happy to talk about she'll decline them, but she said she'll give it a go. I think she's a bit upset about things like that happening in her workplace. She said could you give her a call back after eight this evening and she'll discuss it with you further.'

* * *

I duly rang just after eight. Susie said:

'Ella told me what you'd like to do, and I'm okay to give it a try. I've heard what's just happened at AGRICOZ, and it's very upsetting.

I've been proud of working for the organisation over the years, and I'd hate our name to be spoiled by the actions of whoever did this. I know the place isn't perfect – nowhere is – but it does achieve a lot of good overall.'

'So where would you like us to meet? Presumably not at AGRICOZ, but would you like to come to the station? Or maybe somewhere neutral?'

'Definitely not AGRICOZ, and probably not at the station either. If this works out between us I can be a lot more use to you if nobody knows we're talking. I assume this is urgent for you. So would tomorrow morning be all right?'

'Fine by me. Where would you like?'

'My suggestion is that we meet over coffee, at ten o'clock at my golf club. Same as Ella's, of course, Federal. At that hour we can sit on the outside terrace overlooking the course, and there should be hardly anyone around to hear. The staff'll be working inside, and anyone else'll be out on the course. It'll just look like a social chit-chat.'

'Sounds good. I'll look forward to it.'

'Me too. And I'll be interested to meet the person Ella married. You can't be as bad as she paints you....'

At least there was a chuckle in her voice as she said that.

* * *

In view of the urgency I called Marcus Wiersma at his home to get his okay for the meeting.

He said: 'Go for it. The more views from other perspectives that you can get the better. Just don't let it get back to the AGRICOZ heavies.'

'Soul of discretion, mate.' I hoped that would turn out to be true...

FEDERAL GOLF CLUB

I turned up a bit early. I hadn't met Susie before so I didn't know who to look for, but there was nobody else around when she appeared on the terrace.

'Good morning. Tony, obviously.'

'Yeah, cops stand out, don't they?'

'Well, there isn't anyone else around here, and Ella's told me enough about you. I'll get the coffees – they're cheaper for members. What would you like?'

'Long black for me, thanks.'

'Okay, find yourself a comfortable seat and I'll be back in a moment.'

I chose a table roughly in the middle of the terrace, with a sunshade over it which would make it feel more private. While waiting I admired the view, which must be one of the best in Canberra. A beautifully green fairway sloped downwards, edged by tall trees, with the Brindabella Mountains in the distance. There were birds everywhere – magpies, parrots and cockatoos, two ducks crossing the fairway with a procession of babies, kookaburras calling – even kangaroos in the shade of some trees. A refreshing contrast to the corpse in the bin.

Susie reappeared with the two coffees. As she sat down she said:

'I'd like to drive the agenda at the start if you don't mind. If I'm to be the most use to you it would help me to know where you're coming from – not just in relation to the case but also about you as a person. How you think, how you go about things and so on. Okay?'

'Okay.' I did wonder exactly where this was going, but I needed her help.

'Right, first off given your name of Mazzini, were you born in Italy?'

'No, I was born just down the road from here in Cooma, actually. But my parents were both Italian-born – father from a small village in the north of Veneto, mother from Ascoli Piceno, a town in the far south of Le Marche, near the border with Abruzzo.'

'Yes, I know Ascoli. A beautiful and historic town. Good food, too.'

That surprised me a little.

'Why did your parents come to Australia?'

'My father was a pastry cook. As I'm sure you'd know that's something that Italians do quite well, but there was too much competition in Italy. He was a baker in Cooma, and my mother got a job in a travel agency there which she did well in. My father died a few years ago, and my mother now lives in Canberra. Still working in travel, now at Qantas.'

'And what motivated you to become a policeman?'

'Actually, I didn't start off with that intention. I've always enjoyed puzzle-solving, and first-off I studied forensic science. I got a graduate qualification in that and I worked as a forensic for about a year and a half, but I found I missed a human aspect in the work. At least live human involvement. I felt that after that first year I knew something about crime, so I applied for the Federal Police. Got trained, and got in.'

'What do you enjoy about being a policeman?'

"I like working with people and interacting with them, and

trying to read them when they're saying one thing to you but meaning something else. I enjoy interrogation, but not the sort you see in crime films where people just get menaced or beaten up. I leave that to some of my colleagues. I like the more subtle approach. And, may I say, I suspect you might like the same because I think I'm being skilfully interrogated here?'

She laughed. 'Yes, I like talking to people as well, and trying to read them. I'm one of AGRICOZ's harassment contact officers – have been for quite a few years.'

'Well, that must give you a lot of insights into the good and bad of AGRICOZ. Which I guess is one of the things I'd hoped to ask you about.'

'The crunch, then. Where would you like to start?'

'Well, you'll have heard that the dead body found in the dung bin was Dr Mervyn Hardcastle. But there's another detail which I hope you haven't heard yet because it's supposed to be highly confidential. It's also very unpleasant. Please, please don't let this go any further than you, but when the pathologist examined the body they found that his penis and testicles had been cut off and stuffed into his mouth. His mouth was then closed with duct tape. That very strongly suggests punishment for a sexual misdemeanour or misdemeanours. I believe it's a classic for such things in Muslim countries, but maybe not only there. I know that as a harassment contact officer you're sworn to secrecy like the Catholic confessional, but can I ask if you think there might be any truth there?'

Susie had gone a bit white. 'I certainly hadn't heard that part of it.' She stared into space and thought for a while. 'I'll guarantee to keep your secret if you'll keep mine. In confidence I'll tell you that Dr Hardcastle was a prize shit. No pun intended on where he was found, but then again maybe that was a deliberate message too. I don't think I've ever met a more unpleasant person in all my life.'

'Might you be able to give me some examples, at least of the sort of behaviour?'

She thought again for a moment. 'Well, he was relatively short in stature and I know he had a bit of a complex about that, because when anyone made a reference to it he became particularly vicious. On behaviour, for a start when he looked at you it always seemed as though he was sneering at you and finding you inferior. I know some people can have an unfortunate face that's set that way, but in his case I think it was genuine. When you saw him when he wasn't talking to someone, he didn't look sneering. He was also particularly demeaning to women. He ignored us where possible, and he never paid any attention to anything a woman told him.

'A string of assistants left his laboratory, most just asking for a transfer to another section. He also regularly made derogatory comments about his senior colleagues. Then the crowning event recently was that he was elected a Fellow of the Australian Academy of Science. That's about the highest accolade a scientist can get in this country apart from winning the Prime Minister's Prize for Science, and didn't he go to town on that one. He crowed to everyone, and he hung the Fellowship certificate in the most prominent position in his office. What particularly galled some of his colleagues is that they were also up for Fellowships and didn't get them. And to them he crowed the hardest.

'He was a Pom and educated at Oxford University, and if you listened to him you'd think that no other university anywhere was worth anything. A Pommie bastard, truly.'

'Yes, fair enough, and calling him a prize shit is putting it mildly. So as potential suspects we have anyone who's jealous, anyone he's demeaned, anyone he may have sexually assaulted, and all women. We prefer it when the field's narrowed down a bit more than that. And that's only people who work in AGRICOZ, of course – there could be others from outside.'

'You're right about that, and I don't doubt there are plenty of people in the wider community who hated his guts. When I first heard about it I thought it had to be an insider because they would have known where the large dung bins were. However, I've just remembered that a few months ago they had an open day for that project, in fact an open weekend. The dung beetles were on full display for most of the Saturday and Sunday, and I heard that many hundreds of people came through. It's always been a project that's caught the public's imagination.'

'Well, that does widen the list of possibles, certainly. On the matter of the dung, would you think it at all likely that it was someone on the dung beetle project who did this?'

'I'd say a pretty firm no, for two reasons. Firstly, I don't think they'd be so stupid as to point the finger directly at themselves, and secondly they're the people who've probably had the least contact with Mervyn. When in Canberra they spend most of their time tending the beetles, and the rest of the time they're travelling round Australia taking beetles to cattle stations for release, or monitoring the success of earlier releases. No doubt Mervyn made disparaging remarks about people who spend all their time in the shit, but they'd be used to that from half of AGRICOZ and they'd just ignore it.'

'You may wish not to answer this, but are you aware of any sexual harassment cases in which Dr Hardcastle was involved as perpetrator?'

She thought for a moment. 'I'll answer that by saying no, he never came up in that regard in any cases I had. Bullying yes, but sexual harassment no. However, I will add that I did hear one or two whisperings and I think it was my colleague, the other contact officer, who fielded them. I don't know any details but you could try asking him. However, he may not tell you. Knowing his opinion of Dr Hardcastle I think he'd be delighted that this has happened and he'd like to give a medal to whoever did it. "Prize shit" wouldn't be his description – it'd be far worse.'

'I heard one comment made that some of the work that goes on in AGRICOZ is sensitive and classified, though I have no idea yet for what reasons. Would you think that there could be any aspect of that sort that could be involved?'

'I have really no idea about that. I'm not high enough up the chain to know about those. All I can say is that my section's work is not that sort at all. It's improving various agricultural crops by conventional methods of crop breeding – not controversial in any way. I guess there could be a possibility, but you'll have to find someone higher up to answer that.'

'Thanks. That could be hard because they clearly don't want to talk to us any more than they have to, but they may just have to.'

'Anyway, I've just that noticed your coffee's finished. Would you like another, or are we done here?'

'I won't have another thanks, and I think we might be done for the moment. I'm really very grateful to you for talking with me as you've done, and it's been most helpful. I can now picture the scene and context far better. I knew there was something when my boss asked the same thing of your DG and his hangers-on, and there was silence while they all looked at each other, but then of course the DG batted it away.'

'My pleasure too. I think this whole thing is horrible. No matter how much a person may have deserved to be taken down a peg, it shouldn't have been in such a vile way. If there's anything more I can do to help, please ask. In confidence, like this meeting.'

'Thanks again, and I'll probably do that. And thank you for the coffee – my shout next time.'

'I also enjoyed finally meeting you, and discovering that you weren't quite as bad as Ella likes to make out…'

There was a twinkle again, this time in her eyes.

'And I could say the same about you… *Arrivederci*!'

'*Arrivederci. Buon viaggio!*'

Maybe we could conduct the next session in Italian. That would be even more private.

* * *

Back at the station I briefed Marcus Wiersma on my chat with Susie, and I stressed the need to keep her involvement totally under wraps.

'Jeez, mate. What a bastard of a mess. I don't think I've ever faced a case where there's so many possible suspects, and no obvious clues at the moment. One line we'll have follow up is the possible sexual harassment aspect, given his prick and balls being cut off and force-fed to him. We're going to have to demand information from the AGRICOZ management on that, and we don't take no for an answer. We also need to find out more on his personal life. Had he received any threatening mail, emails, social media or the like recently? Has he got any sort of criminal record? Were there any sexual misdemeanour charges brought against him in AGRICOZ? – all that sort of thing. We need to get inside his mind and history.'

I said: 'If there's any criminal history our records should be able to do that, together with the national database. For disciplinary charges within AGRICOZ, they'll have to come up with that, and no hedging.'

'We'll also have to check out any areas near the entry gate of AGRICOZ where the car might have parked. I know you said that the car didn't come into the gate CCTV picture, but I don't imagine they'd have wanted to carry a body too far – bodies are pretty heavy. There might just be something in the grass or wherever.'

'I did that already. They were close to the gate but just out of sight. On one side of the gate there were signs in the grass that a car had been there, and a bit of trampling. I drew the examiners' attention to that.'

'Right, the other thing that gives me the creeps is the way his throat was deliberately cut to bleed him out. I can't remember whether the pathologist said the blow to the head killed him or the loss of blood, but either way it was a calculated and vicious act. And somewhere there must be a large amount of shed blood, though I'd doubt we're ever going to find that.'

'Mate, if I could chip in with one more aspect? I asked Susie about a possible security aspect to this, because I've gathered that some of the work that goes on there is classified and kept very much under wraps. She didn't know because she's not high enough to be in that loop, but she said it wasn't impossible.'

'Hell. That's another aspect we'll have to look at, and you can bet there's going to be resistance on that one too. I'll brief the Super on this, and then I think we may have to go to the Assistant Commissioner to get his take on the political side of it all.'

* * *

Back home that evening I said to Ella: 'I survived the meeting with Susie, but I learned some new tips about interrogation. I was the target of much of it at the start.'

Ella gave a deep chuckle. 'She's a bright cookie all right. That's why I enjoy her company so much. She's a very shrewd judge of people. Did she say she was prepared to see you again?'

'She did, and it may well be necessary. She's quite a mine of useful information.'

'Well, you've passed quite a test then. She doesn't suffer fools gladly.'

'She surprised me with one other thing too. She was trying to get a handle on my background and she asked me about family. When I mentioned that Ma was born in Ascoli Piceno, she said "Yes, I know Ascoli. It's very beautiful, and historic." I wasn't expecting someone here to know Ascoli.'

'Well, I told you she was smart. Next time I golf with her I must ask her what she thought of you. I might get some new insights to explain all the bits that puzzle me.'

All I could do was roll my eyes.

AUSTRALIAN FEDERAL POLICE HEADQUARTERS

Next morning I met again with Marcus Wiersma, who looked very stressed. He rubbed his forehead and said:

'Why did I have to be the bunny to cop this case? Or you and me, I should say. The more I think about it the more I realise that there's probably a whole lot of background of which we're totally unaware. I don't think it's going to be a simple murder by a colleague or someone at AGRICOZ. There's got to be a much deeper story.'

'I couldn't agree more. I was lying awake in bed last night thinking exactly the same. And there's a further dimension – we need to know in detail about his scientific work. I got the impression that they're not at all keen to talk about that, and we'll have to come the heavy to get it.'

Marcus said: 'I've already spoken to the Assistant Commissioner about that, and he'll be more than happy to do the necessary if we need pressure.'

'Well, I thought I might meet again with Stella, who dug out Hardcastle's personnel details for me when we were round at AGRICOZ. She seemed to be right across anything to do with administration in AGRICOZ, and I'd like to see if I can get anything more of use from her.'

'Okay, go for it, but don't stir anything up with the senior management.'

'Soul of discretion, mate. I hope….'

AGRICOZ

I contacted AGRICOZ's administration and asked if I could meet with Stella once more to tidy up a few details about Hardcastle's employment. I made it sound as low-key as possible.

They agreed, and Stella said she could meet me later that morning. I started off with a few rather small details, and then asked her politely whether she had anything to add that might help me to find who'd done this horrible deed.

She said nothing for a moment, obviously weighing up whether or not to tell me what she did know.

'I'm not supposed to pass on any details or comments about members of staff under any circumstances, but I think this is almost outside any normal circumstances. It was absolutely horrible, and I wouldn't like to think that someone who could do that might still be wandering around here and working here.'

I didn't tell her that it was very unlikely to be someone from AGRICOZ – I'd rather hear what she had to say.

She said: 'I understand he was a brilliant scientist, but he wasn't very popular with staff. I used to hear him making comments that belittled their work, but he never missed an opportunity to praise his own achievements. Which recently included quite a high honour,

and he made as much as he could out of that. It didn't go down well with his colleagues. They'd have been very happy if the honour had gone to someone else, but not to him. There were some very cool moments in the tea-room when I was there.'

I already knew most of this, but I wanted her to keep talking.

'Was his work internationally regarded?'

'You should probably be asking the senior management about that if you want detail, but I can tell you that he did a lot of overseas travel. I help out as well in the travel section, and we had to arrange a lot of trips for him. Always in Business Class, of course. That's the entitlement for someone of his level in the organisation, but many of them opt to save money and go Economy. Not Dr Hardcastle, however.'

'That's very interesting. What sorts of places did he travel to?'

'Oh, all over the place. To the States and the UK quite often, and places like Rome, Paris and Geneva. But he also went to a number of Asian countries. India, China, Thailand, Malaysia and Japan, I think, and maybe others too. And the Middle East if I remember right.'

'Do you know if he was attending conferences, or visiting laboratories or what on these trips?'

'I can't remember that. But any request for travel has to be signed off by the relevant Chief of Division, or if the relevant Chief isn't around, one of the other Chiefs or the DG or Assistant DG. They have to assess the purpose of the travel, which would be written down in the relevant section of each travel requisition, and they're all filed in my office if you want to see them.'

'That's very kind of you, thanks. I won't do that at the moment, but I'll come back to you if it looks as though it might be relevant to our investigation. Now I wondered whether I might ask you something a bit more delicate? It's supposed to be very confidential but you may have heard that there seemed to be an element of revenge for a personal slight or insult in the murder. Do you know of any specific people either in this organisation or in the wider community who might have a revenge motive for attacking Dr Hardcastle? I need hardly say that I would keep anything you say in absolute confidence, but it might just help us to solve the crime if we knew that.'

I crossed my fingers, but to no avail.

'I'm sorry, I would tell you if I knew anything but I don't. However, what I will say is that I might raise the subject in very general terms with some people who've been here for some years, and see if anyone knows anything. If they do, I'll certainly get back to you.'

'Many thanks, Stella. You clearly know this organisation very well, and you've been a great help.'

She glowed slightly, and said: 'You aren't like most policemen we've had in here. You're very polite.'

'Well, I haven't always been a policeman. I started out as a forensic scientist, but then I decided I preferred working with living people. And I'm sure you guys here feel that scientists are the nicest sorts?' I winked as I said it.

'Not sure that I'd agree with you on a hundred percent of them.'

'Well, you can't win 'em all!

I grinned and took my leave. I reckon Stella might be on my side if I need her help in the future.

* * *

I was just walking away from Stella's building when my phone rang. It was Pete Smith, the head of security, who had both of the nightwatchmen in his office. When I spoke to them they assured me they'd done their full rounds as normal on the night of the murder, and the shorter, chubbier one of the two told me he'd swear on his grandmother's bible that he'd checked the doors at both ends of the dung beetle corridor and they were locked.

They further told me that they kept their master keys on them at all times as they went around the site, and when they went off duty the keys were locked away in a safe in the main Security Office. I'd have to have another session with Pete Smith to find out what master keys existed for the relevant doors, and who had them. However, other things needed to be done first.

AUSTRALIAN FEDERAL POLICE HEADQUARTERS

Bill, Jenny and I sat with Marcus Wiersma to discuss the case. Marcus asked me for comments first.

I said: 'I reckon I at least misjudged this case at the start. I thought it was going to be maybe an aggrieved husband taking bizarre revenge against someone who'd screwed his wife, or something like that. A crime of passion – that sort of thing. A straightforward matter, anyway. However, that doesn't tie up with things that we've been seeing. The placement of the body in the dung bin was carefully planned and executed. And then last night the theft of files from Dr Hardcastle's apartment was equally carefully planned and executed, and an aggrieved husband wouldn't have been interested in them. Our net total of clues from all of that is zero, and the whole thing suggests something quite professional.

'So what could be behind all this? My first perusal of the files that have now disappeared is that there were a whole lot of things that I was surprised to find Dr Hardcastle involved with. I did at least make a note of all the titles, and I accept responsibility for not having brought them all straight back here. I hadn't at the time realised what we were getting ourselves into, and it was a lapse of judgement. At the time I thought a day wouldn't have made any difference because I didn't think anyone would have had access.

'I think we need to go back to AGRICOZ to find out whether those files had any relevance to Dr Hardcastle's work with them. Secondly, I think we need also to go through all the papers that we did bring back with us to get a better idea of what he was involved with. Thirdly, we need to go very carefully through both his computers to see what's in there. And that will include all financial information as well as any other. And last of all, we need someone with relevant technical knowledge to go through the chemicals that we've just brought back and let us know what they might have been doing in his personal storage area. They certainly aren't your average household chemicals.'

'Good summary, Tony – thanks. Anything to add, Jenny or Bill?'

Jenny spoke first. 'Sir, I'd be happy to take on the computer side of it if you'd like. Both are secured by sophisticated security systems, and I think there'll probably be encrypted stuff in them as well. I could give it a first go if you like, though I may need more expert assistance in due course.'

'Go for it, Jenny, and absolutely ask for any other help if you need it. Keep me and Tony in the loop at all times. Bill?'

'Sir, I'd like to say first that I agree absolutely with Tony's assessment of what we're facing. And secondly, I don't think there's anything specific that I could do that Tony or Jenny couldn't, but Tony's going to need a lot of assistance and with your permission I'd like to be part of that.'

Marcus grinned. 'If you're okay with that, Tony, it's fine by me.'

'Well, he's probably no worse a bastard than half of them around here, so fine by me.' I think Bill would have noticed my wink.

'Okay, guys and Jenny. Get to it, and when you've got something to report we'll all convene again. Needless to say give it your top priority, and in the meantime I'll brief the Assistant Commissioner on all of this. I think shit's going to hit a fan fairly soon now, and I'd like to have our heavies waiting in the wings.'

* * *

Back in the office Bill and I sorted out the papers that we'd brought with us. At my suggestion Bill took all the financial stuff, and I took the rest. This included quite a bit of science-related material, and I thought that my background in forensic science might be a small help there. Or at least I might know where to go to get some more expert information.

We all beavered away for some time, and Jenny was the first to report something.

'Guys, in relation to this being a possible sex-related crime, I think you should come and look at this.'

We went over to the larger of the two computers that she'd been working on.

'There's a whole part of the memory that's called Venus. Cute, huh? It's got various things to do with sex. One section's got quite a lot of pictures of nude men, mostly with large penises. Do you know if Dr Hardcastle had an inferiority complex in that area?'

'I don't know myself because I wasn't at the post mortem, but the pathologist who did it could tell us straight out. He fished the relevant item out of the guy's mouth. I'll go and call him now.'

It didn't take long to find out. 'The doc said that he was perfectly normal – in fact slightly above average, so he shouldn't have been feeling inferior.'

'Okay, well that's one theory gone. I've got another section to work through now. I'll call you if there's anything else.'

We met again when Bill went and got us all coffee. Jenny said: 'I'll be glad when this part of the work's over. It's pretty disgusting, some of it. By the way, do you have a photo of Dr Hardcastle by any chance?'

'I do. I'll go and get it.'

I came back with it and showed it to Jenny, who said: 'Yeah, that's him all right. You won't believe this but there's a video on the computer of him having live sex with a woman. I think I should show you, not for you to perv on but it might just tell you something relevant about the guy.'

We sat and watched the clip, which showed a straightforward act of sexual intercourse, but when the face of the female partner came into view Bill exclaimed: 'That's Lulu!'

I gaped at him. 'She's a friend of yours?'

'No, but I know her quite well. She's worked for years at Birds of Passage, which is one of the brothels in Fyshwick. Before I joined Murder I used to be in the Vice Squad, and the Fyshwick and Mitchell brothels were in our bailiwick. I got to know a number of the girls because we had to interview them at various times, and Lulu was one of the more sensible and helpful ones. She's quite a nice lass in normal life. I don't know why she had to get into the sex trade – she never told me.

'It's interesting because as I've been going through Dr Hardcastle's finance records he seems to have made a sizeable number of payments over the years to Birds of Passage, so he must have been a regular there. I don't know how often it would have been Lulu, but I could go and ask her about the guy. She might remember him if he'd been a regular with her.'

'Could be very helpful, Bill. Ask her what her judgement of him as a person was. We've been told that he was an absolute shit, but maybe she saw a sweeter side of him. Maybe....'

Jenny was screwing up her face, but said nothing.

Bill said: 'I'll go and give the owner a call. She knows me well enough, and I can probably get a time with Lulu. Don't look at me like that, Jenny. This'll be a purely work assignment. I know too much about brothels to get involved with them in any other way.

'By the way, in case it's relevant, among the financial records there was also a single payment to Daughters of Satan, which is another brothel in Fyshwick that specialises in S and M. My guess is that he gave that a go once and didn't want to do it again. I only mention this in relation to indicating what his character may have been. Mainstream sex rather than anything else.'

'Okay, thanks to both of you for this, and to Jenny for pursuing what must have been quite distasteful. I wouldn't mention any of this around the place here – you know what some of them would make of it. I'll take any responsibility if it's needed.'

* * *

Bill got an appointment to meet with Lulu next day, mid-morning. Obviously a quiet time for brothels, and they weren't going to get any money from his visit. He came back to report just before lunch.

'Lulu remembers Dr Hardcastle quite well. She reckoned that he came to see her for company as much as for sex. He told her that other people didn't understand him – how often have I heard that before? She said that sometimes he seemed to be preoccupied, and just recently he'd been saying to her that he was becoming fright- ened by something he'd got himself into with work, but he didn't elaborate any further. He said that he thought that Pepe was after him, but when she asked who or what Pepe was, he wouldn't say any more.

'I did ask her, by the way, how come there was a video of him having sex with her on his computer, and she said that that was an extra service that Birds of Passage provides to its customers for a further charge. I must have looked a bit sceptical because she said: "You'd be surprised at how many people ask for that. You should give it a go yourself one day – you'd be surprised at what you see then.". I suggested that I mightn't be taking her up on that, and she just grinned and said: "Chicken!".'

'Thanks for doing that, Bill. Rather you than me. Anybody got any thoughts, by the way, on who or what Pepe might be?'

Blank looks all around. Something to follow up on, though.

* * *

Meanwhile I started going through the various sets of papers that had been in the locked desk drawers. A fairly large number related to plant diseases, some related to specific crops and others more general, on the structures of the diseases themselves and their mechanisms of attack on plant tissues. Of those, a proportion were on how to combat the harmful effects, but others more worryingly were on how to increase the harmful effect. I couldn't imagine why anyone would want to do that except as a form of aggression against crop plant growers. Though the DG had also said something about using pathogens to control noxious weeds. I guess that they'd need to be as pathogenic as possible for that, but would you then be able to control them in the wider environment?

There were also some studies on toxicity to mammals. That was fair enough because users would have to be careful not to poison the spray operators or the local fauna, but what was more worrying were some hints of biological warfare relevance. Anything like that could explain why we seemed to be dealing with some very professional opposition.

I started sorting the papers into the broad subjects. I could do anything in English and Italian, but some were in languages that I didn't know. I could make a reasonable stab at the topics of ones in Spanish, and a bit less with German, but I wasn't up to French and I didn't have a hope with the ones that were in Cyrillic script. My guess was that it would be Russian, so I'd have to find someone who could read them.

I thought about going to Marcus with all that, but I felt I needed some more concrete information before I did so. It would raise a big furore, and if Hardcastle had been doing that work with official authorisation we might have one or more of the security services down on us. Heavily.

It occurred to me that Bill might also find some financial transactions that were relevant. I'd need to get him to keep an eye open for that sort of aspect.

MOUNT MUGGA MUGGA
NATURE RESERVE

Finally we had a stroke of luck, thanks to Fritz the German Shepherd dog. Fritz's owner, Dieter Junghans, was exercising Fritz on one of the walking tracks on Mount Mugga Mugga when Fritz went on the alert with his nose in the air, and then rushed off the track and part way up a hillside. Dieter tried to call Fritz back but he paid no attention, so Dieter followed him. He found Fritz with his nose down in some heavily discoloured earth, digging at it with his paws. On closer inspection Dieter began to suspect that the discoloration might have been due to blood on the ground. He quickly fastened Fritz's lead on and dragged the dog back, much to Fritz's displeasure.

There was not only the possible blood but there were signs that there might have been a struggle – scuffed earth and some drag marks. Dieter always carried a mobile phone with him, so he phoned triple zero to report this. He was told to wait there while the police came, which was easier said than done because Fritz was a large and powerful dog and didn't easily take no for an answer. Dieter had to walk him back and forth vigorously to pacify him.

Good luck prevailed for once when Dieter's call came in, because the operator who took the call knew of our investigations into the Hardcastle murder, and that a lot of blood could be involved, so she immediately called Bill Hansen to go and look at the scene.

When Bill got there he realised the possible relevance to Hardcastle's death straight away. He phoned back to get a forensic team on the spot as fast as possible, and then asked Dieter Junghans about what he'd noted when he came across the scene. That wasn't a great deal because Dieter had been more concerned to keep the dog out of what he'd guessed might be a crime scene, but at least it meant that the spot was fairly intact.

Bill then let Dieter go, and he took some photos of the scene from all angles with his mobile. He noticed that there were a number of cigarette butts lying around on the ground, and they looked reasonably fresh. He stood guard until the forensics arrived, and then left them to it and came back to the AFP to let me know what had been found.

When he showed me his photos I agreed with him that this looked very promising, and we were both busting to get the forensic report. Interestingly, the location was off Mugga Lane, and it was not all that far from the side gate of the AGRICOZ site where the body had been carried in. The cigarette butts suggested that whoever had been there had spent some time, which might have included cutting off Hardcastle's genitals and sealing them in his mouth. They would also have wanted rigor mortis to set in so that they could do the spectacular immersion in the dung bin, and that would have taken several hours.

The cigarette butts were the first lapse from complete professionalism, however. If we're lucky they'll have traces of DNA detectable on them. Probably the perpetrators didn't expect that the site in the bush would ever be discovered.

AUSTRALIAN ACADEMY
OF SCIENCE

While the forensics were working on the Mugga Mugga material, I went back to the documents from the files locked in Hardcastle's desk. In addition to the ones directly on plant diseases there was a group of papers describing what other countries were doing in those lines of work, and some of them were countries that Australia would regard as unfriendly. I was already worrying that we might get tangled up with Australian security services over some of this work, and that concern was growing further.

What I was going to need was someone with much greater expertise on plant pathology who could explain the significance of all these papers to me in detail. The only trouble was that I didn't know who to approach. AGRICOZ would undoubtedly have people, but they would be too close to Dr Hardcastle. I needed someone totally independent. And I had a sudden flash of inspiration – why not the Australian Academy of Science, who'd recently recognised Dr Hardcastle for his work?

I thought of phoning, but I've found that it can sometimes be easier with a rather delicate question to ask it face to face with the person, so I drove round to the Academy. I parked near the spectacular dome of the Academy, which is one of Canberra's best-known buildings. In the embassy city of Canberra, it's sometimes referred to as the Martian Embassy or the Eskimo legation, and once again I could see why. It's certainly shaped like a large flying saucer, or an igloo. I crossed the little moat that surrounded it and went in, but was promptly redirected to the main office which was in the adjacent Ian Potter House. I asked the receptionist if I could see the chief executive, and after a quick phone call I was shown into a neat and comfortable office.

Behind an enormous desk was a very small woman, who introduced herself as Professor Mary McDougall. I introduced myself in return, and explained what I was after.

'I imagine that you'll have heard of the death of one of your Fellows, Dr Mervyn Hardcastle. I have the rather unenviable task of investigating what happened, and to do that I need some help from someone who has strong expertise in plant pathology, preferably with experience of its international dimensions as well as just the science. I thought that if anyone might know of a name it would be you here.'

'I have indeed heard about the death, and what I learned was horrible. I'd love to be able to help you find the culprit myself, but I'm afraid my own subject's nuclear physics. International, yes, but plant pathology related, definitely not. But we do have a Fellow who's probably one of the world's top experts in what you want – Professor Yeva Thompson of the Australian National University. She's an Emeritus Professor now and quite old, but she's still very much on the ball, and also very well-connected internationally. She lives at University House these days, just over the way from here. I'll give you her phone number. When you call her, please feel free to tell her that I recommended her to you.'

PROFESSOR YEVA THOMPSON

I don't usually get nervous going to interview witnesses, but this was a senior fellow of the Australian Academy of Science and a Professor of ANU, and I was a rather lowly ex-forensic scientist, now a cop. However, I did need her expertise, and when I phoned her she said she'd be happy to meet with me, at ten o'clock the next morning.

Her rooms were in University House, the residential institution at ANU that's built like a college in Oxford or Cambridge University – a central quadrangle with staircases leading up from all the sides. When I arrived I found a very pleasant pair of rooms overlooking greenery, with birds audible in the trees around.

I also found a tall and slightly stooping woman, who gave me a penetrating look when she opened the door. However, she greeted me quite warmly, invited me in and waved me to a chair.

'I'm about to make myself a cup of coffee. May I get you one as well?'

'That's very kind, thank you. I'd love a long black.'

She gazed at me again and then said: 'Mazzini sounds Italian, and you look Italian. So not an espresso or something?' Her slight smile made it a question, not a criticism.

'Born in Cooma, actually, but my parents were both Italian. And a long black coffee will still be fine, thanks.'

As she made the coffee at a side table I made my own appraisal of her. She had rather wild hair, but that suited her strong features. She had the papery skin of the very old, but she moved easily around the room. She had hooded eyes, but the most notable of her features was a large and downcurved nose. The combination of the two made her look like rather like a bird of prey.

That nose in my experience could only indicate one ancestry.

'Since you were enquiring about my ethnic origins, may I politely ask about yours? If I had to guess I would say that you might have Armenian descent?'

She laughed. 'Trust a policeman! I suppose it's the nose that's the giveaway?'

'That was one feature, yes. But when I heard that I was visiting Professor Thompson I hadn't expected that.'

'Ah, well. Thompson was my married name. I was married in an era when women took their husband's name on marriage. Not like now. But before that my name was Vardanyan. My Christian name, Yeva, is Armenian. It's the Armenian version of Eva.'

'Thank you. My apologies for being intrusive.'

'Not at all, and now that I'm retired it's nice to have someone to talk to about such things. Since you started this line of talk, have you ever heard the story of how Armenians came to have noses like this one?'

I shook my head.

'For this, you have to remember that Armenians are good business people as well as having the noses. Think Gulbenkian the shipping magnate, amongst others.

'Anyway, when God was creating the world, He came to the time for noses to be allocated to the different nations. He first called a Frenchman and said: "What sort of nose would you like?" The Frenchman waved his hands delicately in the air, and replied: "We would like a nose that can fully appreciate the scent of a beautiful woman." So God gave them that.

'Next God called a German and asked him. The German waved a fist in the air, and said: "We would like a nose that can best enjoy the smell of good schnapps." And so they received that one.

'Then he called an Armenian and asked him what sort of nose he wanted. The Armenian looked at God suspiciously, and after a moment said: "How much are they?"

'God looked rather startled and said: "Well, they're free, of course. There's no cost."

'The Armenian thought for a moment, and then said: "We'll take two…."'

'Ah, I love it. I wish there was something Italian I could offer in return.'

'I think Italy has given plenty to the world in other ways. Healthy and delicious cuisine, for one. Nearly as good as Armenian…. Anyway, I know you didn't come to talk about noses or cuisine. How can I help you?'

'I'm sure you'll have heard of the very unpleasant murder of Dr Mervyn Hardcastle, and I'm here about that.'

'I had indeed heard, and it was disgusting. But I'm not an expert on murder, so what aspects of Dr Hardcastle would you like to ask about?'

'I'd like to ask about his work in plant pathology, which I know is your own discipline, but even before that I'd like to ask what your opinion of Dr Hardcastle as a person was. It is relevant to our enquiry, I can assure you.'

There was quite a pause, which I'd expected. Everyone hesitated when they were faced with that particular question.

'I didn't know him all that well as a person. I found that he could be somewhat abrupt, and I've heard that he could be demeaning to women scientists which annoyed me considerably. I know he was disliked by a number of colleagues, including some who are

Fellows of my Academy. However, I try not to be too prejudiced by the opinions of others.'

'I understand that despite such feelings he was recently elected a Fellow of the Academy.'

'And to that I would have to say that such feelings don't come into it. Election to the Fellowship is purely on academic achievement. And I might mention that I chaired the panel that considered his nomination, so I can speak from authority. His work over a number of years has been quite outstanding.'

'Okay, thank you and I'm sorry to have had to ask that. Now I'd like to come to his academic achievements, and in the circumstances you'll obviously be very well across those.'

She nodded, and she didn't look too upset at any of these questions.

'There are many plant pathologists around Australia, but Dr Hardcastle's speciality was the modes of action of pathogens in harming or killing their plant hosts. If you can understand the mechanisms you may be able to reduce damage or stop it altogether. Dr Hardcastle had had significant success with management of Black Sigatoka disease of bananas, which devastates whole banana plantations when it gets into them, and as you'd know bananas are an important crop for Australia. He'd also made progress against several other diseases, which I can list if it's relevant to your investigation.'

'No, I think at the moment that's fine. I have a heap of papers that were found in his desk and I'm about to go through them, but I thought it would help me if I knew roughly what I was reading about.'

'Well, please let me know if you need further help. I don't do all that much work any longer, and it would be nice to exercise my brain a bit more than I get a chance to do these days. But without wishing to insult you, I would say that you might need a bit of background in plant pathology to make head or tail of some of the papers.'

'You don't insult me at all, but I'll just mention that for a year and a half before I became a policeman I worked as a student forensic scientist. My pathology then was human rather than plant, but I had to do basic general science before I could graduate in forensic science.'

'Well, well – a policeman who's a scientist as well as knowing about Armenian noses. You must be an asset to the AFP. And I'm not being sarcastic, by the way – I do mean it genuinely.'

'I think I'll soon be discovering my limitations, but I'm very grateful for your offer of help. I think the best thing might be for me to go back and gather up the most important papers on which I'd like an opinion, together with questions that I'd like to ask about each, and then I could bring them round to you. However, not all are in English. I can do ones with Italian, and a bit with one or two other European languages, but some are in a Cyrillic language which I can't do. I'd guess that it's Russian.'

'Well, I'd have no trouble if it's Russian.' She must have seen my look of surprise, because she added: 'Maybe you forget that Armenia was part of Russia when I was born. We were one SSR of the USSR – we were the Armenian Soviet Socialist Republic. We were only supposed to read and speak Russian, and of course we were taught in it. That only changed when the USSR broke up. Armenia didn't become independent until 1991.'

'Now that you mention it, it does ring a bell but I'd forgotten it. That must have been rather awful being under Russian domination.'

'In many ways yes. There was strict surveillance at all times, and no freedom of speech. However, there were a few pluses as well. There was some economic development that probably wouldn't have happened without the Russians, and they also suppressed the war between Armenia and Azerbaijan which had been going on for years. I don't think many regretted it when the Russians went, but they weren't the worst of the nations that ruled Armenia over the centuries.

'Since the earliest days we had Romans, Greeks, Persians, Byzantines, Arabs, Mongols and Turks over us at times, and the Turks were the worst. But don't get me started on them.'

'Another day, maybe. Anyway, I'd better get back to my office to sort out the publications for you.' I said hooroo and went back to my office to assemble the papers.

* * *

I was back in her rooms a couple of days later, and I had the impression that she'd been looking forward to a return visit. She must be a bit desperate for company if even a copper's welcome, but maybe it was just that she wanted to see all the papers. Either way, it was fine by me.

I'd made a selection of particular types of papers, and I presented each of them to her with a brief comment. At the end she said:

'May I keep these for a couple of days? I will guarantee to hold them very safely, but it would help me to help you if I could actually read the papers first.'

'I'd certainly be happy to leave these with you. I've made a list of all of them so I could get further copies of any if I needed them before you're finished. But these are the others that I'd like to show you if I may.' I dug out the papers in Cyrillic script and handed them to her.

She took a quick look at each. 'These are definitely all in Russian. I was worried that some might have been in Bulgarian, which also uses a Cyrillic script. There's a scientist in Bulgaria who works on plant pathology and I couldn't have read the Bulgarian, but these are all Russian. I can read them for you and give you a précis.'

* * *

That evening Ella and I were sitting over dinner when I told her about my couple of meetings with Professor Thompson.

'She sounds quite a lady. I'd love to meet her if there's ever a chance.'

'I'd like you to meet her too. I'm sure she wouldn't mind, in fact I'm sure she likes meeting new people these days. I've had the impression that she sits in her college room most of the time otherwise. I owe her a bit of a favour for doing all this work for us. I was wondering if you might be able to bake a few of your Sicilian biscuits or something? We could take them to her to say thank you.'

'I'd be more than happy to do that. You know I always love showing off Sicilian cuisine. I was going to make some *reginelle* again soon, so that'd be a good excuse.'

'I'll probably have to leave her for a couple of days or so to go through what I left with her, and then I'll contact her again.'

'No problem. Just give me the nod. They're quick to bake.'

MOUNT MUGGA MUGGA
FORENSICS

The forensic report from the site on Mount Mugga Mugga had arrived, and Marcus Wiersma called us to a meeting.

'Right guys, this is Fergus Green who'll give us the details of what was found on Mount Mugga Mugga. Go Fergus.'

'Morning all. We first looked over the whole area to gauge what might physically have happened there. There were some depressions in the soil that looked as though a body may have lain there. There were also some patches where the soil had been churned up a bit. Our view was that someone on the ground might have been struggling there, though some of it of course was due to the dog that found the blood-soak. We took extensive samples of soil from the blood-soaked area, plus some samples from soil around there where there was no apparent blood on it or in it. We also took imprints of several shoeprints in the churned-up soil. Unfortunately they looked pretty common in type and pattern.

'The soil that looked blood-soaked was exactly that. The blood type was the same as Dr Hardcastle's, and we recovered DNA from the samples that showed that it was his. In several places there were fragments of skin, presumably from when he was beaten about the head, and they were his also.

'The soil that didn't look contaminated contained nothing unusual, apart from one small bit in a depression that was under a stone. There was a wet patch that appeared to have slight traces of chloroform in it. Chloroform would normally evaporate quickly and totally from soil, but we think the stone preserved it in that spot.

'As you know, a number of cigarette butts were found at the site, eight in total. We've managed to get DNA from several of them. All were from the same person, and that person is not in our database. We're currently polling international crime databases, but nothing's come back yet. We've logged it into the national database in case it comes up anywhere again.

'Finally there were a number of spots around the overall area, behind trees, where urine had soaked into the soil. The people who'd been there had obviously pissed there. It's almost impossible to get DNA from piss, at least if it's been in soil for a while, but two of the samples contained glucose and ketones in addition to the urine, suggesting that the person was diabetic. Not that that narrows it down all that much in the general population. The other thing that those samples tell us is that the people must have been there for several hours to have pissed that many times.

'And that's it, Marcus.'

'Thanks, Fergus. Questions, anybody?'

There was silence from us, and then Bill Hansen piped up. 'If there aren't any questions for Fergus, I'd like to add a bit about access to the site in question. The spot where the blood was found is not all that far from one of the fire trails that provide access to Mount Mugga Mugga. We searched along that trail back to the main road access, which was Mugga Lane. There were some reasonably fresh tyre marks in one or two spots, and we've got imprints of the treads. They don't look anything out of the ordinary, however, like the shoeprints that Fergus got.

'When we saw the tyremarks we wondered how they would have got vehicle access. All the fire trails are secured by a metal gate, which swings open wide enough to allow access by a fire truck if there's a bushfire. The gate's secured by a padlock, and all the padlocks are keyed alike. The firies, and the rangers who patrol the parks, all have keys to the locks. We assumed that the perpetrators must have somehow acquired one of the keys.

'We had one of the keys from a ranger, and when we tried it the lock wouldn't open. It turned out that the original padlock must have been cut away, and they'd then re-locked the gate with their own padlock so that it didn't look as though anything had happened. That indicates a fair bit of advance planning. They must have done a thorough recce of the whole area, and then brought a serious bolt-cutter with them to get the padlock off.'

'Thanks, Bill and Fergus. Any questions from anyone?'

There was general shaking of heads and otherwise silence, so we adjourned.

DR HARDCASTLE'S FINANCES

A day later Bill Hansen emailed me to say that he needed to talk about what he was finding – and not finding – in all of Hardcastle's financial records. He set himself up in one of the interview rooms so that he had room to spread the material out to show me.

'Okay, first off there's the usual stuff – bank statements, details of bills paid like electricity, water, body corporate fees – that sort of stuff. I've looked at it all carefully and I don't think there's anything hidden in that. He has one cheque account at the National Australia Bank, and two credit cards – a NAB Visa and an ANZ Bank Mastercard. I've looked very carefully through it all, and none of that looks dodgy in any way.

'However, he also has an account with a bank in the Cayman Islands, which is probably not something that your average Australian scientist has. The bank is the Cayman Palms Bank, located in Georgetown which is the capital on Grand Cayman Island. Address 29 Royal Bank Avenue, in a building called Grand Towers. There are regular payments into Hardcastle's account from a company called Greenhaven Investments. The only information I've been able to find on Greenhaven suggests that it's some sort of shell company, but it's all very vague. There's absolutely no indication of why Greenhaven would be giving money to Hardcastle.

'The balance in that account went up and down, so he must have been spending the money on something or transferring it to another account, but I can't find any details of what or where. All I can say is it doesn't seem to have gone into his NAB cheque account in Australia.

'Any thoughts about all of that?'

'Well, big-time dodgy for a start, but how we find out more I'm not sure at this stage. I have two thoughts. One is that Jenny may find something in one of the computers that gives clues on this. The second is that we can approach the US experts on dodgy finances and see if they can winkle out any further information. I'm pretty sure the Cayman Islands will be high on their list, and they'll have sources that we don't have. I suggest you go to our finance team and get their thoughts, which'll probably be better than yours or mine, and they should also be able to give you a name in the States that you could contact.

'Meantime I'll tell Jenny to look out for anything relevant to all this too.'

PROFESSOR YEVA THOMPSON

The next day I had a call from Professor Thompson.

'Sergeant Mazzini, I've had an initial look through those papers that you brought me, and I'd like to raise a few points and questions with you. Would it be possible for you to come round some time? Maybe tomorrow afternoon? I've got a few things on until then, but if that suits you it would be good.'

'Thanks, Professor Thompson. I could manage at about half past three if that's all right by you.'

'Fine, and I'll look forward to seeing you then.'

* * *

That evening I told Ella about my forthcoming visit to Professor Thompson and asked if she'd like to come along briefly just to meet the professor, but she said she had a work meeting that would run later than mine. No problem – I'm sure there'll be more opportunities.

The next afternoon I was back at University House. I declined an offer of wine that early in the afternoon, much as I'd have been interested to see what Professor Thompson might serve, but I accepted a cup of coffee. I must find out what coffee she buys – it's good.

'I've been through all the papers that you brought me, in reasonable detail. This pile here covers individual diseases of crops, and is fairly standard plant pathology. Descriptions of the disease organisms, symptoms, in some cases methods of control and so on.

'This next heap has each paper on a specific crop, with lists of all the diseases, and in some cases pests as well, that attack that crop. Again this is all fairly routine plant pathology.

'Then in this heap there are studies on the modes of action of the pathogens – how they invade the plant tissues, what they do to the plant cells when they're inside and so on. That's also fairly standard pathology, but what are interesting are the marks and notes that Dr Hardcastle's put on some of them. He's specifically marked parts that describe highly damaging effects on cells, and he's annotated things like: "could be of some use" and "potential value as attack agent". The latter in particular I would find hard to explain, except with some slightly sinister motive, perhaps? Does this fit with anything that you've been working on in your investigation?'

'That's extremely interesting. I'll have to give you two answers to your question. Firstly, we've had it suggested to us that Dr Hardcastle was looking at biological control agents for noxious weeds, and clearly there would be some advantage then in increasing the pathogenicity. However, we've also picked up a few hints from his computer of something more sinister. So the overall answer is that we can't say yet what the motive might be, but we're beginning to suspect that there might be something deeper in all of this than we first thought.'

Professor Thompson was frowning. 'On your comment about increasing the pathogenicity of biocontrol agents, it might make sense on one level, but I think it would be irresponsible and probably highly dangerous to release something like that into the environment. Biological control generally requires saturation of the environment with the pathogen. Many weeds – probably most, in fact – have relatives that are useful plants, like garden plants or even crops, and there'd be no way to be sure that they wouldn't be attacked as well. I very much doubt that the regulatory authorities would ever give approval for such a release.'

'I take your point. Anyway, our thinking on Dr Hardcastle's death is changing by the day. Our very first idea was maybe a sort of ritual murder to avenge a sexual crime. Then we thought that it was some other murder for a reason as yet unknown, and the murderer had simply gone to bizarre lengths to throw us off any possible scent. However, we're now beginning to wonder if Dr Hardcastle was involved in something nefarious, maybe even with security dimensions, and for whatever reason someone is eliminating him from the field. The elaborate window-dressing of the murder may have been a warning to others also involved in the wider field. That's just a gut feeling at the moment, but it's beginning to feel at least possible, and I think your comments have gone a little way towards saying that we might be right.'

'Right, well I'm glad this may be helping a little. Now I'd like to come to this last pile, and I think that may help you further still. It contains papers that are political more than scientific, and they're about the use of biological agents as tools of warfare. Germ warfare is the major part of that pile, but there are also papers on the potential for using aggressive plant diseases to destroy the crops of enemy countries.

'Now this in itself may not be alarming because Dr Hardcastle may have been studying this on behalf of Australia's security services or something like that. I'm not aware that that was the case, but I'd imagine that it would be kept secret so I wouldn't hear about it anyway. I can't of course enquire further on that, but I imagine your people could check that out.'

'Phew. I have to admit that in my quick read of the papers I hadn't come across those ones, and I'm most grateful to you for drawing all this to my attention. I'll follow it up at our end, and I'll give you as much feedback as I'm allowed to. I certainly owe you that much.

'Now, if it's not stretching the friendship too much further, I have some more papers with me and I wondered if you'd be prepared to give a comment on those as well?'

'I'd be more than happy to do so. I have to admit that it's given me quite a boost, being able to feel that I'm doing some useful work once again. Please give me as many as you'd like, and we can meet again when I've studied them.'

AUSTRALIAN FEDERAL POLICE
HEADQUARTERS

Jenny McIlroy came to my office. 'Tony, we need to talk about what I'm finding on Dr Hardcastle's computer – the one that was in the locked drawer, not the one in the safe. The safe one's going to take a lot more time to get open, and I may have to get help with it. However, I'm already finding stuff on the other one.

'I haven't done many of the emails yet because there's a large number and it'll take me a while, but I've been through the stored documents. A lot of them just look like scientific papers about plant diseases and they don't look dodgy, but there are some that are about biological warfare. There are also some about specific countries and their involvement with biological agents in warfare. Maybe he's been working with our security services on stuff like that, but I'd reckon we need to check that out.'

'Well, that's really interesting you should say that, because I was just with a professor at ANU who's been looking through the papers that we got from Hardcastle's desk and she found the same in them. But I'm afraid I don't have any relevant contacts in the security services that I could go to. I'll have to refer this one to Marcus.'

* * *

That afternoon briefed Marcus on the fact that there could be a security aspect to Hardcastle's murder, and that it might involve dangerous plant diseases. I asked for his advice on which agencies here would know who was doing what in that sort of field, and whether or not they themselves might be involved.

He thought for a minute or two, then said: 'If you want to know about threat evaluation, ASIO would be doing it for threats to Australia, and ASIS for information on what other countries might be doing. But if you want to find out who might be sponsoring that sort of research in this country, I really don't know who might be doing that. I know the Department of Health has a small section that deals with security aspects of health. It might be worth your while to chat to them. But before you do anything I'll brief the Assistant Commissioner on all of this. I'll get an authorisation from him which'll make it a hell of a lot easier for you to approach all these agencies.

'And while I'm loading you with more work, there's one thing I wanted to raise with you. I'd like you to take on one more person in this investigation, and that's Layla Mackenzie. Have you heard of her?'

'Can't say the name rings a bell.'

'Well, she's been working in the anti-terrorism branch for a while, and I think her experience there might be useful to you in this investigation. Now, I'm going to ask you one more thing – do you feel you can trust me?'

I thought: what the hell's going on here?

'I've always found you to be totally straight with me, mate, so yes.'

'So I'm going to add, because you may hear it around the traps, that there's a reason that Layla has to be moved out of where she is, but I will swear to you on my life that this is not a negative about her, and it won't in any way impact on your section and work. You have my word on that.'

Rather mystifying, but I'll live with it. I hope.

A VISIT TO UNIVERSITY HOUSE

Professor Thompson had called again for a consultation about the papers, so I asked Ella if she'd like to come with me at least at the start to meet Professor Thompson. She was very keen, and said she'd make a batch of *reginelle* to bring along.

When we got to the Professor's room I knocked, and when she came to the door I said: 'I hope you don't mind, but my wife was very keen to meet you, so I've brought her along to say a brief hello.'

'I'm delighted! Please both of you come in.'

'So this is my wife Ella, or more correctly I should say Antonella.'

'Ah, so you would be Italian as well?'

'Yes, but I'm authentic. I was born there, not in Cooma. Though I should probably say that I'm Sicilian, not Italian. We respect our history, which was a lot different from the rest of Italy.'

'You must tell me about it, but please sit down first and I'll make some coffee. Now do Sicilians choose espresso, or long black like Italians from Cooma?'

'Absolutely espresso, please. And to go with it I've brought a few *reginelle* to leave with you. They're a Sicilian speciality – sweet sesame biscuits. They originated in Palermo, but you find them all over Sicily now. Other Italians have copied them, but the Sicilian are of course the best.'

Both parties were grinning in this exchange, so it wasn't being taken too seriously.

The coffees came, and the biscuits went down very well. Then Professor Thompson said:

'So tell me about how Sicily differs from mainland Italy?'

'Well, we were frequently not Italian at all. That came relatively recently, when Italy was unified and took a rather reluctant Sicily with it. But in previous times we were ruled by Phoenicians, Carthaginians, Greeks, Romans, Byzantines, Arabs, Normans, Southern Germans, Aragonese, Spaniards and Bourbons, and each of them contributed something to Sicily's culture. I suppose under the Romans you could say we were Italian, but certainly not with the rest.'

'My goodness, that's on a par with the history of my own country, Armenia. So which part of Sicily did you come from?'

'I was born near Marsala, on the far western coast.'

'A beautiful part of Sicily. Your island's the only part of Italy that I've ever visited, and I loved it.'

'Do you remember Trapani, just north of Marsala?'

'The place with the huge salt pans? They were just harvesting the salt when we were there.'

'Well, my father came from Trapani, and I was born there and lived there till I was nine. Then we came to Australia. But my mother was born in Taormina on the east coast of Sicily, in the shadow of Mount Etna. And her house there looked over a town called Giardini Naxos, which is a relic of the time when Sicily was Greek. The name translates as Gardens of Naxos, and it was a Greek settlement which grew food that was then shipped to Greece.'

'May I ask what you're doing these days?'

'I'm a data analyst.'

Professor Thompson gave her a long look, and then said: 'Am I allowed to ask what sort of data you analyse?'

'I work for the Office of National Intelligence.'

'Ah well, then I know that I shouldn't ask any further. I've worked with the Office a couple of times – Office of National Assessments it was in the days when I was involved. I know that your work is security classified.'

'Well, much of it is but my present work actually isn't. You'd probably know that in recent times Australia's been cutting back on its overseas aid program. Any time the government wants to make financial savings it cuts aid first because that's popular with the electorate. Most people think that aid's just giving their money away to other countries, with no benefit to Australia. But as well as hopefully doing some good in poorer countries, the aid buys friendship with Australia which translates into votes at the United Nations and elsewhere in ways that we'd like. As we've pulled back on our aid, China's stepped in to replace us, so the UN votes are now in China's favour. My colleague and I are trying to analyse the economics and politics of all this, and report back to the government.'

'Well, good luck with that. It sounds like it needs to be done.'

The coffee was finished, and Ella farewelled Professor Thompson, leaving the remaining *reginelle* with her. And she and I got down to work.

* * *

Professor Thompson gave me another of her penetrating looks. 'I've looked at the new papers that you brought me last time, and I'm even more concerned now at what might have been going on with Dr Hardcastle.

'I mentioned last time that he'd had some papers dealing with biological agents including plant pathogens as tools of warfare, including the use of aggressive plant pathogens to destroy enemy crops. I've found a few more on similar subjects, but far and away the most worrying are the detailed papers on ergot that I've found.

Did your forensic work ever involve ergot? Do you know what it is?'

'I've heard of it but I don't know much detail. It's a cereal disease, isn't it?'

'It's a genus of fungus called *Claviceps*, and the various species attack cereals and grasses. The most serious is *C. purpurea*, which mainly attacks rye, though it can also affect triticale, wheat and barley.'

'It's rather nasty if you ingest any of the infected cereal, isn't it?'

'That's the understatement of the year. The person who eats infected grain suffers what was called St Anthony's Fire. They have severe burning sensations in their limbs, with muscle spasms, fever and hallucinations. They can become manic, or they may become paralysed. The toxin also causes vasoconstriction which can cause gangrene, and even loss of limbs.

'I've never seen anyone who's had the effects, but I know someone who has and he said it was a real screaming agony for the victim. On the hallucination side, it's interesting that the chemical involved is fairly closely related to LSD.

'Anyway, Dr Hardcastle had made some quite detailed notes on aspects of ergot in relation to how it could be used as an aggressive agent in warfare, and this is truly worrying. I did say earlier that it's just possible that he was doing this on behalf of the Australian security services – have you had a chance to check yet if this was so?'

'No, I'm sorry that we haven't, but in the light of what you say we should probably now do that as a matter of urgency.'

'I couldn't agree more. My worry would be that Dr Hardcastle couldn't have been doing this just as a private venture. If it wasn't with our security services, then it would have been with someone potentially very dangerous who is presumably still out there.'

'Thank you again for bringing all this to our attention. Were there yet more horrors in the papers I brought?'

'A few more on subjects of that type, but that was by far the worst.'

'Well, unless there's anything else I'd better get back and follow up with security. I'm sorry that after the pleasant interlude with Antonella we've had to finish up with something like this, but thank you again for your hospitality.'

'My pleasure, and I'd be interested to know what security says, unless you won't be allowed to tell me.'

'I'm sure I'll at least be able to say whether or not he was with them – just not the detail, perhaps.'

PLANT PATHOGENS FOR
GERM WARFARE?

Back in the office I told Marcus about this new information, and he agreed we should follow up quickly with Australian security. However, he said the request for information should come through the Assistant Commissioner to ensure that we got quick cooperation and detailed information. I prepared a detailed brief, which Marcus took upstairs.

The request from the AC went to ASIO, ASIS and the Department of Health. ASIO replied fairly quickly to say that the broad subject was one on which they had a watching brief for hostile acts against Australia, but nobody was doing anything active against us at the moment. At least not that they knew of. And Dr Hardcastle had not in any way been involved with any of their activities, nor was he on their radar for anything.

The Department of Health replied to say that they had once used Dr Hardcastle to identify a pathogen in a batch of vegetables from a farm in Victoria that had caused an outbreak of food poisoning, but he had not been involved with them in any other way, including any research studies. When we checked further they assured us that the pathogen had not been ergot.

ASIS took longer to reply, but they also sent us a more comprehensive brief on the subject from their point of view. They are actively monitoring several countries that are believed to be developing pathogens for germ warfare, but these are human pathogens. They gave us details of the various projects, and nothing rang any bells with our investigations. They didn't know of any country doing similar things with plant pathogens, but said that if we found out anything they would very much like to know. And finally they said that Dr Hardcastle hadn't been on their radar either.

Time for more research at our end on Dr Hardcastle.

STELLA

One of the first things we need now is more information about Hardcastle's overseas travel for AGRICOZ, so I got in touch with my earlier contact in the organisation, Stella.

We fixed a meeting for that afternoon, and when I arrived she grinned at me and said: 'I was wondering when you'd be coming to ask this. I thought you'd have been here sooner.'

'And why would you have expected me more quickly?'

'Because as I think I told you earlier, Mervyn did a huge amount of travel compared to almost anyone else in the organisation, and there had to be some reason for that beyond just the science. In my view anyway.'

'Hm. If they ever sack you here, we could probably find a place for you in the AFP. So that means that there's going to be an awful lot of records for you to have to look up?'

'It shouldn't be much of a problem really. I think I mentioned to you before that for any travel in this organisation the traveller's had to fill in a form detailing dates, how they would be travelling and the reason for the trip. Until quite recently the form was a paper one – it went electronic about eighteen months ago, but the completed form still had to be printed out and signed off by Admin for accountability. We've always been very careful here because our travel bill's very high, and parliamentary scrutiny's pretty frequent. All the requisitions have been kept filed for the same reason, so all I have to do for you is photocopy all of Mervyn's travel requests and give them to you. After that you've got the much harder job of analysing all the detail.'

'Well, I hadn't expected it to be as straightforward as that. If you could do that it'd be great, and I'll enquire about the job at the AFP if you're interested!'

'Thanks but no thanks. I'm actually quite happy here, apart from this horrible business. But I'll be very glad to do anything to help you sort this out. I'll start copying the papers now, but it'll probably take me about an hour. I'll give you a call when they're ready.'

'Thanks a lot, Stella. If it's easiest, just email them to me.' I wrote down the email address on a slip of paper for her.

'Okay, will do.'

LAYLA MACKENZIE

My new staff member arrived this morning, and I'd been wondering what she would be like, given Marcus's odd comments about her.

The door opened, and she looked in rather tentatively. 'Sergeant Mazzini?'

'Yes, but it's Tony to you if you're going to work here. Welcome, and have a seat.' I waved at the chair in front of me. 'Okay, tell me a bit about your background. How long have you been with the AFP?'

'Six and a half years – all with counter-terrorism.'

'And before that?'

'I did a Law degree at ANU – honours. I got a good result, which helped me to get into one of the good law firms in Canberra – Raleigh, Coutts and Sharpe. I'd always enjoyed Law as a student, but practising it in a firm was actually rather boring. I worked there for about six months, but it never got any better. I wanted something a bit closer to criminal action, but it would have been years before that happened, if ever. Then I saw a recruitment drive by the AFP, and I thought that would take me closer to some sort of action, so I applied and I was picked for the intake.'

'And in counter-terrorism you were doing what?'

'I was mostly analysing paperwork and computer records taken from suspected terrorists, overtly and covertly. We were trying to work out who was plotting what, with whom, where, how – that sort of thing. I loved it. I've always enjoyed puzzle-solving, and that seemed to be the ultimate challenge for a puzzler.'

'But now you've been uprooted and placed with me?'

'Yes, but I'll be happy to work with you.'

She didn't sound a hundred percent confident about that, so I thought I'd probe a bit more – gently.

'Inspector Wiersma told me that it was a forced move, but he said he respected your privacy and he didn't tell me why. He did say that in absolutely no way did it reflect on you or your ability to work in this section. I will also respect your privacy and not ask you, but I will just offer you the chance to say more if you'd like to. But if not, absolutely no problem.'

'Well, it wouldn't be any invasion of my privacy if I tell you, and if you know it might help us to work better together in the future because then there won't be any suspicion between us.

'I got married just over three years ago. Two months ago my husband was driving to Parkes along the Newell Highway to visit his mother who was dying. A semi-trailer crossed to the wrong side of the road and smashed into his car, then overturned and spread itself all over the road. Both drivers were killed instantly. I had to identify my husband's body, and it was the most awful thing I've ever had to do. The injuries were so horrible that they would only let me see his face, but I could sense the rest.

'The shock of that killed his mother almost straight away. I've had a bit of time to process it. I can't say that I'll ever be the same as I was before, but I've had other tragedies in my life when both my parents died, and I've managed to come to terms with it. And in one way it made me even more determined to work to defeat terrorists, who commit similar butchery on people.'

'But now you've been taken away from that. Did they think you'd become too personally involved or something?'

'No, it wasn't that at all. My immediate supervisor couldn't cope with the thought of the grief that I was going through.'

She must have seen my look of incredulity, because she then added: 'It wasn't his fault. He'd had two postings to Afghanistan, and he'd come back with post-traumatic stress disorder. He'd seen colleagues shot beside him, blown to pieces in front of him, and the carnage when a truck bomb goes off in a crowded market place. He just couldn't handle the thought of what I was going through. Ironic, though, that I got moved because he was the one who couldn't handle my grief.'

'Layla, I'm deeply sorry to hear all of this – the terrible death of your husband, and then those events afterwards. You have my fullest sympathy because I've had tragedies as well, and I can understand all of this. In my case it was when I was a teenager and my older sister developed a brain tumour. It was inoperable, but it dragged on for ages. She was in horrible pain, and her behaviour altered in bizarre ways towards the end. It was an awful thing for a boy to see and be absolutely unable to do anything about. So I say again that I do know where you're coming from, and I thank you for being so frank with me.

'I'll add one final thing. The investigation here that we're working on has elements that certainly seem to have security aspects, and it's not impossible that there's a terrorism element too. We're also trying to analyse papers and computer data, so we'll be very glad of your experience and you may not be as far removed from your original field as you might have expected. I reckon you and I should be able to work well together, so once again welcome to the section.

'We weren't expecting you quite as quickly as this and we haven't got your desk organised yet, but it will be by early this afternoon. Come back with your gear at about half past two, and we'll have a little arvo tea for you to meet the rest of the troops. Then you can settle in after that.'

* * *

That timing gave me a chance to get Jenny and Bill in to alert them to the new arrival. I gave them the background on why Layla had been moved, but stressed that it was only so that they didn't say something unfortunate when they first met her. And I told them that they were coming to arvo tea to meet her – not negotiable. I wanted us all to get back on with work as fast as possible.

We have a Nespresso machine that makes good coffee, and we also keep in some good quality teas. In addition I brought out some *reginelle* that Ella had baked. They were intended as another gift for Professor Thompson, but I figured that when Ella heard what they'd actually been used for, she'd forgive me and bake some more.

The expanded team seemed to get on well in chatting, but the clincher came when Jenny and Layla started talking about hockey. It turned out that Layla grew up in Inverell in northern New South Wales, and played hockey when she was at school. Her school used to play in inter-school hockey tournaments against other local schools, one of which was in Glen Innes, and then we discovered that Jenny was at the Glen Innes school and had played hockey there. Not at the same time, of course, because she was older than Layla, but it gave them a common bond.

As they chatted I rolled my eyes at Bill and said: 'Looks like we're on the outer here, Bill.'

'You'd better believe it, Tony,' said Jenny, grinning at me. 'Us girls stick together. We have to in this place!'

The arvo tea over, I let Layla get sorted out at her new desk, and then called her in for a briefing.

'I need to get you up to speed with what we've been doing so far, but first I'd like to ask you one more personal question if you don't mind. Your surname Mackenzie – is that your family name or your married one?'

'My family one. We decided I'd keep my own name after we got married.'

'So does that indicate that you have Scottish ancestry?'

'Yes. Three generations back, but it's there and I'm proud of it. My great-grandfather came out from the highlands and settled on a property just outside of Inverell. My family's been raising cattle there ever since. And I love the bush, and cattle.'

'That's good. I have great admiration for the Scots – a lot of them, anyway. Sound common sense, and they don't suffer fools gladly. But I've also got a special family reason for liking Scots. Have you ever heard of the Italian Chapel in Orkney in Scotland?'

'No, that's a new one on me.'

'It was built by Italian prisoners of war captured in North Africa during the Second World War. They were taken to Orkney, and made to build what were called the Churchill barriers. These were walls across entrances to a bay in which Allied warships anchored, and they were to keep out marauding German submarines. The Italian prisoners wanted their own place of worship, and they were given a Nissen hut and allowed to make it into a chapel. The prisoners decorated it most beautifully, and when the authorities saw how much effort and feeling had gone into it, they provided further materials and a good relationship developed between the Italians and the Scots.

'The little chapel became famous, and later – a long time after the war ended – when it began to decay some of the original Italian prisoners returned to Orkney to repair it. My particular interest in this is that one of the prisoners was my great great uncle on my mother's side. So I've always respected the Scots for being pragmatic and down-to-earth people. I've never been to Orkney or Scotland, but I hope to go one day.'

'I've never been either, despite my heritage. Hope to one day. And since we're on personal subjects, do you mind if I ask you if you're any relation of Antonella Mazzini?'

I looked a little surprised. 'Well, in one sense yes. I'm her husband. Why, do you know her?'

'Well, I wouldn't really say I know her, but she came to work with us one time when we were cooperating with ONI, and she impressed me very much with her work and her approach. Please say hi to her from me – she might remember me.'

'I certainly will. Typical Canberra – everyone knows everyone else here. Anyway, back to crime.'

I filled her in on all the details of the murder, and then the various bits of evidence that we'd so far gathered which wouldn't piece together.

'We've got toxic plant diseases, with evidence that the deceased had been reading about biological warfare aspects. We've got some very heavily encrypted material on a laptop, at security levels that are most unusual for a private individual and which we're still trying to get into. Jenny's our expert at lock-picking and getting into locked computers, but she's been beaten by this one and we're about to get the Signals Directorate to help.

'Then we've got multiple payments over a number of years into the deceased's accounts that come from unidentifiable sources in the Cayman Islands, and anything involving the Caymans is always suspicious. And finally we've got Pepe. We have no idea who or what Pepe is, but we've been told that soon before he was killed the victim expressed worry about his safety in relation to Pepe. And I'd better give you the full story on that one. We were told this, or rather Bill was, by a prostitute who works at the Birds of Passage brothel in Fyshwick. And before you get any wrong ideas, we picked her up as a contact from a video on Hardcastle's computer and Bill recognised her because he used to be in the Vice Squad. The brothels were part of their responsibility. Hardcastle was a regular customer of hers, and he told her about his increasing worry about Pepe. Bill says she should be a reliable witness on that, but neither she nor we have the faintest idea who or what Pepe is.

'On the matter of the papers on plant diseases that may relate to biological warfare, I've got a plant disease expert who's advising on the scientific side, but she wouldn't be across possible political or terrorism aspects. However, I'm wondering whether I've now acquired a colleague who just might be?'

"I'd certainly be prepared to look through it all and see whether anything strikes me. I might just have a different perspective from you guys. Not saying better in any way – just different.'

She raised her eyebrows a little when she saw the volume of material, though I'd sorted it into two piles.

'This larger pile is more general background stuff, and this smaller heap is directly on biological warfare aspects. I suggest if you like you could do the small pile first, and use the other as background if you need it.'

'Very happy to give it all a go. I'll let you know in a bit how it's panning out.'

I left her to it.

* * *

At home that evening I mentioned to Ella that Layla Mackenzie had just joined our section, and why.

'Oh, you're in luck then! Yes, I remember her well. She was in a team that was looking at the emergence of right-wing terrorism in Australia, and we at ONI had some background information from a previous study that we shared with them. I think you're very lucky to have been given her. I thought she was very bright. She never hogged the limelight, but she was always up there doing things quietly, and better than half the guys, I'd have to say.

'One thing she seemed very good at was interrogation. She wasn't obviously confrontational, but she asked all the right questions and was very firm in making sure that she got an answer. And she didn't suffer fools.'

'She comes from Scottish ancestors. That's where she gets all those characteristics.'

'Well, I wouldn't mind saying hi to her again some time, if there's a chance.'

'I'm sure we can make an occasion.'

DR HARDCASTLE'S TRAVELS

Next morning I found an email from Stella with a table listing all of Dr Hardcastle's official overseas travel. She wasn't a lady to waste time.

My first impression was that AGRICOZ must have plenty of funding, because Hardcastle had certainly done a lot of travelling. The list read:

Dates	Destination	Reason for travel
14-28/06/2012	Atlanta, Ga, USA	Attend International Symposium on Weed Control with Plant Diseases
7-22/10/2012	London, UK	Attend International Congress of Plant Pathology
	Oxford, UK	Liaise with UK weed scientists
11-19/02/2013	Montpellier, France	Discussions with French and Australian weed scientists
4-13/07/2013	Berlin, Germany	Present paper at International Convention on Biocontrol
28/11-07/12/2013	Pretoria, S. Africa	Discuss cooperation with South African Dept of Agriculture plant pathologists

19-28/03/2014	Dallas, Tx, USA	Discussion with USDA plant pathologists and weed scientists
2-14/09/2014	Shanghai, China	Participate in Review of Chinese weed control science
27/10-08/11/2014	Porton Down, UK	Discussion on safety of dangerous plant pathogens
03-17/03/2015	Montreal, Canada	Attend International Congress of Biological Sciences
19-30/04/2015	Tehran, Iran	Discuss possible cooperation with Iranian weed scientists
12-25/08/2015	Singapore	Attend Symposium on control of weeds in Asia and Australasia
18-29/11/2015	Baton Rouge, USA	Discussions with USDA plant pathologists
02-18/02/2016	Oxford, UK	Chair review of UK weed control operations
15-27/05/2016	Stockholm, Sweden	Attend Congress on Peaceful Uses of Plant Pathology
08-14/07/2016	Vienna, Austria	Visit International Atomic Energy Agency to discuss radiation control
05-13/11/2016	Dubai, UAE	Participate in discussions with Middle East weed scientists
14-28/02/2017	Shanghai, China	Attend Chinese National Symposium on plant pathogens for weed control
26/08-03/09/2017	Atlanta, Ga, USA	Discussions with USDA plant pathologists and weed scientists
11-26/11/2017	Rio de Janeiro, Brazil	Attend meeting on weed control in South American countries
29/01-09/02/2018	Paris, France	Attend meeting on international protocols for safe use of plant pathogens
10-17/02/2018	Montpellier, France	Discussions with French weed scientists
16-25/05/2018	Atlanta, Ga, USA	Discussions with USDA plant pathologists

Apart from the cost to the taxpayer it looked to be a reasonable list, though I thought I might show it to Professor Thompson at some stage in case she has any useful comments on it. She must have been to plenty of meetings like that in her time, and might have a different perspective from mine.

The surprising thing in Stella's email was that all she'd been able to send was a consolidated list of dates, destinations and purposes. She said that at this stage she'd been unable to locate the actual forms that would show who'd approved the travel – she didn't know what had happened to them.

AUSTRALIAN SIGNALS
DIRECTORATE

I got an email from Jenny McIlroy to advise me that she was still having trouble getting into Hardcastle's second computer, so I went to her office to talk about it.

She said: 'This is the toughest nut to crack that I've ever encountered. I've had about four that I couldn't get into in the ten years or so that I've been here, but this one's just impossible. I don't think there's anyone else in the AFP who could do it. You suggested the Signals Directorate the other day. Could you organise it if that's okay with you?'

'Absolutely fine by me. If I remember right you've got a good contact there anyway?'

'Yeah, Fiona Hauptmann. I've already given her an informal call and she can fit it in if we can get the approval organised.'

'All right, I'll let Marcus know. I'll do the paperwork, but it'll have to go through the Assistant Commissioner. I'll keep you posted.'

The Australian Signals Directorate is one of Australia's security services – its main task is to listen in to military and other communications going around the world. However, a subset of it is the Australian Cyber Security Centre, which is where Fiona Hauptmann works.

It took three days, but then we were on. The Signals Directorate itself is in the Russell complex of Defence Department buildings, just up the road from our own HQ across King's Avenue bridge over Lake Burley Griffin. The Cyber Security Centre, however, is a bit further away in the Brindabella Park Buildings next to Canberra Airport. We drove there with the computer securely in the car. At the front desk of CSC we were stripped of our mobile phones, and negotiated a rather tortuous entry to the building through several careful checks. Eventually Fiona came with passes, picked us up from the security desk and took us to her office.

Jenny did the honours. 'Fiona, this is Tony Mazzini who I told you about. He'll brief you on the case we're investigating, and then I'll fill you in on the computer.'

We each of us gave Fiona our spiels, and she then said:

'Thanks for those details. It often does help for clues on what sort of encryption's been used, though I can't guess at this stage what yours might be. Can you leave this with me for a day or two, and I'll get back to you? And I ought to mention at this stage that if it's really difficult I may have to get Louis to help. Louis Chantal's the top among our encryption breakers, but he's also autistic and he's short on communication skills so I won't introduce you to him at this stage. It's more likely to throw him than help.'

'No problem with all of that, and good luck!'

AGRICOZ MASTER KEYS

While Fiona was dealing with Hardcastle's laptop, I wanted to catch up on a few loose ends. I called Pete Smith of AGRICOZ Security to ask if I could come in to get a list of who had what master keys for access around the AGRICOZ site.

As I'd expected, he said the written list was classified and he couldn't give me a copy, but he'd be happy to give me a verbal run-down. I find it odd that all these people think they can withhold potential evidence from the police in a major murder enquiry, but I didn't want to rock any boats until I had to. People cooperate better if you don't have to monster them.

'First the overall master keys that can open any lock on the site. The Director-General of the organisation has one of those master keys, as does the Deputy DG, and the Chief Administrator. I have one as head of Security, and four masters are kept in the safe in the main security office. They're the ones that the nightwatchmen use when they do their night rounds, and they have to be signed in and out.

'After that there are some partial masters that the cleaners use when they go round in the early mornings to clean the corridors and labs. There is one key per shift, which opens just the doors relating to that shift and no others. Each of those keys is also kept in the security office, and signed out and back in for each shift.

'Every other member of staff has a key that just opens the doors relevant to them – no masters. And all the keys are of a type that can only have duplicates cut by an authorised cutter, who will only do it with written authorisation from AGRICOZ. In our case the locksmith is CLASS in Fyshwick, and I've always thought they're pretty trustworthy.'

'Which leaves open the question of what the suspects used to open the corridor to the dung beetle labs, but the vision isn't good enough to see exactly what and how. We'll take that one on notice. Thanks for your help on this, Pete – we'll be in touch further.'

DR HARDCASTLE'S FINANCES

Bill Hansen came to me and said: 'Mate, you know I've been looking through all the financial papers that we got from the apartment in Kingston. There's some things that don't add up. I reckon you need to have a look at them.'

'Fine by me. It might help us to make a bit more progress than we're doing at the moment, which is two-fifths of bugger all.'

'Okay, I already told you that Hardcastle had the usual bank accounts that you and I would have – a cheque account and Visa card with NAB and a Mastercard with ANZ. Since then I've discovered that he also had a savings account with the Bendigo Bank, and an American Express account. I'm talking about Australian accounts, not the Cayman Islands one that I told you about earlier.

'I think the Amex one may have been a corporate card through AGRICOZ, and we can check that but it doesn't really matter because there's nothing odd about most of the transactions in those accounts. He had his salary paid fortnightly into the cheque account. It was a fair amount, but he was a senior scientist so nothing suss there. His credit card transactions were normal, and he settled them up every month from the cheque account.

'What's missing is how he paid for the Kingston apartment.

We know from the papers you found when you first searched his apartment that he owned it, and I reckon the apartment would have cost around four and a half million – maybe even a bit more. There's no payment remotely like that in any account. I reckon we should find out who built that particular block, and how much that particular apartment cost, and then try to find out where the relevant agent received the payment from. In the circumstances they're going to have to tell us. We can stress that we're not implying they're crooked in any way – more that we don't think Hardcastle paid it and we'd like to know who did.'

'No argument there. I'll brief Marcus on this, but go for it. Let me know if you need help in any way. Anything else?'

'There is one more thing. There are a number of payments into the savings account, and they aren't transfers from the cheque account. It could be that he's getting dividends or something from other investments, though I haven't found many papers suggesting that he's got a lot of shares or anything, and the amounts are more than normal share investments would yield, and a bit more often. There's no indication in his records of the source of these, and I think we should heavy the Bendigo Bank to find out where they came from. Again no suggestion that they did anything wrong – just that we need that as background for a murder case.'

'Go for this too, Bill. Any more again?'

'If I went through the accounts with an even finer toothcomb I might find that some other things don't appear to have been paid for by him, like some of his furniture for example. But I think we should follow up first on the apartment and the savings account. They're so far ahead of anything else we may not need the finer detail.'

'Okay. I suggest you contact All Homes to find out who built the apartment block and who the selling agents were, and then contact all the names that you get. The polite approach just asking for help in an enquiry – we can come the heavy later if there's resistance.'

'Will do, straight away. I'll keep you posted.'

MORE COFFEE AT THE
FEDERAL GOLF CLUB

Ella phoned me from work to say that she'd just had a text on her phone from her friend Susie, who'd given me a lot of help with background on aspects of AGRICOZ. The message had said: "Would like to have another coffee at Federal. Suggest 1030 tomorrow if OK. Pls advise. Love Susie."

Ella said: 'I'm sure she isn't after coffee with me at that hour. It sounds as though she's after you, but doesn't want anyone to know she's meeting with you. Sounds a bit ominous if you ask me. Can I send her an acceptance, or are you tied up then?'

'No, I'll be fine for then, and I think I'd like to hear what's happened. Could you send her an okay, please?'

'Will do. See you tonight.'

* * *

I got to the Federal Golf Club first again, and was once more enjoying the scene when Susie arrived. When she arrived she sat down in a hurry and said:

'I desperately need a cup of coffee. It's your shout – take my membership card and you'll get the discount. I'll have a strong black, thanks. Then we can talk.'

Coffees served, she said: 'I don't know what the hell's going on at AGRICOZ, and I'm worried. Apparently Dr Stephen Harrington, who was Mervyn Hardcastle's immediate superior, has suddenly been told that he's going on extended leave, and a placement has been arranged for him at a laboratory in Montpellier in France. They do research of various sorts on weed control there and Harrington's a weed scientist, so the placement makes sense, but not the sudden rush. It sounds as though the management's trying to get him out of the way. For what reason I can't begin to guess, but it worries me. This is not the organisation that I've been proud to work for.'

She handed me a card with details of the French laboratory on it. 'This might be handy in case you want to follow up on this, though I don't know quite what you can do.'

'This is a bit of a shock to me too. We hadn't been homing in on Dr Harrington yet but we would have, and I don't like being pre-empted like that. I'll discuss it with my boss, but thank you very much for bringing it to my attention. Do you know Dr Harrington well enough to say what sort of a bloke he is?'

She took a long draught of her coffee, then said: 'I don't really know him because he isn't the sort of person who communicates much with others at AGRICOZ. You know how some people chat happily in the canteen or wherever to all sorts of other staff. Well, he's never been one of them, and he's always seemed a bit surly if one tried. Surly or maybe just shy, but I thought surly.'

'I can't at this stage guess what he might have known that AGRICOZ wouldn't want us to hear. I don't suppose you've got any thoughts on that?'

'Probably no more than you would. Maybe he knew something that Dr Hardcastle had been doing that he wasn't supposed to, but what's more mysterious is why the senior management would then try to hide it. And just a further thought – please be careful if you take this up with the management that there's no clue that I told you about it. I'd be out of a job, but you'd also be losing one of your contacts inside the place.'

'Don't worry about that, Susie. We may be plodding coppers, but not quite that bad. We can simply go to management and ask to meet with Dr Hardcastle's superior officer, and when they say he's no longer there we ask where we could find him. And it might be interesting in the light of your comments to see what their response to that is.'

'Thanks, Tony. And thanks for the coffee – I needed it today. This sort of thing really isn't my cup of tea. Sorry, no joke intended!'

* * *

After Susie had gone I sat for a moment longer and thought about this new development. There absolutely had to be something on the nose about this, and I very much need to know firstly why and secondly who is behind it. I certainly will go to AGRICOZ's management as I'd said to Susie, but maybe I also need to find out more about Dr Hardcastle's overseas jaunts and what went on during them. I recalled that Stella had told me that every scientist who goes on an official trip has to put in a trip report afterwards, so I decided I'd call Stella and ask her to dig those reports out for me.

* * *

When I did ring Stella said: 'I'm sorry, the reception's terrible in here. I'll just go outside into the garden. It may be better there. Can you just hang on?'

This seemed a bit odd because the call sounded loud and clear to me, but when she resumed outside all was explained.

'I'm sorry about that but I couldn't risk being overheard in the office, at least if they'd realised it was you. Just yesterday I was told that I wasn't to provide you with any information about Dr Hard-castle's travel. I said that you'd already asked me for the information on where he'd been, and I'd provided a list of dates and destinations since it was an official police request. I said it was nothing more than a list, but they weren't pleased even about that. Then they took away all the files with his trip reports in them, just in case you asked for those too.'

'Bugger, that's just what I was ringing you to request today.'

'If I thought that something like that might happen I'd have copied them for you, but it never occurred to me. I'm very sorry, and I'm disgusted by this sort of behaviour in an organisation that I'd been proud of up to now. I don't like it happening in my workplace – it's underhanded.'

The same reaction as Susie's to the skulduggery.

'Stella, could I ask you who it was who came to you about this?'

'It was the Chief Administrator, Mr Portillo. However, I'd guess that it wasn't his idea originally. I think he was merely doing the donkey work for someone else.'

'Thank you so much for filling me in on this, Stella. I'm as concerned about it all as you are. We're trying to investigate a very serious crime, and I absolutely can't imagine why anyone at AGRICOZ would want to impede us in that. I'll be taking this further, but in the meantime I can assure you that we'll keep your involvement in all this completely confidential. Just hang in there and act normal – you'll be fine.'

'Okay. One final thing before you hang up. If you do need to contact me again, could you please do it not via work. I remember you gave me your email address earlier, so I'll send you my private phone number and home address shortly. I won't mind you contacting me via either of those – just not through work. I really want to see you sort this horrible mess out.'

'Thanks, Stella. No problems, and I'll guarantee any necessary confidentiality.'

* * *

Back in the office I organised an urgent meeting with Marcus Wiersma and told him about the sudden posting of Hardcastle's superior and then the removal of all of Hardcastle's trip reports. He didn't say anything for a moment – just frowned heavily.

'Well, this is becoming a bugger's muddle all right. What the hell are they playing at over there?'

'I'd like to know what they're playing at, but also who exactly is making these sorts of decisions and why. There's something very fishy that they're trying to hide. But is it the whole management or is it just an individual?'

'Well, I'll leave you to work out what you want to do, but please keep me posted at all times. And if you need any of our heavy guns brought in just let me know. I'm not having us buggered around like this. Who do they think they are?'

'One thing I'd like to get organised is for the guy who's shot off to the south of France to be interviewed by someone from here. I know that'd cost travel funds, but I think it's vital to get his take on all this. He may be as guilty as anyone else, but a skilled interviewer should be able to sort out what's going on.'

AUSTRALIAN FEDERAL POLICE HEADQUARTERS

I called Jenny, Layla and Bill in to my office.

'This case is getting more complicated by the minute, and I think it'd be a good idea if we could meet every day to compare notes and share what's been happening.

'The latest development on my front is that AGRICOZ are up to something very strange and probably dodgy. They've very suddenly posted Dr Hardcastle's superior officer to a weed laboratory in the south of France, and they've confiscated and possibly destroyed copies of Dr Hardcastle's trip reports on all his overseas travel. Presumably they're trying to cover something up, but what and who's behind it I haven't worked out yet.'

Jenny piped up at that stage. 'I may be able to help you on the trip report part. I'm pretty sure that when I went through the computer that I was able to open, there was a folder in Word that was full of what seemed to be travel reports. Maybe he drafted the reports on his computer and then submitted them to his management. I'll go and check after this meeting, and I'll forward them to you if they're there.'

'That'd be fantastic if that's right. I've been thinking we're about due for some luck our way. If you've got them, save them on to a stick and give it to me. I'll look through them as a matter of urgency and see if I can pick what they might be trying to hide. Anything from anyone else?'

Bill chipped in with his bit. 'I've found out that Dr Hardcastle's apartment building was built by Tower Mansions, and the original selling price for his penthouse would have been $4.2 million. As far as we know he bought it new, but I've still got to find out which agent sold that particular unit. Different ones in that block were sold by James Bros, Allied Property, Kingston Real Estate and Location Properties. I'm waiting for that info now from All Homes. They were very helpful with the name of the builder – I hope to get this other soon.'

'Good, keep us all posted. Any more?'

Bill spoke again. 'I've also had an answer from Bendigo Bank about the regular payments into Hardcastle's savings account. They came from the Cayman Islands, and the source name was Greenhaven Investments. That's the same mob that was also paying into Dr Hardcastle's Cayman Island bank account.'

'Jesus, this all sounds mega-dodgy. You'd wonder that the Bendigo Bank didn't look into it themselves from a source like that in the Cayman Islands, but maybe they did and it looked okay. I guess there are some honest people in the Caymans. I'll try to find out a bit more on this Greenhaven mob – I've got a CIA contact in the Department of Defence who could help with that. More from anyone?'

There was nothing so we adjourned.

DR HARDCASTLE'S TRIP REPORTS

Jenny had given me a stick with what were indeed the trip reports from Hardcastle's computer. I plugged it into my computer and settled down with a large cup of black coffee to read them.

The first visit was to a symposium in Atlanta. Hardcastle noted that he'd given a poster presentation, and he made a number of comments on various other presentations at the meeting. He also mentioned being approached by someone from a non-government agency that was trying to promote the use of plant pathogens for weed control as an alternative to harmful chemical weedicides. He said the agency was called CROWD – the Consortium for Research on Weed Diseases.

Out of interest I put that name into my computer to see what came up. A site appeared, but it mainly contained vague generalities and one certainly didn't get any idea of anything practical that they seemed to be doing. It was a bit odd, and it would be interesting to see if they came up again in later reports. The address given for the agency was in Baton Rouge, Louisiana.

The next trip was to London for an International Congress of Plant Pathology, followed by a visit to Oxford to liaise with UK weed scientists. Oxford was Hardcastle's old university and he no doubt spent a bit of time renewing former acquaintances, and if reports were right also whingeing about Australia and Australians. However, none of that made it into the report.

The trip after that was a definite hardship effort – to Montpellier in the south of France. Home to some nice wines and equally good food. He was visiting a weed research laboratory there where both French and Australian weed scientists worked. The Australian scientists were looking for pathogens to control Australian weeds that were of Mediterranean origin, such as Paterson's Curse. That was interesting in that it's also the lab to which Hardcastle's superior officer has very suddenly been shunted off. I'd imagine that he'd be too senior to be doing practical weed control work nowadays, so what's he really there for? We need to find out.

Trips to Berlin and Pretoria didn't throw up anything of great note in the trip reports, but then there was a visit to Dallas in Texas. That was to liaise with plant pathologists and weed scientists in the US Department of Agriculture, but it was interesting that he noted another meeting with CROWD there. Those guys evidently get around.

Next he participated in a review of Chinese weed control, based in Shanghai but they also travelled out to some field sites to see experimental work. That would have been a feather in his cap to have been on such a review mission, and it was probably also an interesting bit of travel. However, the trip after was a grimmer one – to Porton Down, near Salisbury in England. Porton Down is operated by the UK Ministry of Defence and conducts research on chemical and biological warfare. Much of their work has been on chemical agents, but some also on human diseases such as anthrax, botulinum toxin and plague.

None of that is directly relevant to plant diseases, but Hardcastle seems to have discussed aspects of plant diseases that also have human toxicity. However, he didn't put much of that detail into the report – he just noted that he would be giving the DG of AGRICOZ a private briefing on the outcome.

There was nothing of particular note in the next three reports, for Montreal, Tehran and Singapore. Then he went to Baton Rouge in Louisiana to meet with US Department of Agriculture scientists, and again he encountered CROWD there. Maybe not surprising since Baton Rouge is given as the HQ address for CROWD on its web site, but why would Hardcastle keep on meeting with them?

My eyes were glazing over somewhat at this stage, so I had a break for lunch. I looked at the bowls of salad in the cafeteria display counter, and wondered how much weed control had been needed for their production. And what sort....

Then back to the reports. After chairing a review of UK weed control science in Oxford – he was coming up in the world if he was now Chair – Hardcastle went to Stockholm for a congress on the peaceful uses of plant pathogens, and then to the International Atomic Energy Agency in Vienna to talk about radiation control. Again the reports were a bit light on for detail of discussions of both of those visits.

Dubai and Shanghai were next and were straightforward, and then he went to Atlanta again to the US Department of Agriculture. And CROWD yet again, though he seemed to be a bit cooler about them on this occasion. I do need to find out a lot more about that agency.

After a visit to Rio de Janeiro for a meeting on weed science in South America, he went to Paris for meetings of a panel developing international protocols for the safe use of plant pathogens. There was clearly an increasing focus on safety issues in Hardcastle's work, but I'd had a nagging feeling for a while that he could be either a goodie or a baddie in that area.

Two final trip reports – one a straightforward visit to Montpellier again, and finally one back to Atlanta. Again there was a meeting with CROWD, and this time the general tone was quite negative about the organisation. But frustratingly, without any detail on why.

I need to talk all this over with Marcus, but first I've got to find out more about CROWD. I'll call my CIA contact in the Defence Department and ask for advice on tracking down mysterious organisations in the States.

* * *

Chuck Doherty was in his office when I called.

'Hi Chuck. It's Tony Mazzini here.'

'Tony, good to hear from ya. You still with the AFP? The ethics committee hasn't caught up with you yet?'

'They did, and I passed with flying colours. So good in fact that they've given me one of the shittiest cases you could imagine. That's what I'd like to talk to you about, to share the pain. I reckon you might be able to help me with a bit of info.'

'You wouldn't be referring to the case of the dead doctor in the doodoo, would ya? Even the press in the States has been going to town with that one.'

'Right on, unfortunately. I was wondering whether we might meet up for a quick chat? I'll shout you a coffee – maybe at the café just under our building if you're free?'

'I'm free, but I'll suggest a café near here instead. It makes some of the better coffee that you can find in this goddamn country. Kiitos, in the C5 development just past the ASIO building. Meet me at the corner of Constitution and Reg Saunders Way, and we can walk down there.'

'You're on. I'll be there in about fifteen minutes if that suits?'

'Okay by me. See you then.'

I didn't pay any attention to the goddamn country reference. I knew that Chuck was on his second term of posting to Australia, at his own request.

We wandered down Constitution Avenue making small talk, until we got to Kiitos which I hadn't ever seen before. Chuck allowed me to buy the coffees – what a surprise that was – and we sat outside at a table in the sun.

'So why do you need to drag me into the shit along with you? If you'll pardon the expression.'

'Nothing would bring me greater pleasure, believe me, but I'd actually just like your opinion on what an organisation in the States might be. Our victim was a senior scientist who used to go to a lot of conferences and other meetings overseas. A number of them were in the USA, and he seemed to have had a lot to do with an organisation with the initials CROWD. That supposedly stands for the Consortium for Research on Weed Diseases, which sounds like a mickey mouse sort of title. It's not a government organisation, but we can't find out who or what's behind it.'

'Well, I could pass a query on to one of my buddies back home, but it doesn't sound like the sort of thing that'd be high in their target list.'

He sounded sceptical, and I couldn't blame him.

'It gets better, though. Our victim had been receiving regular payments from a bank account or accounts in the Cayman Islands, and I don't have to tell you that we're having a hell of a job tracing back who's making those payments. It's something called Green-haven Investments, but that doesn't really seem to exist.'

'Ah, well now you're getting more relevant. The first thing that suggests to me is drug-trafficking. Any suspicions of that sort of thing?'

'None at all. That was one of our early thoughts too, and although we can't totally rule it out there's absolutely no evidence to link him to any activities of that sort. But somebody was paying him to do something.'

'Any information at all about this CROWD mob?'

'All I can tell you is that their headquarters is in Baton Rouge, and he met with them there once, once also in Dallas, and at least twice in Atlanta.'

'Hm. All southern states, where there's quite a lot of right-wing activity, racial bigotry, that sort of thing. So one other scenario that could suggest itself is something to do with terrorism. Any possible links there?'

'Not that we've been able to find so far. The only other thing I can tell you at this stage is that soon before his death the victim told someone he was becoming increasingly frightened of someone or something called Pepe.'

'Ah, well now you might be getting right back into the drug scenario. That sounds very much like Mexican drug cartels, or similar. Now I will get back to my mates about this – they might be interested to follow up on CROWD if they don't already have the dope on them. If you'll excuse that expression...'

'Thanks, Chuck. And thanks for introducing me to Kiitos – you're right about their coffee.'

'My pleasure. Always good to be able to educate the natives.'

DR HARDCASTLE'S LAKESIDE APARTMENT

Bill Hansen came to me again with some progress on the purchase of Hardcastle's apartment.

'I got hold of a very helpful guy in All Homes. Apparently he'd been wondering about the circumstances of the purchase of Hardcastle's apartment at the time when it went, so he remembered who the selling agent was. The firm was Kingston Real Estate, and the agent who did the deal was Laura Karpinsky.

'So I got an appointment with Laura, and told her what had happened to Hardcastle and that we were trying to get some background on his finances in case it helped to identify his killer. I didn't want her to think that we were in any way looking into dodgy dealings by her, although that could always come out of it.

'I said that we had an idea that somebody other than Hardcastle had paid for the apartment, yet it was put in his name as the outright owner, and that seemed very odd to me.

'She said that it wasn't all that unusual, though in the majority of cases it was a guy buying a place for his mistress. Less often it could be a woman buying it for her toy boy. However, she did accept that

Hardcastle's case was quite unusual, and she says that she enquired quite carefully into the background before the deal went through. The purchaser was a company called Blue Horizon. Laura did say that she couldn't identify what sort of business it was. However, they managed to persuade her that they had the necessary funds, and that they wished to pay and make Hardcastle the owner.

'Laura then wondered whether this was some sort of tax evasion dodge, but they managed to talk their way out of that one as well. They said that it wasn't payment to Hardcastle for work done, which would have attracted tax on what would then be income, but it was just that they were interested in the work that Hardcastle was doing and wished to encourage it.

'So the relevant papers got signed for the purchase from Tower Mansions who had built the apartment, with Hardcastle registered as the owner. Blue Horizon came up with the relevant bank cheque which went through okay, and Laura accepted that there was a sale and that was the end of it. No doubt her commission was in her mind as well – she wouldn't have wanted to torpedo the deal unless it was really dodgy.

'So I think she didn't really act inappropriately, but there's something very suss about it all because I tried to find out more about Blue Horizon and I've drawn a complete blank. I don't know who the hell they are.'

'Thanks, Bill. That's a big help. Yet another thing to investigate further, but we're beginning to pin a few things down now. I'll ask the Fraud Squad if they know anything about Blue Horizon. We might just get lucky.'

LAYLA MACKENZIE

As Layla got to work this morning I called out and asked her to come into my office as soon as she was ready. She frowned slightly, possibly wondering if she was in trouble, but she came in a few minutes later.

'Hi Layla, sorry to grab you so quickly, but I didn't want to miss you. And before I forget it, my wife Ella says hi, and she does remember you well. You obviously made a good impression on her.'

She murmured rather vague thanks, and still looked a bit apprehensive.

'Ella seemed particularly impressed at your skills in interrogation. Does that surprise you?'

'Well, it was kind of her to say that. I don't know that I've had all that much experience, but I quite enjoy doing it. It's a challenge to draw as much information out as you can, and I like that sort of challenge.'

'Well, it so happens that we have a job that needs someone to do some important interrogation, and you might just be the best choice for it. I just have to ask one more thing – how's your French?'

'*Assez bien. Pourquoi demandez-vous?*'

'Right, but you'd better just translate that for me because my

French is shaky. Italian I can do, but I'm not so good with French.'

'What I said was: "Not too bad. Why are you asking?"'

'That's pretty good. How do you come to speak French as well as that?'

'I had several years of it at school which gave me a start, and then I had a French boyfriend at uni for a while, and we chose to speak French quite a bit because I wanted to learn it better. It was also a bit more private when there were lots of other students around.'

'Okay, now we just have to convince Inspector Wiersma that you're the right person, because he doesn't really know you.

'So I'm telling you now that Inspector Wiersma is of Dutch ancestry, and his family collaborated with the Germans during the Second World War. They were strong Nazi sympathisers, and recently evidence has come to light that Inspector Wiersma himself still holds views like that. He's been talking to a Serbian fascist organisation, and to another group that regularly wears swastikas and other Nazi symbols and goes round setting fires in Muslim-owned shops.

'Beyond that, CCTV picked up vision of someone looking very like Inspector Wiersma going into a Halal Grocery in Curtin and threatening the owner to the point where the owner was cowering behind the counter. That was late in the evening of last Saturday.

'What I'd like you to do is to go to Inspector Wiersma and interrogate him on all of this. I'll give you an hour to work out how you'd like to go about it and what questions to ask him. He's been told to expect you in his office at ten o'clock this morning.'

She gulped audibly and was clearly wondering what the hell this was about, but to her credit she didn't ask.

'Okay, Tony – I'll see what I can do. I'd better go and work out some questions pronto. *Tout de suite*, in fact…'

TRANSCRIPT OF INTERVIEW BETWEEN LAYLA MACKENZIE AND MARCUS WIERSMA

MACKENZIE: Good morning, Inspector Wiersma. I've been asked to establish a few pointers about your personal background in relation to your position in this organisation. I believe that you're originally of Dutch ancestry?

WIERSMA (aggressively): I'm a bloody Dutchman, yeah! So what?

MACKENZIE (calmly but firmly): And I'm a Scotswoman and a straight speaker, so nothing. I think the Dutch have given the world a lot, but some of them have held views that are regarded as not politically acceptable in Australia.

Silence for a moment.

WIERSMA (still aggressive): Are you accusing me of something?

MACKENZIE (still calm and firm): I'd be interested to hear your views on extreme right-wing groups in Australia.

WIERSMA (dismissively): There's a lot of exaggeration and bullshit in the socialist press about that sort of thing. I don't think groups like that really exist. There's always been political differences in Australia, but so what?

MACKENZIE (sharp flip): Do you ever shop in places like the Halal Fruits and Vegetables at Mawson?

WIERSMA: What the hell's that got to do with it? No, I wouldn't go into somewhere like that. They have all sorts of unnatural practices. They should never have been let into the country.

MACKENZIE: So what do you think should be done about that?

WIERSMA: Well, the bloody Australian government's never going to do anything about it, so maybe a few loyal Aussies should take some action instead.

MACKENZIE: What sort of action do you think might be possible?

WIERSMA: Oh, putting the frighteners on them for a start. Maybe if things get uncomfortable enough for them here, they might up and off home. A few late-night visits to their shops or homes, a suggestion or two that there might be accidents or something. Nothing illegal of course, just some suggestions.

MACKENZIE: And is this something that you've been helping with yourself?

WIERSMA: No, of course not.

MACKENZIE (sharply): So you wouldn't have been in the Halal Grocery in Curtin late last Saturday, speaking aggressively to the owner behind the counter?

WIERSMA (aggressive again): I told you, I wouldn't go into dumps like that. You never know what you might pick up there. They're dirty in their habits.

MACKENZIE: But we have CCTV footage that shows you inside the shop, doing just that.

WIERSMA: Well, it can't have been me. There's plenty of guys who'd look rather like me. I would have been at home then, anyway.

MACKENZIE: Is there anyone at your home who could confirm that?

WIERSMA: Well, my wife could.

MACKENZIE: So would you mind if we called on her just to verify that fact?

WIERSMA: Well, actually she wasn't in Canberra that day. She was visiting her mother in Sydney.

MACKENZIE: Is there anyone else at your house who could confirm that you were there?

WIERSMA: Nah, all the kids have left home. They've gone overseas. Couldn't get jobs here. The jobs have all been taken by the Muslims, you know.

WIERSMA again: Okay, we can call a halt to all this now. In case you get the wrong idea about me, the only thing that was true about me in all of that was that I do have part-Dutch ancestry, from two generations back. Hence the surname Wiersma, but that ancestor lived in Indonesia as it now is, and he married a local Muslim woman. So I'm certainly not prejudiced against Muslims. You can come in now, Tony.

[END OF TRANSCRIPT]

'Right, Sergeant Mazzini has been listening in to this interrogation. As you've probably now guessed, we just wanted to see how you'd handle an interview like that, with an aggressive subject who also happened to be your superior. I thought you did well, and you didn't seem fazed by my seniority. The questions were well-targeted at getting out what my supposed prejudices were, and they were direct and unambiguous. And Tony, you wouldn't have had the visual aspects, but I can say that Layla looked very directly at me, and I felt pressured into giving some sort of answer. No overt pressure, but I did feel that I had to give an answer.

'Tony, maybe you could take Layla out and explain what we had in mind and check that it's okay with her. And well done, Layla – I'm glad I wasn't really like that because I was actually a bit uncomfortable with where you were taking me.'

* * *

I took Layla back to my office and got coffees for both of us.

'Okay, I'm sure you've guessed what all that was about – Dr Harrington's sudden departure for the south of France. Marcus wants someone to go over there and interview Dr Harrington. We'd like to know what he knew about Dr Hardcastle that might have led to the murder, anything about Hardcastle's background, what he was doing on his very frequent trips. That could also lead into whether or not Harrington knows anything about CROWD, and maybe even PEPE. A further area of questioning would be the money that Hardcastle was receiving from overseas, and behind everything would be the question of why Harrington went off to France at such short notice.

'This would all be helped by skill in framing questions and the sequence in which they get asked, and I can say that after listening to you grilling Inspector Wiersma I think you could do a pretty good job at it. So we'd like to send you to the south of France to have a go at it. Will you?'

Layla gulped slightly. 'If you really think I could I'll be happy to give it a go. I'll work out some questions and maybe float them past you beforehand. But what about backup? If I'm to get anything that may be required as formal evidence later on, there has to be a second observer.'

'We were thinking of Donovan Lewis. Do you know him?'

'I can't say I do, no.'

'He's been working for the AFP, but based in Sydney and liaising with the New South Wales Police. He's asked for a transfer back to Canberra, and Inspector Wiersma thought we could use an extra person in this investigation.

'I don't know him well but I've met him a couple of times. He's level-headed and mature – he joined the AFP relatively late. I think he could be quite a good back-up for you. I'll introduce you to him and you can check him out, then let me know if you'll be okay with him.'

AUSTRALIAN SIGNALS DIRECTORATE

It was three days before Fiona Hauptmann got back to us, but at least it was good news. She called Jenny to say that Hardcastle's small computer was open, so we went straight over to collect it.

Fiona was looking very pleased with herself. 'We didn't think for a while that even we were going to get it open, and it was Louis who finally did it. It seems to have been encrypted by a system developed in America – very sophisticated and hard to crack. The good news is that none of the contents of the computer seem to have been further encrypted, so you'll be able to read all of them. My guess would be that the owner of this wasn't a coding expert himself. I'd be pretty sure that somebody else set it up for him, and he just ran it after that. And it would have been someone very professional who did it, so you might like to enquire about that too.'

'Thanks big time, Fiona. You guys probably justify the huge amount that the taxpayers shell out for you.'

She grinned. 'Can you say that about the AFP, though?'

'Probably not, but Jenny here makes up for it.'

'By the way, when we were running through the computer to

check that nothing else was encrypted, I noticed that there was a great deal of stuff dealing with some science laboratory in Georgia in the USA. As I said, it seemed to be an American system of encryption that was used so you might like to check out any deeper association there. It might be just coincidence, but I thought I'd mention it.'

'Yeah, thanks. If you're ever looking for a transfer, there might be a spot for you in the AFP.'

'God, I hope I'm never that desperate...'

THE SMALL COMPUTER

My next most urgent task was to see what was on Hardcastle's small computer. I settled down in my office with a large black coffee, and opened the machine up.

There were quite a few different folders in the directory. One that immediately caught my eye was "Personal notes on overseas trips." There was a document for each trip, and it was a sort of personal diary of anything that struck him particularly that probably wouldn't have gone into the official trip report.

I went through them in date order of the trips, so the first was when he attended a weed control symposium in Atlanta, Georgia. He noted that he'd been contacted by a representative of CROWD, which he identified as the Consortium for Research on Weed Diseases. He was told that they were very interested in his work on the use of pathogens for weed control, and they offered him some extra personal funding for him to assemble a dossier of pathogens available, their plant hosts and their degrees of pathogenicity. He accepted the offer, and gave them bank account details for a transfer of funds. However, CROWD indicated that it would be easier for them to set him up with his own account at their bank in the Cayman Islands, and he could then do his own transfers from that as it suited him.

I smelled a large rat here, but Hardcastle evidently didn't.

The next trip was to an International Congress of Plant Pathology in London, and Hardcastle noted that there had also been a representative of CROWD there – a different person from the one in Atlanta, but this one seemed to know all about Hardcastle's work.

The next visits to Oxford and Montpellier had no significant comments in this diary, but then there was Hardcastle's attendance at an International Convention on Biological Control in Berlin. Again CROWD had a person there, and Hardcastle noted that this time the person was a bit more demanding of the information that CROWD had paid for. He told them that he was assembling it but it was a big task. However, he offered to send them what he had so far gathered.

Next came a visit to Pretoria which had no special comments, followed by a visit to the US Department of Agriculture in Dallas, Texas. CROWD was again there, and this time they asked him for a side meeting with several of their representatives to discuss their funding and its results in more detail. The meeting took place with four people from CROWD, and Hardcastle noted that he was a bit puzzled by the people who didn't seem to have much detailed understanding of the science of plant pathology. He queried them on this, and they said that they weren't so much scientists as benefactors for the human race. Their motivation was to get various sorts of science, in this case plant pathology, applied to benefit humanity, and this was why they needed the real specialists like himself to do the actual work.

The smell of the rat was getting quite strong by this stage, but not apparently to Hardcastle, though he did sound a bit muted in his enthusiasm this time.

The next trip to Shanghai to conduct a review of Chinese weed science had no special comments, but the one after certainly did. It was to the Defence Science and Technology Laboratory of the UK

Ministry of Defence at Porton Down near Salisbury. The lab was set up during World War I to research chemical weapons such as mustard gas, and it later expanded to other chemicals such as sarin and other equally toxic agents. There was also research on biological agents, initially anthrax and botulinum toxin.

Hardcastle didn't record all of his discussions there, but he noted that in 1942 there had been broad-scale testing of anthrax on Gruinard Island just off the west coast of Scotland. Eighty sheep were taken to the island, and anthrax bombs were then detonated on the island as a result of which the sheep died. Even worse, the island was so contaminated that it had to be quarantined from 1945 to 1990, and it was only in 1990 that public pressure forced the government to decontaminate the island so that it became safe again.

Hardcastle discussed this work with the Porton Down scientists in relation to his work towards large-scale field release of pathogens to control weeds over a broad area, and as a result of the talks he obviously began to have some doubts about how well the strategy might work – or at least how safely. He noted that he would need to inform CROWD of this.

His opportunity came on his next trip, which was to a Biological Science Congress in Montreal. A representative of CROWD was once more there, and was quite concerned at Hardcastle's news. He said that CROWD had been providing significant support to Hardcastle, and they wanted some practical results for their investment. This evidently at last rang some alarm bells for Hardcastle, from the tone as much as the content of what CROWD had said, and back in his motel room he checked the Cayman Islands bank account that CROWD had set up for him.

To his initial surprise, and then dismay, he found that a considerable amount of extra funding had been deposited there. He began to wonder if he might be accused of something unethical or illegal if that came out, and he wondered whether he could refund the money to CROWD. But he suspected that that would be difficult, and he began to be alarmed at what they might do if he tried.

* * *

I had to stop reading at that point. There was a knock on the door and Bill Hansen said: 'Your mate Chuck from Defence would like to have a chat to you. He said you'd need to do it today because he's going back to the States for the next three weeks, and you need to hear what he's got before he goes. He said three o'clock at the same café as before, if you can make it.'

'Tell him I'll be there.'

That would certainly be too important to wait.

* * *

I had to buy the coffees again, but I was expecting that.

Chuck was looking a bit more excited than usual. 'Man, have you stirred something up with your enquiry. You can forget anything to do with drugs, like I said it might be last time we met. It looks as though it's white supremacists.

'My pal in the FBI knew this CROWD mob in Baton Rouge, but he said that the letters didn't stand for Consortium for Research on Weed Diseases like you said – they call themselves the Campaign for Restoration of White Democracy. Some of 'em even say Campaign for Restoration of White Domination. A lot of Southern gen'l'men who reckon that the Ku Klux Klan has lost its way and they want to get some action going again. The core organisation is PEP, which stands for People for Ethnic Purity, and they have Enforcers each of who's known as a PEPE. So your Pepe's no drug cartel guy, but he's probably just as nasty.'

'Christ, I was afraid of something like this. I've just been going through some notes that the victim made on his private computer, and that's the picture that's beginning to emerge from the notes.'

'Anyway, the FBI's also interested in the financial dealings of this mob and they'd be keen to share notes with you on that. They've got someone in the Embassy here who's the local FBI rep, and she'd like to talk with you. Mo Summers is her name.'

'I'm more than happy to do that. Give me her contact number and I'll fix a meeting.'

* * *

Mo Summers couldn't meet me until the next day, so I went back to Hardcastle's personal notes on his trips.

The next trips were to Tehran and Singapore. There were no issues of great note in either, except that Hardcastle had felt a bit uncomfortable in the Islamic atmosphere of Tehran. However the next one, which was to Baton Rouge, provoked quite a long essay in Hardcastle's computer.

Hardcastle had had a confrontation with the organisers of CROWD. He told them that he wasn't happy with the sort of work that they seemed to be expecting him to do, and he wanted out. They told him in no uncertain terms that he'd accepted money from them and they now wanted delivery for their money. Hardcastle offered to refund the money in full, and they said that that was not acceptable. And they pointed out that there was a lot of their money in his Caymans account, and they could publicise that fact widely. They suggested that that would not enhance his reputation in the scientific world. It finished with a stalemate, and an increasingly worried Hardcastle.

He next had to chair a review of weed control science and operations in the United Kingdom. It would have been a feather in his cap to have been given such a prestigious position, especially as a UK graduate himself, but he must have had in the back of his mind the worry about his association with CROWD being publicised.

Ironically the trip after that was to Stockholm, to attend a

Congress on the Peaceful Uses of Plant Pathology. A bit two-faced for someone at least unintentionally involved in some uses of the subject that were far from peaceful.

Trips to Vienna, Dubai and Shanghai didn't raise any significant issues, but then he went again to Atlanta – a key centre for CROWD. On this occasion CROWD told him that he had to start organising some trials of wide-scale release of plant pathogens to destroy crops. They told him about one area of rundown farmland in Georgia that they had secured for such a trial. They would pay for labour and materials, but Hardcastle had to instruct them on how a large enough quantity of the pathogen could be prepared, and in detail on the strategy for application. They would do the rest, except that Hardcastle would be required to attend after the trial was conducted to assess the results.

By this time Hardcastle appeared to have succumbed to the pressure. He agreed that when he was back in Canberra he would write out all that was required and send it to CROWD. His private comment in the trip notes was that maybe it wouldn't do any harm to run such a trial because it would almost certainly show CROWD that it would never work in practice as a means of aggression against other nations.

There were no personal notes on his next trip to Rio, but the trip after that was to Paris to discuss international protocols for the safe use of plant pathogens. Ironical again, considering that he was planning to help CROWD to conduct trials that were likely to be anything but safe.

The next trip was to Montpellier and there were no personal notes, but after that he went again to Atlanta. He must in the meantime have sent CROWD some detailed instructions for a field trial, because when he met with them in Atlanta they described the results of the trial to him. It had not gone well. He told them that that was probably because they didn't have enough direct experience at that sort of work, to which they replied that they had been paying him a lot of money and they expected better service than that. Much better.

There was clearly a major argument, which finished with Hardcastle saying that the whole idea was crazy, he would refund their money however he could, and he intended to get out. He then walked out of the meeting. He noted further that for the rest of his time in Atlanta he kept an eye open for his safety, but there was no overt threat or action.

And there were no further personal notes on that part of the computer because Hardcastle took no further trips. By then he was dead.

MO SUMMERS

Mo Summers had agreed to come over to my office for a discussion. By a stroke of luck Ella had just baked a new sort of Sicilian biscuit the night before, and I conned a few from her to offer to Mo Summers.

When Mo arrived she wasn't what I'd expected – she was small and motherly-looking. However, she had dark and piercing eyes that belied the motherly bit, and I soon discovered that one didn't mess her around.

She accepted an offer of coffee, and I served Ella's new biscuits with it. Mo looked at the biscuits and said:

'San Pietro?'

'Wow, you know more than me on this. My wife baked them, and she said they were *Chiavi di San Pietro*, or Keys of St Peter. She said they're a recipe from Palermo that her mother used to bake. They used to be made for the feast of St Peter, and they represented the keys to heaven that were held by St Peter. How come you know them?'

'I was based in the Embassy in Rome for a while, and my local bistro used to have them. Rome was my favourite posting. Plenty of scope for someone investigating money laundering over there, with all the varieties of the Mafia that exist in Italy.'

'Including in Sicily,' I murmured.

'Indeed. From your name, might you be Sicilian?'

'No, but my wife is. I was born just down the road from here, but my parents were Italian. Not Mafiosi, though.'

Mo grinned. 'No, of course not! Okay, on to the money. From what Chuck said I'm guessing that your main interest in this case is who killed your scientist guy. My part of the FBI tracks dirty money of all sorts, and how it's laundered and through where. My brief here's mostly drug money in Australia, but my colleagues are very keen to follow up on what Chuck says you've been finding on this white supremacist group back home. You wanna give me all the background on where you're at?'

I filled Mo in as briefly as I could on the weed background and the possible use of pathogens to destroy crops, and then Hardcastle's increasing worry about the true intentions of CROWD. After that I described his murder, and then what we'd so far found out about money transfers to Hardcastle.

'He'd been receiving regular payments from something called Greenhaven Investments, from an account in the Cayman Palms Bank, Grand Towers Building, 29 Royal Bank Avenue, Georgetown, on Grand Cayman Island. The account was set up in his name by this CROWD mob. We haven't managed to find anything out about Greenhaven yet.'

'Well, it sounds like a typical Cayman Islands sort of set-up. I've had a number of cases involving the Caymans but I don't recall either the Cayman Palms Bank or Greenhaven Investments. However, we've got a local rep over there and I'll send him all your details and get him to investigate further. There'll be plenty of interest if it gives us a handle on a right-wing terror group. I'll give you a call as soon as I've got something.'

'That'd be great – we'll welcome anything you can come up with. There is one other thing that I'll mention. Our victim had a very expensive apartment purchased for him by something called Blue Horizon – they paid for it and put the apartment in his name as the owner. The agent queried the deal at the time because she was worried that it was tax evasion, but they said that they wished to encourage Dr Hardcastle's work and it was a gift. But we've been chasing up on Blue Horizon and they don't seem to exist. They were able to present a bank cheque for the purchase, but that's all we know. If you happen to come across them in your chase after dodgy finance, we'd love to know.'

'Okay, I'll take that one on notice too.'

'Thanks, Mo. And my wife'll be happy to know that someone actually recognised her Keys of St Peter!'

DONOVAN LEWIS

Donovan Lewis arrived today, and I introduced him to the troops, explaining that he and Layla were to go to France to interview Dr Harrington. I was pleased to see that he blended in quickly and easily with the others. I told him that Layla had come to us from Anti-Terrorism, and he said that while he was in Sydney he'd had some contact with their Sydney operation and was impressed with it.

He told us that he was a relatively recent recruit to the AFP, and Layla asked what he'd been doing before that. He said that he had an agricultural background from a family canola farm in New South Wales, but he'd felt he wanted to do something a bit more adventurous so he tried to get a position with the Food and Agriculture Organisation of the UN.

'They were going to get me to go to Afghanistan to provide training and assistance to farmers, and a requirement was that you had to undergo security and safety training before you went. They've developed a series of special CDs for this. Each one has lectures on different types of security threat, and then a series of scenarios that test out what you've learned. They set you up with a visual scenario, and you have to work your way through it without being shot, blown up or whatever. You have to get to the end of each scenario without making a mistake, and if you get everything right you get a code number which you submit back to FAO. No code number, no job.

'The scenarios are visual. The one I did showed a winding road in a desert sort of area, and I had to plan and take a convoy of twelve trucks along the road from A to B. The first thing you have to do for that is split the convoy up. No more than four trucks in a group, so that if there's an attack only one small group is taken out.

'Then you have to look for possible ambush points. I recognised the low-level bridge over a dry wadi that might have explosives under the bridge, and I took the convoy through the wadi away from the bridge.

'After that there were blind corners around which an ambush might have been laid, high points where snipers could lurk, waiting for passing traffic – things like that, and you have to dodge all of them. I thought I'd negotiated every one of them perfectly, but I failed to spot a place in the road where the gravel surface had been a bit scratched up. That was where an improvised explosive device had been buried, so I was blown to smithereens along with my truck.

'So I didn't get a code for that, but they do allow you one more go. The next CD had a different scenario but similar sorts of threats. I concentrated really hard, and I made it safely to the edge of the town that was the final destination without being shot or blown up. And then I was shot dead by a sniper hiding in the first building of the town. Apparently I shouldn't have gone in through the main entrance to the town.

'Anyway, I didn't get a code and I couldn't try again, but I'd already decided that the daily stress level would be higher than I was prepared to cope with, so I looked around for something else and the AFP came up as an appealing option. I signed up, and I haven't regretted it. And one thing the experience did do for me was give me the greatest admiration for those who are prepared to take on that sort of job. I can certainly understand how too much of it can give someone post-traumatic stress. That's an absolutely real thing.'

I glanced at Layla as he said that, and she gave me a rather grim nod.

ANALYSIS OF OBSTRUCTION

Marcus was becoming increasingly agitated about our relative lack of progress in this case. He called us together and said:

'One thing that's been bugging me increasingly about this whole thing is the attitude of AGRICOZ. I think all of us who were at the briefing first thing after the body was discovered saw their evasiveness on various issues. They've been saying "Oh, it's all to do with confidentiality", but we're the police, for God's sake, not their commercial competitors. And they're legally bound to give us all the information they can when we're investigating a murder.

'It goes beyond that, too. They deliberately withheld and in fact destroyed information in their computers relating to Hardcastle's travel, trying to obstruct Tony's investigations. We were lucky there in that all the information was in Hardcastle's own computer anyway, and some of it was quite revealing.

'And then there was the attempt to prevent us interviewing Hardcastle's senior officer, Dr Harrington, by sending him at almost zero notice to the south of France, and making out to us that this was a trip that had been planned long before. I have serious doubts about that, and Layla and Donovan will be investigating it further very soon.

'There has to be somebody inside AGRICOZ who's associated with this mob and is actively helping them. So one thing we need to do urgently is find out who in AGRICOZ wants to hide what from us, and why, but I'm in two minds about how to do this. I'd originally thought that we should go in with all guns blazing, read the riot act and demand the answers, that sort of thing, but now I'm thinking that all that might do is shut the key people up and we won't then be able to identify them. We might stand a better chance if we look as though we're still ignorant, but go in quietly and firmly to ask questions of various of the staff. Any thoughts from any of you on that?'

I was the first to chip in. 'I have a contact inside the organisation who's already provided some useful information. She's middle level so she mightn't be privy to everything that goes on there, but she's also been in AGRICOZ for a long time. Furthermore, she's very pissed off about how AGRICOZ has been acting in all of this. I can talk to her again and see what I can find out. I think she'd be prepared to let me know anything she does have, but we're also going to need information on the high-ups there and I don't think she'll be so useful for that. You'd need someone at a higher level.'

'Thanks, Tony. Go for it with your contact, but I agree that we'll need the higher-level information. I'm convinced that someone there is a problem. Any thoughts from anyone else?'

There was silence for a moment, then Layla spoke up.

'I've got an alternative suggestion to going in and asking questions of the senior staff. You know I used to be with the anti-terrorism branch, and we had good contacts also with ASIO working on the same. They'd actually be very keen for their own purposes to know who was doing what if there's someone in AGRICOZ who's related to domestic terrorism, and they have ways of accessing information from an organisation's computers, and people's personal computers. You don't want to ask how, but it can happen. I could sound out a relevant person if you like, and we could take it from there.'

Marcus said: 'I think that's a great idea, Layla. Get a list of the senior staff at AGRICOZ, and go for it as quick as you can, before you leave for France. Anyone else?'

I said: 'I can quickly do the list of the senior positions in AGRICOZ and the names of the current holders of each position. I've already got some of it, and it should be on their web site as well. I'll put it together asap and send it to all of you. Layla – tic-tac with me on this.'

AGRICOZ SENIOR STAFF LIST

It didn't take me long to pull the names off the web site. Each also had a short spiel on the person's background and specialities:

Director General – Dr Harcourt Johnson
> Degrees in Economics and Politics; various senior positions in Federal Departments including Science; basically a very senior public servant, up to Secretary level, but not an agriculturalist.

Deputy Director General – Dr Ratko Petković
> Environmental engineer, originally from Bosnia. Lectureship at University of Sydney; specialised in treatment options for animal waste.

Assistant Director General 1 – Dr Barbara Plumley
> Fruit fly specialist; worked for Queensland Department of Primary Industries, and then Australian Quarantine.

Assistant Director General 2 – position currently vacant

Chief Administrator – Frank Portillo
> Various administrative positions in Australian Public Service.

Assistant Chief Administrator – Remy Marchand
Born in Réunion; worked for French Ministry of Agriculture in several administrative positions.

Chief Security Officer – Pete Smith
Australian Army, then worked for Securicor and other security companies.

Chief Personnel Officer – Frank Arbuckle
Previously Chief of Personnel with a large confectionery company.

Chief of Animal and Veterinary Science – Dr John Newman
Animal physiologist; graduate of Cambridge University; previously Reader in Animal Physiology at University of Reading, UK.

Chief of Plant Science – Professor Claudia Thomson
Graduate of Sydney University, specialising in various methods of crop improvement through plant breeding, including genetic engineering. Joint Professorship at University of New South Wales.

Chief of Pest Management – Dr Rafael Paulsen
Graduate of Cambridge University, where he then became Lecturer in Plant Pathology. Moved to private laboratory in USA, then to AGRICOZ in Australia. Specialist on fungal diseases of crops, but has also researched virus diseases.

Chief of Soil Science – Dr Peter Forsyth
Graduate of Flinders University; specialist on fertiliser science.

Chief of Molecular Science – Dr Ronald Varghese
Graduate of Melbourne University in Physical Sciences; switched to molecular science at Berkeley University, California. Speciality: application of molecular science to genetic engineering.

Chief of Environmental Science – Dr Helena Sweetman
    Graduate of Harvard University, originally in entomology.
    Then became interested in alternatives to chemical control
    of pests and diseases, and overall improvement and safety of
    inputs to agriculture.

Dr Harrington wasn't high enough up to be on the list, but he was only one level below Dr Paulsen, and in the same Division.

I looked at each entry, considering whether any might have a background that could suggest right-wing terrorism. I couldn't think of any directly, but could there be a slight pointer or two? Dr Paulsen has worked on fungal diseases of crops and also worked in a private lab in the USA. Some sort of right-wing place? Dr Varghese and Dr Sweetman also have American connections. Dr Petković could have a background with Eastern European terrorism? We need more detailed biographical information on all of these.

I put these names and thoughts together and emailed the list to the whole group, including Marcus, and suggested that we meet again as soon as they'd looked at the list.

When we met, Layla was the first to speak.

'If I'm not jumping the gun, I'd like to kick this off if you don't mind because it's very much what I was doing in Counter-Terrorism before I came over here.

'It'll sound like a textbook lecture, but it's the lecture I was given when I joined Counter-Terrorism and I reckon it's good background. There are currently two main sorts of terrorist threat in this country. One is Islamic and the other is right-wing or neo-Nazi. Everybody's aware of the Islamic terrorist threat – Muslims wanting to kill infidels and set up Islam as the state religion. Fewer people are aware of the right-wing threat, and until recently it hasn't been all that large. There was the Ustasha Croatian group in the 1960s, but that was specifically aimed against Yugoslav migrants in Australia, not the whole community. It was also Croatians training to go home and fight Serbs. They used to meet in remote forest areas, particularly in Victoria and Western Australia, and do various sorts of military training. They had potential for harm, but not much really came of it.

'However, in the last few years there's been an expansion of the right-wing groups, and they're becoming very much more threatening. Some people think that they're just a reaction to Islamic terrorism, but there's only a handful for whom that'd be true. The majority are males whose creed is neo-Nazism. They want to become a dominant master race. They set themselves up with banners with swastikas on them, they arm themselves, they undertake military training in remote areas like the Ustasha did, and they work hard to recruit other males who'd be susceptible to their master-race thinking.

'They've been going for the longest time in the United States, and you've probably heard of some of them. The Proud Boys is one of the better-known ones, but there are others. They and others have been actively working to recruit susceptible males in other countries like Canada, the UK and Australia, and they're having some success. The CROWD mob that Dr Hardcastle was involved with would be one of these organisations.

'One neo-Nazi organisation in Australia's already been banned – it was the one called Sonnenkrieg Division. It promoted white male supremacy, the killing of any people with mixed race partners, any women who were ethnic mixtures, anyone who is Jewish, raping of female police officers – the list goes on. And there are others that haven't been banned yet.

'I'll finish with one of the nastiest bits. Amongst other ways of showing their male dominance, some of the men abduct young women, rape them multiple times, and then carve swastikas into the flesh of the women's abdomens. So now you know the sorts of people you may be dealing with.'

There was a stunned silence after this last bit, then Marcus said:

'Well, in case you need motivation there it is. So let's look at AGRICOZ specifically. I'm increasingly sure that this isn't just an outside crime aimed at AGRICOZ and Dr Hardcastle. I reckon there's at least one person and maybe more inside that mob who's sympathetic to CROWD and what it stands for. These people could have lined Hardcastle up with CROWD, and fed CROWD with information on how he was going. We need to find out who they are.'

Nobody spoke, so Marcus said: 'Layla, you're our counter-terrorism expert. I'd welcome your views on this.'

Layla gulped slightly, and said: 'I'll give you a few thoughts, but please remember that I wasn't very far up the pecking order in counter-terrorism. But I can make a start.

'I reckon you're spot on in suspecting there's at least one person in AGRICOZ who's involved, and maybe more than one. And I also reckon that it would have to be someone pretty high up in the organisation – middle or lower people wouldn't have the power and authority that would be needed.

'My other reason for saying that it's someone senior is the very sudden shunting of Dr Harrington to the south of France – that could only have been done by someone well up the ranks. So I think we should look at the senior staff carefully first.'

'Okay, let's start at the top. The DG, Harcourt Johnson?'

I spoke up here. 'Talking to people in AGRICOZ I've had the impression that he's a figurehead more than anything. We did see him at the first meeting with AGRICOZ after the murder was discovered, but I think he simply had to put in an appearance then. He was formerly Secretary of the Department of Science, but he's been in that sort of position in various departments. His background is politics and economics, and he isn't a scientist himself. I think he's in his position mainly for political clout and influence, and I doubt he would do specifics like scientific programs or movements of staff. Bear him in mind by all means, but others could come first.'

'Right, the Deputy DG, Ratko Petković.'

Layla said: 'The name suggests eastern European ancestry. That can certainly be a factor towards right-wing terrorism.'

'Agreed. Could you ask your mates in the counter-terrorism branch to look into him, please?'

'I've already passed them the list of names of senior staff because they were quite keen, but I can ask them to look at him particularly.'

'Well, let's see first if there are more. Assistant DGs – there's only one at the moment – the other position's vacant. Though we should check when the vacancy occurred. If it's recent the previous person could have been involved. Tony – will you follow up on that please.'

'Will do.'

'The one who is there, Barbara Plumley. Any thoughts on her?'

'No pre-disposing factors there, and we've said that women are less likely to be into right-wing terrorism. Her field of work used to be fruit flies – nothing to do with crop diseases. I think we can count her out for the moment.'

'Then we have the Chief Administrator, Frank Portillo, and the Assistant Chief, Remy Marchand. I can't really see anyone in their positions being able to unilaterally shunt Harrington off to France. Nor the Chief Personnel Officer. What about the Chief Security guy?'

I said: 'I think he was in the army before he joined AGRICOZ. If he served in Afghanistan he might be strongly anti-Muslim. Is that fair, Layla?'

'It can certainly happen with some Afghanistan vets, yes.'

'Okay, please check further on that. However, I still think that people in those positions wouldn't be influencing the scientific research programs, and couldn't just shunt a senior scientist off to another country suddenly.'

'That then leaves us with the Chief Scientists – the heads of each scientific division. Two are women, and we've agreed that they're probably not so likely. We don't know much about the men, but I would note that two have had connections with the United States, and we should look at that further. They are the molecular scientist, Ronald Varghese, and the Pest Management guy, Rafael Paulsen. Paulsen spent some time at a private lab in the States – we should find out a bit more about that.

'As a general comment, I'd note that someone at that level would have the authority to get Dr Harrington offshore quickly, and probably also to get Dr Hardcastle involved with the CROWD mob. I'd also note that Paulsen was presumably Hardcastle's overall director. Tony and Layla, could you follow up on all of this, please?'

'Will do, Marcus. I'll pass the names on to my FBI contact as well. One or more of them might just ring a bell at her end too.'

Layla spoke up. 'You're right in general about women being less inclined towards this sort of activity, but I note that Helena Sweetman is originally from America, and according to Tony's notes she's involved with control of pests and diseases by ways other than chemicals. That's sort of related to what Dr Hardcastle was doing. I think we should at least keep her on our radar.'

'Good thinking, Layla. One final point. All those comments are based on the slenderest of evidence, so I think we actually have to leave everyone in the frame at this stage, and go more deeply into each. Tony – can you get on to your contact inside AGRICOZ and see if you can get any greater depth on any of our names?'

'Will do, Marcus.'

'That's probably it for the moment, but let's all get together again the moment any positive info comes in. We've got to make some hard progress on this quickly.'

How true that is.

To get things moving I got Ella to ring Susie and suggest coffee at the Federal Golf Club again. I'm becoming wary that someone in AGRICOZ may listen in and blow my contacts there, but I didn't think anyone would suspect one golf mate lining up another for a coffee. Unfortunately Susie said she couldn't do it the next day because she would be harvesting an experiment all day, but she offered ten o'clock the day after. Yet another frustrating delay, but there wasn't really an option.

* * *

I emailed Stella at her home address to ask her for the name of the person who'd been in the second Assistant Director position before it became empty, what their field of work was, and how long the position had been empty. Layla meantime had contacted people in the Counter-Terrorism unit, and they would be following up while she and Donovan travelled to the south of France – which was due to happen in a couple of days' time.

Meanwhile I hoped to make some progress with my coffee with Susie.

SUSIE

We met once more at the Federal Golf Club, and it was my shout for coffee again. Then we got going.

'Susie, thanks for meeting with me yet again. We're not making as much progress as we'd like with this investigation, and I need a bit more background on some of the people in AGRICOZ. Same rules as before – if you're not happy about saying anything you don't have to, but if you can it might well help me.'

Susie just nodded, and sipped her coffee.

'We have an increasing suspicion that Dr Hardcastle may have got himself mixed up with a right-wing terror group, and it's just possible that someone inside AGRICOZ may have that sort of association.' I didn't want to frighten her off at this stage by making firm accusations.

'We're beginning to profile people who may have been in a position to influence what Dr Hardcastle did, and also to have Dr Harrington shunted off to the south of France at short notice.

'The first person I'd like to ask you about is your Assistant Director General, Ratko Petković.'

Susie frowned at me. 'What exactly would you like to know?'

'What sort of person is he? Is he very authoritarian, for example?'

She snorted slightly, and said: 'You're a long way off the mark there. He would have to be one of the nicest people there is in AGRICOZ. His main role in the organisation is smoothing out problems created by other people, not least the DG. He's the nice guy who talks to people sympathetically and sorts the messes out.

'I'm pretty sure about this judgement because I've had a lot of contact with him. You know I said I'm one of the harassment contact officers in AGRICOZ. I've been to him quite a few times to consult with him on how to handle problems that I've been faced with. I couldn't of course tell him exact details because contact officers have to keep any cases confidential – it's up to counsellors to sort them out. But I used to give Ko the broad outline and just get his take on how I should react, and I always found him wise and helpful.'

'You called him Ko. Does that mean he's generally approachable? It doesn't sound like he stands on dignity too much.'

'Everybody calls him Ko around the place, and I'd say he's pretty much everybody's friend.'

'Okay, I obviously didn't pick the best name to start with. The next category that I wanted to ask you about is the heads of each scientific area. Do you know much about any of them?'

'Well, I know my own of course. Claudia Thomson's Director of Plant science, which covers plant improvement which is my area. She's a very nice person, straight and decent, and I would find it hard to believe that she's involved in anything untoward. For the rest of them, I don't really know them because I don't move in those elevated circles. I did meet Dr Newman, the animal scientist, once when we had a joint trial of his cattle eating my new strain of feed wheat. He also seemed a decent sort of person, but I wouldn't say I saw enough of him for a good judgement. A good friend of mine plays bridge regularly with Helena Sweetman, the environmental scientist. I could ask her casually what sort of person Helena is if you like. For the rest of them I can't really help you.'

'I would certainly be interested to get someone else's view of

Dr Sweetman. And then I guess the other person I should ask you about is the Director General, though I know he's more of a figurehead than an involved scientist.'

'Hm, I'm not sure that I'd call him just a figurehead. You're right that he's not a scientist himself, but he does take a fairly close interest in what goes on. As far as what sort of person he is, I haven't really heard because he doesn't seem to associate much with AGRICOZ staff. People don't seem to find him very friendly, and there have been one or two complaints about bullying. But he seems to be away from AGRICOZ a lot of the time. Probably lining up his next Secretaryship in another department. I suspect he's quite ambitious.'

'Well, thanks for all of that, Susie. It's orienting me much better on who's what at AGRICOZ. Now it's up to us to do some of our own research.'

* * *

That evening I had an email at home from Stella, who said that the second position of Assistant Director had been vacant for over six months. The original incumbent had been a livestock scientist called Malcolm Robins, who'd been on sick leave for several months before he left the position. It didn't sound as though he'd have had any involvement in the present goings-on.

SENIOR CONSTABLE
LAYLA MACKENZIE

INTERVIEW IN MONTPELLIER

I'm trying not to be daunted by this assignment – it's the most important one I've been given since I joined the AFP. You only get one chance like this, and failure's not an option. Sergeant Mazzini would shunt me on somewhere, which would be a pity since I enjoy working with him.

I discussed the whole operation with him before I left Australia, but there's only so much you can plan in advance. With interviews like this one you've just got to go where the interview takes you.

We're going to interview Dr Stephen Harrington, the immediate supervisor of Dr Hardcastle who was murdered. He was very hastily and suspiciously packed off to Montpellier in France when we – meaning the AFP – started asking questions into the background of Dr Hardcastle's activities at AGRICOZ. Behaviour of that sort by official bodies like AGRICOZ gives me the shits, so Dr Harrington will need to be forthcoming. It may not have been his decision or fault, but I'd like to know why.

You have to have a separate observer with this sort of interview, and I've been given Donovan Lewis as my back-up. He's slightly junior to me even though he's several years older. Tony said that Donovan joined the AFP late, so I don't think it's a sign that he's dumb. I'd only met him briefly during the initial meeting that Tony set up between us, but he didn't seem too bad a guy compared to some I could have been given. He'll be doing the recording of the interview, as well as being a second listener to what Harrington has to say.

* * *

The journey over was tedious – Sydney, Singapore, Paris and then Montpellier. Donovan and I sat separately, which was fine by me – we just met up during the changeover of flights in Singapore and Paris.

Montpellier was a pleasant relief, not just to be finished with flying but we'd been booked into a pleasant hotel – not pretentious, but comfortable and well-run. It also seemed to be in a fun part of Montpellier, though it was too late that evening to explore that side of it – we both crashed after all the travel.

We'd been told to have a day off after arrival to recover from jet-lag so we were fresh and alert for the interview, and we both spent the day on separate explorations of Montpellier. We'd agreed to have dinner together in the hotel that evening so we could discuss the forthcoming interview.

The restaurant was busy when we got there, but Donovan had thought to book a table. One up to him for that – I should have thought of it. We ordered our meals, and then Donovan said to me:

'I discovered today that we're in the Pays d'Oc here.'

That didn't take me much further. 'And that would be?'

'Just one of the largest wine-growing areas of France. It may not produce the top wines like the famous clarets and red burgundies, but it produces a huge amount of wine, and some of it's quite good.'

'I have to admit that I'm not an expert on wines. I know some Australian ones moderately well because I've got an uncle who works at a winery in the Hunter, but that's about it.'

'Which winery would that be?'

'Tyrrell's. My uncle works in the bottling part of the winery. I went into the bottling area once, and it was fascinating. I didn't realise how fast they could bottle wine.'

'Coincidence – I went to a tasting of some Tyrrell's wines a few nights ago. They were pretty good, too.'

'So you know a fair bit about wines, then?'

'Not much, really – I'm still learning. But my dad was an enthusiast. He used to buy all sorts of different wines, and he got us kids to try them all from quite a young age. The kids I mean, not the age of the wines. Just as well I wasn't with the police then – I'd have had to dob him in for encouraging under-age drinking. But we never had much of it – just enough to learn something about them.'

'Okay, given what I've just ordered for the meal, which wine off this list should I be getting a glass of?'

He looked down the list and said: 'If you'd like two glasses over the space of the whole meal, you could try this white for your entrée – should be nice and crisp for seafood. Then maybe this Minervois for your main. I've bought that from Dan Murphy's back home, and it's not bad.'

'*Oui, ça va bien.* Sorry, I forgot you don't speak French – that was "she'll be right, mate". And what's an expert picking for himself?'

'I'm not an expert, but I thought I'd have this white with my entrée and this red blend with my main. Never had that combination before and I'm interested to try it. And if you'd like to try a small amount more, you'd be very welcome to have a sip from each of mine if you'd like. It wouldn't ruin you for tomorrow.'

I tried to look a bit neutral on that – I'd wait and see.

The first wines were served, and as we were waiting for the food we discussed tomorrow's interview. I said: 'As we agreed in Canberra, I'll take the lead at least at first. I guarantee the first thing he'll ask is why we didn't give him any notice that we were coming. I'll try to fluff my way through that without sounding suspicious – maybe some sort of dumb or ditsy female act if I have to. Then I'll start asking about Hardcastle's activities, friends if any, enemies if any – did Harrington notice anything odd about Hardcastle's manner or activities towards the end – that sort of thing.

'After that I'll get on to some of the things we were finding on Hardcastle's computer, and I'll introduce them bit by bit. That will certainly include his focus on hostile use of plant pathogens. Then I'll ask if Harrington knows anything about CROWD, and whether he's ever had contact with them. And somewhere about there I'll also mention the Cayman Islands bank account and the large sums that Hardcastle had been receiving. I'll try to do all of that while sounding as though he, Harrington, is completely on our side and we're just looking for help from a better-informed person.

'At some stage I'll mention his rather quick departure from Canberra and how disappointed we were that he hadn't been kept there while we were still investigating, but what I'm not sure about yet is how to try to get out of him is if there's anyone else in AGRICOZ who's a white supremacist, including who engineered his sudden departure from Canberra. I'll play that one by ear according to how the interview goes.

'Any thoughts about all of that?'

'That all sounds pretty good. What part or parts would you like me to play?'

'I'd like you to have the recorder running all the time, but as inconspicuously as possible. I'll have to mention it to him, but just say it's routine. You might like also to have a notepad in front of you, but I suggest you don't take many written notes. I don't want him to think this is a very formal interview – more a search for helpful information from someone who might know. If you'd like to ask any questions at any time feel free, but if possible not too many. I think if one person keeps up continual questioning it puts more pressure on the person being interviewed.'

'No problem – I'll be very tactful!'

At that stage the entrees arrived and we ate. The food was good, and I gave my wine consultant good marks for the wine choices. In the end I couldn't resist having a small sip of each of his wines, and they were good as well. I need to learn a bit more about wines myself...

INTERVIEW WITH
DR STEPHEN HARRINGTON

We went round to the plant research laboratory on the edge of Montpellier, where Dr Harrington is supposed to be working, just after nine in the morning. We fronted up to the reception desk and I asked in French if we could meet with Dr Harrington. The receptionist raised her eyebrows at us, and asked if we were expected. I told her that we didn't have an appointment, but we needed to speak to him about something urgent that had come up in Australia. I asked her to phone Dr Harrington, and I said that I would speak and explain to him.

In the event I didn't get to do that – she said that Dr Harrington would be down at Reception shortly. I wanted to be able to speak to him in private in his office where he couldn't just walk away easily, and it was going to need a bit of nifty negotiation to achieve that. In the meantime the receptionist got us to sign in at a Register of Visitors.

Dr Harrington appeared – a tall and slightly unkempt man, who was frowning at us.

'Good morning. Dr Harrington?'

He frowned more deeply. 'Yes. And you are?'

'I'm Senior Constable Layla Mackenzie of the Australian Federal Police, and this is my colleague Constable Donovan Lewis.' I handed him our business cards. 'We're enquiring into the murder of one of your colleagues, Dr Mervyn Hardcastle.'

'It would have been courteous of you to have advised me that you were coming, and made an appointment.'

'And I could equally say that AGRICOZ could and should have advised us that you were about to travel overseas, when we were investigating a murder that both the AFP and AGRICOZ want solved as soon as possible. The profile of this case has been embarrassingly high, and we've been told to spare no efforts. And we felt that you may well be a key witness for us since you were Dr Hardcastle's immediate superior in AGRICOZ.'

'Well, I suppose we'd better talk then. There's a meeting room just up this corridor where we can sit.' He sounded as unenthusiastic as anyone could be, but we were going to get our interview.

He didn't offer us any refreshment, so I launched straight into it.

'We would very much like to know whether you had any indication that Dr Hardcastle had enemies of any sort who might have committed a crime like this?'

'That's an amazing thing to say about an eminent Australian research scientist.'

He was obviously going to make this as difficult as possible.

'It's an amazing thing for an eminent scientist to be murdered in such a calculated and brutal way. I don't imagine there's ever been anything like it in the history of Australian science, and there must be reasons behind it.'

'Well, I can only say that I am not aware of anyone like that in his life. I should point out that I was his scientific supervisor, as much as Dr Hardcastle ever let anyone supervise him. I wasn't a personal friend of his, and I didn't mix with him socially.'

'Did he mix socially with anyone in particular at AGRICOZ?'

'Again I don't really know that.'

Try again. 'How popular was he with his colleagues?'

'I don't think he was very popular. He tended to make himself out to be better than many of them, and that wasn't appreciated. However, that's a reason maybe to shun a person, but not to kill them.'

'In recent weeks Dr Hardcastle had expressed concern to one of his social contacts that he was in some sort of danger, but he wouldn't elaborate on that. I don't suppose you might know what that could have been?'

'No idea at all.'

'You are a weed scientist yourself. Do you know of an organisation that calls itself CROWD, standing for Consortium for Research on Weed Diseases?'

'I can't say I've ever heard of it, no.'

'It seems to be a rather nebulous organisation, and we suspect that there may be more to it than just research on weed diseases.'

'I still don't know anything about it.'

His answers were as brief and unhelpful as he could make them, and he hadn't thawed out at all. Time for a bit of a push.

'We recovered two laptop computers from Dr Hardcastle's apartment, and we've been going through the material stored in them. They indicate amongst other things that Dr Hardcastle had an account with a bank in the Cayman Islands, and regular sums of money were paid into that. At the time of his death Dr Hardcastle had many tens of thousands of US dollars in the account. Such accounts are popular with people like drug dealers, but also a wide variety of other people who wish to keep some of their activities secret. Would you have any idea of what Dr Hardcastle was doing with such an account?'

Dr Harrington had finally gone a bit pale. 'You shock me with that, and I'm afraid I can't offer any sort of explanation. Can't you find out who was paying the funds into his account?'

'We certainly have been trying to do that, very hard and with assistance from FBI experts who work on that sort of money laundering, or whatever it is. Unfortunately there are multiple layers of shell companies behind which the originators of the payments can hide, and even the FBI hasn't managed to crack it yet.'

I hope that he's finally beginning to realise that we aren't just nuisances sent to annoy him, so I thought I'd add one other comment. 'You may be able to see now why AGRICOZ is so keen to have this case wrapped up as quickly as possible. You are a member of that organisation, and it's part of our nation's prestige. It reflects very poorly on all of us when this sort of thing continues to be aired very publicly.

'We can probably conclude this shortly now, but I would like to ask you one further thing. Are you aware of any sort of racial or ethnic prejudice within AGRICOZ, either directed against specific individuals or just a general sort of atmosphere?'

Dr Harrington thought for a moment, probably considering what reply would get rid of us soonest rather than whether he knew any answers to our question.

'I am not aware of anything of that sort in AGRICOZ, either general or specific. I find it surprising that anyone would suggest that of the organisation. We have a multi-ethnic staff, and as far as I've been able to tell, all of them work well and harmoniously together.'

The pious prat – time for a bit of education. 'In relation to that I will simply comment that the organisation called CROWD, with which Dr Hardcastle had some sort of relationship, appears to be a front for a neo-Nazi organisation dedicated to restoring what they call ethnic purity. It uses the letters to read Consortium for Research on Weed Diseases at times, but also to read Campaign for Restoration of White Democracy, or in some cases Campaign for Restoration of White Domination. To his credit Dr Hardcastle appears to have tried to distance himself from CROWD later on, and it's possible that his death may be somehow linked to that organisation. However, we have absolutely no evidence to take this idea further. You can perhaps see now why we're going round asking for help from anyone at all connected to Dr Hardcastle, including yourself.'

'With all that in mind, do you have anything more that you'd like to add to what you've said?'

'I don't think so, but I will say that if anything does come to mind I will contact you again. I have your cards.' He waved at the couple of cards on the table.

'Constable Lewis, is there anything you'd like to add or to ask?'

'No, ma'am.'

'It occurs to me that I do need to ask one further question. There was consternation in the AFP in Canberra when we learned that one of the people who was high on the list to be interviewed, namely yourself, had suddenly gone off to southern France and was therefore not available. My superiors had a distinct feeling that this was done to prevent you saying things to the investigators that AGRICOZ, or someone in that organisation, did not want to be said. I will be asked about this when we return, so please tell me, is there any truth in that?'

'My response to that rather insulting suggestion is that it is completely untrue. This trip of mine was planned some time ago, and it would not have been convenient for my French hosts to delay the visit further. It is not as though I was not available for interview – you yourselves are here and you prove that.'

'Well, thank you for your time, Dr Harrington. Next time we'll try to make a more formal appointment….'

We went back to the reception hall, and I said to Donovan: 'What an arsehole. We've got one more call to make while we're here, but I think I need a coffee first. We can try this cafeteria – it should be okay. I'll shout to celebrate the first time anyone's ever called me "Ma'am"!' I winked at him, and got a faint grin back.

* * *

Coffee over, we went back to the receptionist. I asked her in my best French if she'd mind calling the lab of the two AGRICOZ scientists who've been based at this research station for a couple of years now. It was answered by Stavro Ioannides, who said: 'You'd be most welcome to come up and see our place here. We don't get too many visitors from home! I'll come and collect you. You wouldn't find your way here.' A pleasant change from the frosty reception that we had earlier.

Stavro may have had a Greek name, but he sounded a hundred per cent Oz. He led us around various paths through the grounds of the research station – the effect reminded me of the layout of AGRICOZ back in Canberra.

We went into a neat lab and Stavro spread around some chairs. 'My other half, Ray Summers, is currently picking up some freight from the railway station, but he should be back soon. However, let me introduce you to Clémence who does all the real work around here. She's our guide, guardian, general factotum and everything. We wouldn't survive without her.'

A motherly, middle-aged French lady came forward, gave me a lovely hug and greeted both of us. I thanked her in my best French for her warm welcome, and that went down very well. I had trouble following the torrent of French that ensued.

We shouldn't have had the coffee in the reception area, because Clémence insisted on making us some more, and she dug out some *sablé* biscuits to go with it. She'd quite likely made them herself. I glanced at Donovan to see if he would be able to go another coffee and he gave a slight nod. And while we were drinking that and chatting about Canberra these days, Ray Summers arrived back.

That gave me a chance to raise the reason for our visit to France. I asked them if they'd heard of what happened to Dr Hardcastle, and they said they'd picked up a bit but not much. I filled them in and then asked:

'Did you have a great deal to do with Dr Hardcastle at AGRICOZ?'

Ray looked at Stavro. 'Certainly not me. I don't move in those rarefied circles. Did you, Stavro?'

Stavro shook his head. 'I didn't either, and from what I heard from some at AGRICOZ, that was all to the good. He didn't seem to be very much liked.'

'Did you ever hear that his life might be in danger?'

'No, again we weren't up at that level. There might have been one or two around the place who wouldn't have grieved, but I don't think anyone there would have done it in such a vile manner. It sounded vile from what you said, anyway.'

'Have you had a lot to do with Dr Harrington since he's joined you out here?'

'I'm not sure that I'd have used the phrase "joined us". We've hardly seen hide nor hair of him since he's arrived.'

'Do you know what he is actually doing here?'

'We heard something vague like drawing up a strategy for the management of Mediterranean weeds in Australia, which is something our section drew up about six years ago, and we're out here actively implementing it at this moment. So that sounds like some sort of bullshit, and I can't answer you. Stavro?'

'Nope, not me either.'

I had a sudden idea. 'Clémence is probably well in with the management of this research station. I wonder whether she'd be prepared to ask a question of them from me?'

'Mate, Clémence is practically royalty as far as this place is concerned. I'm sure she'd get an answer if she's prepared to ask. Why don't you ask her for yourself – in French. She seemed pretty impressed at your French before!'

So I put together my best French to ask her if she'd mind asking the administration of the research station how long ago they'd had a request for Dr Harrington to come out here on his present assignment.

She beamed at me, said: '*Bien sûr!*', and went off to the lab phone. A fair amount of voluble French followed, and when she came back she told me that the request had come out of the blue, just a few weeks ago. In other words, soon after Dr Hardcastle had died, and we'd started asking questions of everybody at AGRICOZ. That confirmed what Tony Mazzini had suspected, and he was going to be very interested to hear it.

'*Merçi beaucoup, Clémence – c'est bien aimable de votre part!*'

Another broad beam. '*De rien!*'

I thought it wouldn't hurt to get a bit more background on Mediterranean weeds in case it was relevant, so I asked the guys to elaborate. Stavro said:

'Well, the best known one's probably Paterson's Curse, as it's called in the eastern states. It's a serious weed of pastures there, but in some parts like South Australia it's called Salvation Jane because stock eat it when there's nothing else edible. It can poison livestock, though. If you've ever been near the Mugga Lane tip, sorry, waste recycling centre, in Canberra you've probably seen it in all the paddocks. It gets really thick in late spring and early summer – purply-blue flowers everywhere. Actually, if you'd like to see some, come through here.'

He led us through the lab into a glasshouse, where there were rows of pots containing plants with blue flowers. Donovan said: 'Yeah, I know this stuff. My sister keeps horses in Canberra, and she regularly swears about it when it gets in her paddocks. She's tried spraying it but there's too much of it.'

'That's right. There are chemicals that kill it, but there are so many of the plants that you can never get an adequate coverage, and it just keeps coming back.'

'So what alternative are you trying?'

'Biological control. There are various bugs that eat it in areas like around here where it's native, and our idea is to bring them to Australia and try to establish them there. If they thrive they'll manage the weed without any further need for humans to do anything. The thing we have to be careful of is that they don't eat other useful plants as well, so what we're doing here is testing the bugs' range of diet. Key plants that we don't want eaten are borage, comfrey and forget-me-not. We've found several insects that don't attack them but do eat Paterson's Curse really well.'

'It does sound as though you're well under way with this, so I'm puzzled at what value Dr Harrington's adding?'

'You and us both.'

We went back into the lab, and I thought we were probably done since these guys hadn't really interacted with Dr Hardcastle, so I thanked them for their hospitality, thanked Clémence warmly for her *sablés* which I assured her were the best I'd ever had, and we took our leave.

* * *

We went back to our hotel to debrief, and decide what to do until we had to get the train to Paris. We both said we were coffee-ed out, but it was near enough to lunchtime to have a glass of wine in the bar. I felt we'd earned it after this morning.

Donovan suggested a couple of interesting wines and I signed for them, then said to him:

'Comments on this morning's performance?'

'Yours or Dr Harrington's?' The cheeky bugger was grinning as he said it.

'Both of course. And don't spare any feelings.'

'Right, ma'am! Well, yours first. I thought it was bloody good, and I wouldn't like to be interrogated by you. You weren't putting up with crap, your questions were sharp and to the point. Harrington was doing his best to be negative, and almost insulting, and you kept it all going and hit back as necessary. There were some pretty good serve and volley exchanges, and I reckon you won all the points.

'As for Dr Harrington, we both know what he said, and you were probably watching his body language as much as I was, but I wasn't distracted by having to think what to say next. I detected a significant degree of underlying unease throughout, but especially when it got to the money-laundering part. It got worse again when you told him what CROWD might really stand for. However, I wasn't sure that it was because the news was a shock to him – more that he was dismayed that it was now coming out to people like us.'

'Yes, I think I'd agree with that. I can also point out that right at the end he lied outright about the timing of his trip to here. He either decided himself at extremely short notice, or he was ordered to go by someone at AGRICOZ at very short notice, and we had that confirmed by Clémence. I didn't want to go back and confront him about that, though, because it would give away that someone in AGRICOZ had been talking to us, and we promised not to dob them in. I reckon if he knew we'd been told, he'd have been back to the AGRICOZ management like a shot to find out who the leak was. So how much else of what he said is true? I suspect certainly not all of it – I'm sure he knows at least some of what's been going on.'

'We'll share all this with Tony Mazzini when we get back, and he can work out how we proceed. And thanks for doing the backup for me, and the recording. That all went well, did it?'

'I'll start the tape now if you like. It was still running at the end, so if the first bit's okay it all should be.'

He ran it for a few minutes, and it was all fine.

* * *

When we'd finished our drinks Donovan said: 'Would you be interested to learn a bit more about French wines while you're here? We've got one more evening before we leave, and there's a wine tasting advertised in the Garden Pavilion of our hotel. Starts at four o'clock today. I think it'll be similar wines to those we had with dinner last night, but there'll be a greater variety, and if we're lucky there might be some wines from other regions as well. You don't have to get sloshed – just a sip of each would be enough.'

I thought that sounded like a good way to end this trip. We convened in the Pavilion at five o'clock and sipped a reasonable range of wines – some good and some less so – and then had a simple dinner in the hotel restaurant. I felt we'd earned all that.

SERGEANT TONY MAZZINI

THE TRAVELLERS RETURN

Layla Mackenzie and Donovan Lewis were back in the office this morning, and I told them that Inspector Wiersma would like a debrief on the trip as soon as possible.

As they got their notes and recording together, I lined up Marcus and we all sat in his office.

Marcus immediately asked Layla: 'So are you able to tell me who killed Dr Hardcastle?'

'Sir, I wish we could but we can't. We can, however, tell you that Dr Harrington is now a person of interest, at least in some way. Probably the best way we can brief you is for Don to play the tape that he recorded, and then we can fill you in after that.'

'Okay, shoot.'

I thought to myself, "Don" is it now? Must have been a good trip.

The tape played, and then Layla said: 'The first point to make is that Dr Harrington was being as unhelpful as he possibly could. I think we both thought that he was deliberately trying to stifle us and our questions. And the second point relates to his statement on the tape that he had to leave Canberra because his trip to Montpellier had been arranged a long time ago.

'After we'd interviewed Dr Harrington, or tried to, we went to the lab of the other two AGRICOZ scientists who've been working there for a while. They've had almost zero contact with Dr Harrington since he's been there, which seemed surprising since he's a sort of senior officer of theirs. Don taped them as well and he can play you that one shortly, but first we asked their French assistant if she could ask the lab's central management how much notice they'd had of Dr Harrington's visit. She did that, and the reply we got was that there was almost no notice at all. So that was an outright lie.

'And one other small bit – I think Don'll back me up on this. Dr Harrington became rather pale and very defensive when we raised the possibility of right-wing terrorism possibly being involved with the CROWD mob in the US. We weren't convinced that that came as a surprise to him, and he was clearly worried about being questioned on it. And that's it from me.'

Donovan then played the second tape, after which Marcus said: 'Thanks to both of you. Anything to add from you, Donovan?'

'No sir, I think Senior Constable Mackenzie's covered it pretty fully.'

'Right, so where are we now? My first reaction is that I'm now totally pissed off at the reactions we're getting from AGRICOZ, and the help we're not getting. Somebody there knows a lot more, and we're going to have to get it out of them. We do still have to be aware of their political power, and I think I'll go and discuss how we proceed with the Assistant Commissioner. Then I'll get back to you. The aspect I'd like to pursue as hard as anything is the possible right-wing fanaticism bit. We really don't want that getting any worse here than it already is.'

I said: 'And you want to keep that relatively quiet in the AFP as well. There's more than one amongst us who's got views like that too. I could name one who regularly refers to me as Wog Boy, within my earshot. A bit rich when I come from Cooma and he comes from Dagenham in east London. And he's not the only one.'

'Point taken, Tony.'

Back in the corridor I said: 'Layla, could I have a quick word with you?'

I sat her down in my office and said: 'I'd just be interested to know how you found Donovan Lewis on the trip. I'm not asking you to dob him in or anything. I'm just keen to know for his future how you found him as a cop.'

'Pretty good, actually. He didn't really have to do all that much, but what I was most pleased about was that he kept his mouth shut when I was interviewing and didn't try to butt in. A number of my previous male colleagues wouldn't have been able to do that. And as a result of him letting me get on with it, I think we made a bit more progress than we might otherwise have done. Though I'm still disappointed that I didn't get more.'

'Thanks, Layla, and don't blame yourself for that. I don't think anyone could have done more – I don't think even thumbscrews would have got anything else out. But the very fact that you didn't get more says something. Some people at AGRICOZ are actually hiding something, I'm now sure of it, and it's going to need political pressure to get it. Anyway, thanks for the thoughts on Donovan. My own impression's been pretty positive too, and I hope we can keep him.'

A little bit later that day I got Donovan Lewis in to the office as well, and asked him how he felt Layla went during the trip.

'Mate, I wouldn't want to be interviewed by her. All you heard was the tape, but I saw her live. She bores into the interviewee with her eyes, and her body language is full on. I think she's also very smart and a good detective. You want to make sure you keep her on your team.'

'Thanks, that confirms my own view. And talking of teams, would you be interested in staying on this one if I can work it? Layla gave you a pretty fair rap too, and we can use an extra body.' I grinned as I said the bit about Layla in case he took it too seriously.

'If there's any chance that I could, it'd be great by me. There's good vibes in this team.'

'I'll see what I can do. And if you do get to stay, I'll tell you one other thing just for background.' I told him briefly about why Layla had been moved here, just so he didn't put his foot in it. For all I knew she'd already told him during the trip. It wasn't something she was trying to keep quiet.

A DNA MATCH

We had a possible small breakthrough this morning. A New South Wales Police team investigating a case of arson at a Halal restaurant in Sydney found blood stains and small pieces of tissue on a wooden pillar that hadn't been damaged by the fire. When they entered the DNA details from the samples into the national DNA database they got a hit with our sample from the cigarette ends on Mount Mugga Mugga, where our victim was killed and mutilated.

We still didn't have a name for the person, but it was interesting that what was being treated as an anti-Islamic attack should have the same person. It suggested that our thoughts on right-wing terrorism in our case might be right.

The NSW Police strongly asked us to keep the information confidential, because they also had some other evidence that they were following up, and they didn't want the perpetrators to know they had this evidence. That would play into our hands too if they could name someone, so we were more than happy to oblige.

SENIOR STAFF OF AGRICOZ

I wanted to get Layla's take on the involvement of one or more of the staff in AGRICOZ, in both Dr Hardcastle's murder and right-wing activities more generally, so I called her into my office.

'Layla, your work in the south of France has now got Dr Harrington as a person of importance in this whole affair, but he can't be the only one in AGRICOZ. He couldn't just be acting alone, and somebody else ordered him to go to France. Would you like to have a look over this list of the AGRICOZ senior staff and give me any thoughts that you have?'

She looked carefully through the list and thought for some moments, then said: 'I think that there would only be a few people who would have the authority to send Dr Harrington off to the south of France as they did. The possible people could be the heads of the six divisions of AGRICOZ, and the Director General and his Deputy. I doubt that anyone else would be able to do it.

'The most likely might be the head of Dr Hardcastle's own division, Pest Management, who's Dr Paulsen, and he's already on our list of persons of interest. But others who may be additionally involved – at least to some extent – might be Plant Science, Molecular Science which is probably relevant to just about anyone in the organisation, and just maybe Environmental Science. I don't see Animal Science being likely, and probably not Soil Science though maybe it is. So we really ought to suss out or interview those four or maybe five, plus the two top people.'

'That's pretty much my thinking too. But what I'm having more trouble with is how we go about interviews like that. I wouldn't want to alert them to what we've been finding out, at least in the early stage, because that'll just shut any guilty person up. No doubt Dr Harrington will have got back to them about the interview, which will have sounded the alert to an extent, but I don't want to make it worse yet.'

'Maybe you could get back to your contact in AGRICOZ and ask her to check which person signed the authorisation for all of Dr Hardcastle's travel? Didn't anyone wonder why he had to go to America quite as often as he did, and to those southern states a lot? We could then just hint rather vaguely in the interview that there seemed to be some issues with Dr Hardcastle's activities in America, and did the authorising person not wonder about what he was doing there so often?'

'Good thinking, Layla. I'll get on to my contact there immediately.'

* * *

I emailed Stella's home email to ask her about signatures on Dr Hardcastle's travel authorisations, but she emailed straight back to say that she wouldn't be able to give the exact details because the actual forms had gone missing. She said that it was likely to have been Dr Paulsen for most of them because he was of sufficient seniority, but some might have been done by Dr Petković or even the DG if Dr Paulsen hadn't been available. That didn't really take us much further forward. There might have been deliberate moves to involve Dr Hardcastle, but equally well it might be that for such senior scientists the requisitions were effectively just rubber-stamped.

MO SUMMERS

Mo Summers called me to say that she'd got some more info on our Cayman Islands finances, and I invited her round to my office. I didn't have any biscuits this time, but it turned out that she came with some herself.

'These are to thank you for Saint Peter's keys the last time, and for pointing us at Greenhaven Investments. These cookies, by the way, are American brownies – the real stuff.

'Now, Greenhaven Investments. It's a shell company. It has a nameplate on the wall at the address that you gave me, but no actual office there. It has a relationship with Major Holdings, which is another shell company, same address and same other details. They're both related to Nautilus Investments, which doesn't appear to invest anything but lives at the same address. And the list goes on.

'The Caymans regulatory office for financial affairs lists all of the companies, and has directors' names for each of them – in many cases the same names for more than one of the companies. However, when we tried to track down the directors, none of 'em seemed to exist. And I'd have to say that that's pretty standard for anything to do with finance in the Caymans.

'However, we did have one bit of luck, thanks to your hint

about right wing terrorism. Chuck had already told you that the organisation isn't the weed research one but a mob working towards right wing white domination of America, and the core of it is PEP – Patriots for Ethnic Purity. The FBI had managed to track down some of their finances, but not all those accounts in the Caymans, and they're going to concentrate some resources on that now.

'We're currently putting together a list of the main guys behind PEP, and I'll pass that to you as soon as it's ready. As far as we knew they were all in the States, a lot in the southern states but certainly not only there. What we hadn't realised was that they were also trying to involve people in other countries, like your science guy. So maybe they have a key operator in Australia, and that person organised the murder of the scientist, but we've got nothing on that and if you can find anything out we'd be very grateful. We'll beaver away to look for something, but I reckon you'll need to try from this end as well if you're going to get any answers.'

SURVEILLANCE

As Mo Summers had said, we needed to get some more closely focused work going at our end.

Counter-terrorism had started preliminary investigations on several of the names that we had given them. They'd undertaken surveillance of communication systems used by Dr Paulsen and Dr Varghese, and they'd asked the French counter-terrorism services to do the same with Dr Harrington in Montpellier. They'd also made a start with Dr Helena Sweetman here.

So far nothing dodgy had been found with Dr Varghese, but Dr Paulsen was doing a lot of traffic via the dark web. Material going out and coming in was heavily encrypted, and they were working at the moment to decipher it. They had, however, intercepted a few messages nominating times for meetings, with no places or purposes specified. A number of the messages mentioned a person who was just referred to as 'R' – full name never given – and there were references to a "warehouse" – no other details given.

Another puzzling feature was that all the messages had a mysterious thing like a logo design at the top, which appeared to mean nothing. It was a rectangle outlined by a thick black line, and an empty white space inside the it. Underneath the rectangle was printed in bold capitals the word "BLANK", and nothing else.

BLANK

The rectangle was indeed blank, but why anyone would pick such a plain design was not obvious. Extremists often develop their own logos, but they usually come with aggressive symbols – daggers, swastikas, lightning bolts like those on Nazi SS collars – that sort of thing. This one was so plain that it couldn't have been less threatening if it had tried.

Counter-terrorism had also made a general check on Ratko Petković, given the Eastern European name and the fact that there had been Eastern Europeans in Australia who had become terrorists in the past. However, he got a clean bill of health. The surname could be Croatian, Serbian, Bosnian or Montenegrin. The first name of Ratko could come from various Slavic nations, but checks showed that he was of Croatian origin, which is regarded as neutral for terrorism likelihood, and he came to Australia at the age of nine and has had a totally clean record since. They suggested that we drop him from our list of possibles in AGRICOZ, but his first name does begin with an 'R' and I'd rather keep him in our sights for a bit longer.

There were two others with 'R' names – Rafael Paulsen, who was already fully in our sights, and Ronald Varghese. We'd already wondered a little about Ronald Varghese, and we noted that Rafael Paulsen mentioned 'R' as being a separate person, so maybe Varghese was involved as well. Both also worth considering.

It would also be useful to know more about the meetings mentioned in the "BLANK" memos, and we decided that the only way we would find out more might be direct surveillance, initially of Dr Paulsen. I put in a request to Marcus for this surveillance, and he agreed and applied to the Assistant Commissioner for an experienced team to be made available.

MO SUMMERS

M o Summers of the FBI came back to me with some more in-formation about the finances of CROWD, and more widely the Cayman Islands. As far as anyone was able to untangle that convoluted network.

'We've traced through from Greenhaven Investments via a number of other companies to a root source. The various companies, if you can call them that, are just names that serve to confuse any trail of funds to the end point. The end point appears to be a reclusive billionaire called Tucker Sjöstedt. At least that's the name that we have for him. Not sure whether that's the one he would have been born with, but that's what he calls himself now. He made his money trading in commodities, mainly precious minerals and petroleum products. He lives in Tennessee in a palatial home, heavily fortified and guarded by hand-picked goons. He must pay them well because they're loyal, but they probably also know what would happen if they defected. We've tried to get some to defect, but with no luck.

'The mansion he lives in is called Valhalla – cute, huh? I won't go into the detail, but the important bits are that it's a huge and majestic hall mentioned in Norse mythology, where the bravest Norse warriors go to be rewarded after they've fallen in battle.

Think white men, dominant above all others. Sjöstedt's known to hate Jews, Muslims, Latinos and various other ethnic groups. He's probably not keen on what he'd call Eye-talians, either, so you'd be gone.

'We're fairly sure that he's a big-time funder of neo-Nazi type terrorism, but we're having trouble getting hard evidence. A lot of transactions go through the dark web, and although we've got our ways into that to monitor some of it, we can't pin Sjöstedt down yet. But it does look as though some of his money flows through to Greenhaven and funds CROWD. Of course he'd say that that's a philanthropic exercise, promoting safer and better weed management in the world, but that's why the story with Dr Hardcastle is so significant to us, because it's showing the other purposes to which funding like that's being put. So my colleagues back home are pretty pleased with all of this.'

ANOTHER DNA MATCH

We received a second match this morning to the DNA from the cigarette butts found on Mount Mugga Mugga where Hardcastle's body was mutilated. We'd already had the earlier match from DNA found in an arson attack at a Halal restaurant in Sydney, but the culprit in that had not been identified. A second call had just come in from the New South Wales Police, who'd had a further match.

That still wasn't as positive as we'd hoped, because the DNA came from a corpse and the corpse was as yet unidentified. The police had responded to a report of an armed holdup in a bottle shop in Punchbowl. When they arrived there was a firefight, in the course of which a police sergeant and a young policewoman were injured, and one robber was shot dead. The robber was our match.

The police had no ID for the man, but they also arrested two other robbers, and they have strong hopes of persuading the two to give the name of the dead man. Given that two police were injured, I'd guess that the persuasion will be firm.

I spoke to the policeman who phoned this in to us, and he didn't seem to think that there was any Islamic involvement or hint of right-wing terrorism in this last case. The store was one of the national liquor chain, Dan Murphy's, and he said that robbers tend to go for that sort of target because they often hold large amounts of cash. Maybe the guy was just a general thug for hire – let's see if we do get a name.

* * *

A day later they had a name – sort of. The man who was shot dead was known as Mustafa. He had arrived in Australia six months earlier from Lebanon, under the name of Mustafa Aboud. Checks of the documentation that allowed him into the country showed that his name was very unlikely to be Mustafa Aboud, and he gained access to Australia through corruption in the border force or immigration. There has been evidence for a while that organised crime pays some people in the border force to allow in undesirables who can then become hitmen or whatever for the organised crime, and this appeared to be one example. The NSW Police were following further with border force and Immigration to sort out where the corruption is. They were of the opinion that Mustafa was just a general gun for hire since he'd turned up in two different cases, so he wasn't a direct lead to the AGRICOZ-related mob. However, it showed that those associated with AGRICOZ were quite prepared to use muscle like that for something like the Mount Mugga Mugga murder, and they knew where to recruit it.

DR HARDCASTLE'S LAPTOPS REVISITED

In the light of what we now knew and suspected, I decided to go carefully through Dr Hardcastle's two laptops once again. It seemed possible that we'd missed something significant the first time because we didn't know its importance.

Most of the material didn't reveal anything new, but there were a few cryptic annotations amongst his personal thoughts on his trips that we didn't focus on when we first read them. He'd clearly been a bit concerned at some of the people involved with CROWD and what their motivations were, though not worried enough to stop his own involvement. Unless of course he couldn't.

But the most significant thing that we found was a short document entitled: *Read This in the Event of my Death*, which somehow we'd overlooked before. I opened it and read the following:

> If I die in suspicious circumstances, check out the activities of my Chief of Division, Dr Rafael Paulsen. It was he who introduced me to CROWD, telling me that it supported control of weeds using pathogens for general environmental and human

good, and he encouraged me to work with them and accept financial support for my work from them.

However, this picture is at odds with the way they have treated me recently, coercing me into undertaking experiments that I did not wish to do. But they said they would expose the fact that they had paid me (personally) a lot of money if I didn't cooperate.

I cannot believe that Dr Paulsen did not know that this would happen. I have also heard him make negative comments about non-white people, and similarly fascist statements. I am trying to find ways to neutralise my personal situation, and CROWD seems to be getting increasingly impatient. Should anything happen to me, please investigate.

Please!

I printed this out and took it straight to Marcus. His comment was: 'At last a chance to nail the bastards. I knew there had to be somebody in AGRICOZ, but we just couldn't get a clear handle on who. Now we can start some focused and intensive surveillance.'

'I agree, but we mustn't lose sight of the fact that there could be at least a few others in the organisation as well.'

'That's true. Let's hope the surveillance of Paulsen will lead us to the others as well. Outside AGRICOZ as well.'

'And maybe it'll eventually tell us what all the BLANK symbolism means.'

Marcus looked at me. 'What blank symbolism?'

'Shit, I forgot that you weren't there when we were discussing that.' I showed him a picture of the empty rectangle and BLANK written underneath it, and I said I found it odd because it didn't seem to mean anything.

Marcus looked at it for a moment, then said: 'You should have asked a bloody Dutchman. My ancestry doesn't often come in useful, but I reckon it does for this. Dutch has two words that can be used for "white". One is "wit", and the other's "blank". It's similar in Afrikaans. I remember seeing some photos that my uncle took one time when he visited South Africa in apartheid days. They showed signs on toilets and door entrances saying "*slegs blankes*" and "*slegs nie-blankes*". Whites only and Non-Whites only. It horrified me that they needed to separate people that way. And I guess there's also *blanc* in French, so I'm guessing that this one might be the name for a White-focused organisation. Surprise, surprise!'

Maybe I should have guessed too. White is *bianco* or *bianca* in Italian – not so different. I'm getting slow in my old age.

ALWAYS LISTEN TO YOUR MOTHER

When I was a little kid my mother drummed into me the importance of being neat. Neat in dress, but also neat and tidy with one's belongings in the bedroom and elsewhere. She must have really had an impact because I still do it – only half consciously these days but it's still there.

Which I can now thank her for sincerely, because without that training I'd never have noticed that someone had been through the papers and other things on my work desk. I'd sat down and was staring into space, wondering where next to go in the investigation, when I saw that things weren't quite as I'd left them the evening before. The files on the right of the desk were not straight with the edge of the desk, and the pile was slightly skewed. The chair was also pulled out further than I'd left it.

My office is always locked overnight, and no cleaners are scheduled to come in during that time. Somebody had been snooping, carefully but not carefully enough. I got up gingerly, avoiding touching anything, went outside and locked the door again. I called in to Marcus's office to tell him about the intrusion, and he summoned a fingerprint and examination team to go over the office.

The results were interesting. There were no fingerprints at all on the tops of the file covers, nothing on the surface of the desk, and nothing on any of the filing cabinet drawers. On the desk chair there were my fingerprints from this morning, but no others. There should have been a number of other ones of mine from previous days. Likewise on the office door there was just one set of mine from today. Somebody had obviously carefully wiped every surface after the search.

The filing cabinet had been locked overnight. While the fingerprint team was here I unlocked the cabinet. No files appeared to be missing, which was something. My neatness didn't extend to inside the filing drawers, so I couldn't really tell if anything had been moved around. However, the team carefully removed the files and dusted the covers. Same result as with the other surfaces – they'd been wiped clean.

There was no CCTV camera in a position that would record who went into my specific office overnight. There were various people moving along corridors in the general area, so I noted their names for future relevance. Then in discussion with Marcus we decided that we would install a hidden camera to record anyone who went into my office when the camera was activated as I went home.

Marcus decided that we should alert the rest of the team to this event, so we got everyone together. He described what we'd found so far, then said:

'This had to have been an inside job – nobody could have come in from outside, found the office and done that without a lot of prior knowledge. Internal security has thought for some while that there's more than one right-wing sympathiser in the AFP. I'm not going to name names at the moment, but I would like you all to be vigilant within your own desk areas. In particular, don't leave any compromising material at all visible, and watch for signs that anything's been tampered with. If you think it has, don't touch it and we'll get the fingerprint team back to have a further look. And keep Tony and me briefed on anything like that at all times.'

General nodding all round. They all looked quite startled at the news – I think it'll bring it home that we're not in an amateur league with this one.

After the meeting Layla asked if she could see me for a moment.

'Tony, you know that I was with the counter-terrorism guys for a while before I came here. Well, after a while you get a sense of smell about some people, and I've noticed one or two around here who might be a bit suss. I didn't want to say anything in front of Inspector Wiersma at this stage because I'm not at all sure, but I thought I'd at least mention it to you.'

'Would you like to mention a name or two?'

'Well, the first is Allen Briggs from down the corridor. I've heard him more than once making racist comments about people, some quite nasty and certainly inappropriate for supposed upholders of the law. He's also got a nice line in sneering expressions. That can sometimes indicate an unfortunate set of the face, but not in his case I think.'

'Interesting that you say that because he's the person I've heard more than once refer to me as wog boy. And he can't even get that right. I should be a wop, not a wog.'

Layla just rolled her eyes.

'Briggs has a sidekick called Ray Coombs, and I've seen them chatting together with an awful lot of smirking. I'd be looking at him too.'

'Okay, I hadn't picked that one up. Anyone else?'

'Not from my end, but I'm keeping my eyes open. And my ears.'

'Well, I'll add from my end, just for your ears at this stage, Pedro Sanchez and Mark Ziegler in the transnational serious and organised crime unit. They have a lot of overseas contact and liaison, and I've had a slight suspicion for a while that not all of their contacting is for the benefit of the AFP.'

Layla made a note of the names then said: 'So it's you and me up for an interview with Dr Paulsen of AGRICOZ tomorrow?'

'Right on, and I reckon he'll be another name that we can put straight on the list. But let's not get ahead of ourselves – open mind and all that.'

Layla nodded and left.

* * *

I needed now to go back to the files that someone had obviously looked at in my filing cabinet, to see what they might have read. In particular I needed to know whether or not either Susie or Stella might be compromised as sources of our information.

Susie wasn't likely because my contact with her had been purely verbal – nothing had been written down, and there was nothing in any file. Stella was mentioned, but only as having sent a list of trips that Dr Hardcastle had gone on, which was at our official request and AGRICOZ knew that it had been sent.

There were notes in two files about Dr Hardcastle's affairs and financial dealings, but no more than Layla had already disclosed in the interview with Dr Harrington in Montpellier. Fortunately there was nothing about Mo's and Chuck's disclosures about American connections, so I hope that that's remained confidential to us.

I'm wondering if there might be some benefit in dropping a few red herrings, but I'll have to clear that with Marcus first. In the mean-time I thought I'd have a chat with one more person of relevance – Jimmy Carroll who's one of our early intake of Aboriginal policemen. He and I have always got on well because he comes from Cooma like me, though I never knew him there. I arranged to meet him outside in the gardens of the nearby National Gallery – no prying eyes or listening ears there.

'Jimmy, I need your thoughts on something that's getting to us at the moment. You've probably had a number of cops who've made comments about abos or boongs when they know you've been able to hear?'

'No secret about that, for sure.' He was looking at me, obviously wondering where this was going.

'Yeah, and I get comments about wops as well when they know I can hear. I've got a few names of top performers at that, but I'd welcome any that you'd like to dob in to me. And I'll explain why. My guys are investigating a crime that looks as though it may involve white supremacists, or fascist thugs or something like that, and we're getting vibes that someone in the AFP is more than casually interested in this. We need to be on the alert so they don't pick up exactly what we're doing. I thought you of all people might be sympathetic to helping us in that.'

'Jeez, mate. Yeah, I'll help for sure. The most offensive one I can think of straight off is Sergeant Pickering in Protection Operations, and he's got a couple of mates who're about as bad – Barry Schneider and Frank Rawlins. If Pickering behaved on the streets like he does in the office you could have him up on a charge. I could probably think of a few more. I'll pass the names on to you if you like. Oh, and there's a sheila in Special Investigations as well, but I don't know her name. Short, with black hair, and a permanent sneer any time that I'm around. Not much help, probably.'

'No that's all good, mate. If you do think of any more I'd be glad to know. With a bit of luck we might be able to get rid of some of these people from the force.'

We went back to the HQ, and I started getting some thoughts together for the interview with Dr Paulsen tomorrow.

STELLA

I contacted Stella using my home email. I didn't want anyone at AGRICOZ picking up that she was in touch with the AFP. I suggested that we meet at Kiitos, the place that Chuck had introduced me to. It was well away from AGRICOZ, and it had good coffee.

When we met I got some coffees in, and then said: 'Stella, I'll tell you where we're currently at with our investigation, or rather not at because we're getting some obstruction from higher quarters. We don't know exactly who, or exactly why. It's preventing us from finding out who killed Dr Hardcastle, which is upsetting to us and I suspect also to you.

'So in that light I'd like to ask you a few questions about AGRICOZ and some of the staff. I promise you it will be in the overall interests of AGRICOZ, which I admire as an organisation, and if you don't want to answer any of the questions feel free to say so.

'The first thing I'd like to ask is what the layout of offices is in your part of the organisation. The reason for that is to get an idea of the level of interaction between the various staff in the area. Start with your office if you like.'

'Well, I'm in an open area to one side of the offices of some of the senior administrators. We're a sort of admin nucleus for the organisation. The central part has the DG and the Deputy DG. There's an outer office for each where their secretary sits, and then their office immediately behind it. Then on the other side of that central part there are the offices of the two Assistant DGs, and on either side of them the Chief Administrator, Frank Portillo, and the Assistant Chief Administrator, Remy Marchand. They each have an outer secretary's office and then theirs, though those offices are smaller than those of the DG and the Deputy DG.'

'So from your open plan office area you'd be able to see who comes and goes to the DG and the others quite well?'

'Yes, we've got ringside seats for all of that.'

'The Chief Security Officer would be there as well?'

'No, his office is next to the main security office, which is a bit of a way away. The main part of that's a common area like where I sit, and Pete's office is just off that. He doesn't get his own secretary – there's just a general one for all of security.'

'That's most helpful, Stella – it gives me a better idea of the dynamics of the area.' I didn't say that I had a very specific reason for finding that out. It wouldn't have mattered to her, but it was a bit complicated to explain at this stage.

'Since we're talking, could I also ask you how you find the senior people in that area?'

'Well, my favourite is Dr Petković. He's really nice, and he keeps the peace if things ever get a bit heated. He seems to be a sort of trouble-shooter for AGRICOZ.'

Interesting that that's what Susie said too.

'And the DG himself?'

There was silence for a moment, then Stella said: 'I don't have much to do with him. I don't think he talks to mere mortals all that much, and he's actually away from the office quite a lot. When I've had any contact I've found him a bit cold. I suspect he doesn't like women all that much, but that may be unfair. I could ask his secretary Patricia, who goes to the same Pilates class as me. I know she was really fond of the previous DG, but I don't know about this one.'

'Do you ever have much contact with the Chiefs of the Divisions?'

'Not normally – only if they want some specific paperwork or records or something.'

'So you couldn't really tell me what any of them are like?'

'I don't think I should really say anything about most because I just don't know them well enough. The only one I do know about is Claudia Thomson because she lives in the same street as me, just a few doors down. She's really nice, and I think most people around AGRICOZ like her.'

'Thank you very much, Stella – that's most helpful. There is just one other thing I'd like to say. We're about to stir the pot a bit to try to make some progress. That may result in someone coming round in rather a hurry and maybe agitation to see the top management. We'd love to know who comes and who they see. If we do stir up anything I'd like to text you to alert you, and if you'd be prepared to let me know who and what I'd be most grateful. My text will just say "Auntie's okay" so it doesn't look suspicious. If you're not at your desk no problem, and again if you don't want to do this that's fine, but if you could it would help a great deal. You could phone me or email me at home later in the evening.'

She looked a little doubtful, but she said: 'Yes, I could do that.'

'Thanks a million. I'll see if I can get further towards solving this horrible mess now.'

INTERVIEW WITH
DR RAFAEL PAULSEN

We met with the head of Dr Hardcastle's Division, Dr Rafael Paulsen, in a small meeting room at AGRICOZ. Layla Mackenzie was to do the interview, with me operating a recorder. Layla started.

'Good morning Dr Paulsen. I'll just do an introduction to start us off. Interview between Dr Rafael Paulsen of AGRICOZ and Senior Constable Layla Mackenzie of the Australian Federal Police. Also in attendance is Sergeant Antonio Mazzini of the Australian Federal Police. The interview is being recorded for purposes of subsequent verification if required.'

We were being really formal with the Antonio, and I liked that Layla pronounced Mazzini the correct Italian way – Mat-seeny not Mazz-eeny like most Aussies do.

'Dr Paulsen, you were Dr Hardcastle's senior officer. I'd like to ask you if you were ever aware that he had any enemies or threats to his life?'

'None. This whole affair has come as a shock to all of us.'

'Dr Hardcastle travelled overseas a great deal in the course of his work. When we read his trip reports....'

She was interrupted by Dr Paulsen who started saying: 'I thought you didn't have access....' He stopped as he obviously realised what he was saying.

Layla left a moment's silence, then said: 'You were saying...?'

'Well, what I meant to say was that when I looked for one of the reports just recently they weren't there, so I assumed that you hadn't been able to read them.' He tailed off bit lamely.

'We are aware that the trip reports have gone missing, which must raise a question of accountability at AGRICOZ. There are also indications that someone may have deliberately removed them, which begs the question of who, and why. Also missing are the original requisitions for travel, which would have indicated who signed approval for each of Dr Hardcastle's trips.

'However, we have in fact read all of the trip reports because they were on Dr Hardcastle's laptop which we took from his apartment when we searched it after his murder. In the trip reports there was mention of an organisation with the initials CROWD, which Dr Hardcastle met with regularly when he was in the United States. Do you know anything about that organisation?'

'No, I know nothing at all about it.'

'But I presume that you would have read Dr Hardcastle's trip reports each time he submitted them after a trip. Did it not occur to you to wonder what CROWD was?'

'I wouldn't have followed up on every detail of a report, just anything that seemed particularly significant.'

'Dr Hardcastle believed that CROWD stood for Consortium for Research on Weed Diseases, at least when he first met with them. We have been advised by the US Federal Bureau of Investigation that CROWD more commonly stands for Campaign for Restoration of White Democracy, or at times Campaign for Restoration of White Domination. Would you have any idea of why Dr Hardcastle would associate with an organisation like that?'

'None whatsoever, and you shock me with all of this.'

'Yet he was under your supervision…'

'My Division is quite large, and I have many scientists and staff under my supervision. I couldn't possibly monitor every aspect of the behaviour of all of them.'

'Were you the person who removed all of Dr Hardcastle's trip reports from the official files?'

'Certainly not, and I resent the fact that you are asking.'

'Well, somebody did and we would like to know who.' Pause. 'And why.'

I could sense Layla's eyes boring into Dr Paulsen, but he said nothing so after a moment she continued.

'Dr Hardcastle was receiving regular payments from CROWD, some quite substantial, paid into an account that he held in the Cayman Islands, a notorious tax haven. Would you have any idea of the purpose of those payments?'

'I'm afraid I have no idea at all, and this all shocks me. Dr Hardcastle was regarded as a brilliant scientist, and his work was supported by official funds generously. I can't imagine why he would need more, or what they would have been spent on.'

'Well, most of it was not spent. It's still in the Cayman Islands.'

Dr Paulsen just shook his head.

'I think this has exhausted the questions that we wish to ask you at this stage, but there may be more in the future. Thank you for your time. Interview terminated at 11.38 am.'

Dr Paulsen left the room, and I quickly sent my "Auntie's okay" text to Stella.

* * *

I had a phone call at home that evening from Stella.

'I was at my desk this morning when there was a kerfuffle – would have been about midday. Dr Paulsen, the head of the Pest Management

Division, rushed in and straight into the DG's secretary's office. I could hear him asking – or more or less demanding – to see the DG. Patricia told him that the DG was out – I think he was speaking to some parliamentary committee or other about funding. Dr Paulsen said he needed to see the DG as soon as possible and could Patricia summon him the moment the DG was back. Then he stormed out again, and charged into poor Mr Marchand's office.

'Patricia came out of her office shortly afterwards, and said "What a rude man!" to all of us. She must have realised that we could all hear.'

'Thanks again, Stella. That's a huge help once more.'

Things are beginning to play out.

SURVEILLANCE OF SOME AGRICOZ STAFF

I met with Layla to discuss further our interview with Dr Paulsen. Layla said: 'I'm convinced that he knows all about what's been going on, and if I was a betting person I'd lay big money on him being the one who took all the travel documentation and trip reports, and hid them or destroyed them. However, we have to find out if there are others involved in AGRICOZ as well. My suggestion is that we get the counter-terrorism branch to monitor communications and see if we can pick up who's involved.'

'I'm right with you on this. I'd nominate Dr Paulsen and maybe the DG, Dr Harcourt Johnson for a start. Maybe we could also include the Deputy DG, Dr Petković, as well, though some of the staff seem to give him a good rap.'

'I don't think you want to ask counter-terrorism for too much – they're pretty busy all the time. Maybe just the first two for a start. You can always add others later, particularly if someone else comes up as involved from the first two.'

'Okay, we'll stick to two, with Dr Paulsen as tops. For the second, I'd say it's between the DG and Dr Varghese, who's worked in the

USA for a while. I still wonder about the DG, who's not really a scientist. You know the counter-terrorism people – would you like to sound them out to see what they could do?'

'Yes, I do know them but I think in the particular circumstances that might actually be a negative. Just remember why I'm now here, because they couldn't handle my bereavement. I wouldn't want to bring in any sort of negative, even if it's not directly related. Could I suggest one of the others in the team? It can't be Jenny because she's off with the sprained wrist for a bit still, but you could ask either Bill Hansen or Don Lewis if they'd be prepared to approach them? They're both smart guys but quite low-key in their approaches. They wouldn't rub anyone up the wrong way, and they should be able to get them onside with this. We can point out to them that we may be uncovering another terrorism operation in Australia through this, unless it's something they're already on to. Though even then we may be providing them with more information.'

'Sounds good, Layla. Let's get Bill and Donovan in and ask them.'

In the event Bill said he was still ploughing through the financial records and making useful progress, but Donovan said he'd be happy to take it on.

'Great, mate. I'll get this going as quickly as I can, but to make it work we're going to have to get it set up at a high level, so there's no argument from anyone. I'll get Marcus to involve the top brass – the sooner the better.'

TOP BRASS

Marcus went up the line quickly, and a meeting was chaired by no less than the Deputy Commissioner for Investigations – only one below the top. He was Philip Ferguson, who was widely regarded as a tough but fair operator, and one who didn't suffer fools. He summoned one of the Commanders for Counter-Terrorism Operations, Sean Smith, and a second Commander for Covert and Technical Operations, Hamish McKay. Sean Smith in turn brought along one of his specialists on right-wing terrorism, Steve Fontelle. None of those had been directly involved with Layla when she was in that area, which was good.

Ferguson introduced everybody, and then outlined the situation very succinctly.

'Sergeant Mazzini here has been leading the investigation of the gruesome murder associated with AGRICOZ. You'll all know about it – the press has had a field day, and complains regularly that we're making no progress towards solving it. Not a good image, but at least there's been no leak of the fact that we believe there's a link to an organised right-wing terrorism group or groups, and any leak might prejudice that side of the investigation.

'It appears that the victim, Dr Mervyn Hardcastle, was offered research funding from a group that he believed was working towards his own goal of improved weed control using weed diseases. By the time he realised that the group actually wanted the disease organisms for attacking crops in countries that they didn't approve of, he was hopelessly compromised. He tried to extricate himself, but the group pointed out that he'd received a lot of money from them and out was not an option. In the end he told them he was walking away, and he died. Gruesomely, probably as a warning to anyone else who tried to do the same.

'Sergeant Mazzini's team has been working very hard to find exactly who Hardcastle was associating with, and somewhat surprisingly there are signs that one or more top people in AGRICOZ may also be involved with the funding organisation. Sergeant Mazzini's team has conducted interviews with two of the staff, and they were clearly dodging questions and hiding information. Important documents have also suddenly gone missing from AGRICOZ's records.

'I'll leave Sergeant Mazzini to fill you in on the details after I've finished here. What I wanted to say now is that further interviews are not likely to produce much more of use at this stage, and may lead to yet more evidence being covered up, so we need a different approach. The method most likely to produce useful information is surveillance of all communications to and from the key figures in AGRICOZ – at least the present suspects, but maybe a few more in case we've not spotted all of them yet. Mazzini will give you the names. You guys in Counter-Terrorism know what to do to achieve that. Please tic-tac with Mazzini's group when you have anything at all, and make sure the dialogue's going at all times. In both directions, and I expect to be kept posted as well. The AFP's name is involved here, as well, as nipping some nasty terrorism in the bud.

'I will add one further point which I wish I didn't have to say, and that's that there are possible signs that one or more AFP officers are also involved with the group. Sergeant Mazzini is following up on this at the moment, but I mention it because I consider that your investigations on this should not become widely known or publicised in the AFP. It will help all of us if those involved are not warned about our operations.

'Any questions?'

Heads shook all round, so he said: 'Right, you all know the situation. My suggestion now is that Hamish as the expert on Covert Operations, and Steve Fontelle as an expert on right-wing terrorism, sit with Tony who'll fill you in on who they've identified or pointed the finger at so far. You can all take it from there. Any problems?'

There weren't any, so the three of us shifted to a smaller table, and I gave the others notes that I'd prepared in advance.

'This has got all the names and their positions in AGRICOZ. I've listed email addresses and phone numbers as far as we've been able to find them out. That's all from official records in AGRICOZ. There are some personal email addresses for individuals, but one or two are still missing and they may of course have more than one email account. Especially if they're doing something dodgy.

'And even more so with mobile phones. You've got what AGRICOZ knows about, from one of our helpful contacts in their admin, but I'm sure there'll be others. But I know you guys are experts at locating that sort of thing.

'And the final page has got details of who's been dodging questions, lying to us, possibly destroying evidence – everything that we've got against them so far. If you'd like to discuss that side of it further, I'm happy to do that at any time. I can meet you at any time you ask for, but for the moment I'd like to nominate Donovan Lewis as your everyday contact with our team. He was part of the interview team in France which you'll read about in the notes, and he's well across everything.'

They sat for a few moments reading the summary, then Hamish McKay said: 'This'll give us a great start – thanks, Tony. I'll go away and get a team together to start from our end, and Donovan can come and work with us straight away.'

I couldn't wait to get Donovan there – finally we might be able to make some progress.

* * *

One matter raised during these discussions was the unsatisfactory responses given by Dr Harrington when he was interviewed in Montpellier, and the Deputy Commissioner had suggested that we might consider sending Layla and Donovan over again, this time to demand answers and not to worry about revealing our hand. However, as luck would have it, only a day later we received news from the Australian Consulate in Montpellier that Dr Harrington had died very suddenly. He had apparently fallen from the balcony of the apartment that he'd been renting. It was a sixteenth-floor balcony, and he'd died immediately.

There seemed to be three possible explanations:

- It might have been an accident – possible but not all that likely. He was a fit and healthy person – why would he fall off a balcony?

- He might have been feeling guilty about his lies in relation to his trip to the south of France and committed suicide. Possible, but even less likely than an accident. He didn't seem to be the sort to show remorse for what he did.

- Or he might have been pushed or thrown over the balcony, and if so by whom? That seemed far and away the most likely, with the deed set up by CROWD or a relevant person in AGRICOZ, and carried out by a hired hitman.

We got back to the Australian Consulate in Montpellier and advised them that there were circumstances about this death that needed serious investigation. We told them that we would send them a briefing on the background that would give the salient points of the case, and ask them to request the French Police to investigate urgently.

* * *

The Australian Consulate in Montpellier must have impressed the urgency on the French Police, because a report came back relatively quickly. The investigating police stated that death was due to severe injuries to the head caused by Dr Harrington's fall from his sixteenth-floor balcony. He fell on to a hard courtyard, and the accompanying photographs were gruesome. There was some bruising to his arms which could have been caused in a struggle if he'd been attacked, but given the extent of damage to the body generally it was hard to be sure.

The door to his apartment was closed and locked from the inside when the police attended the scene, but the door latch was one that would lock when the door was pulled shut from the outside, so that meant nothing. The interior of the apartment was reasonably orderly, but the police thought that it was possible that there had been a struggle, and the signs had then been tidied up afterwards. They felt that the arrangement of items had not been quite as they would expect things to have been left. To their credit, they got hold of the woman who did the cleaning in some of the apartments. She had cleaned regularly in Harrington's apartment, and when they showed her the apartment she said that things were not how he normally left them.

The police then questioned some of the other residents in the block, and one reported that he had seen two men standing outside Harrington's door. He noticed that both put their hands quickly into their pockets as he approached, and he thought that they might have had some sort of gloves on their hands but he couldn't be sure. He asked if he could help them and they said no rather abruptly, but he had no good cause to hang around to see what was going on. When he looked out some minutes later the men had disappeared.

Fingerprinting in the apartment revealed only prints from Harrington and the cleaner – none from any visitors. They did think that some surfaces had been cleaned off that would normally have prints of the resident on them, in particular the handles of the door that led out on to the balcony. If Harrington had opened the door to go out on to the balcony those handles should have had his prints on them, but they were totally clean.

Their overall conclusion was that there was no direct evidence of anything criminal, but there were certainly some suspicious circumstances. However, they could find no further aspects that they could follow up.

I discussed it with Marcus and the rest of the team. We all felt it was very likely that Harrington had been thrown off his balcony by two assailants, but we probably weren't going to get any further forward than that. However, the French Police did seem to have tried their best – at least we knew now that there was significant suspicion about it all.

I asked Layla to compose a note of thanks in her best French for the French Police. If the neanderthals down the corridor heard that a Wop had asked a woman to write thanks in French to some Frogs on behalf of the AFP, they might have early heart attacks. With a bit of luck....

BUSTER TO THE RESCUE

Yesterday evening the investigation ramped up to yet another new level. A senior member of the AFP Counter-Terrorism unit, Pierre Fournier, who is involved with some of the surveillance for our case, went with his wife to hear Kate Ceberano singing in the Canberra Theatre. After the show they ran into some friends who'd also been there, and they all went for a drink together.

So they were a bit later than usual getting home, and as they pulled into their driveway they saw a figure on the front lawn crouching over some objects on the grass. As the intruder saw their car he got up and tried to flee round the side of the house. A bad move, since there was a quite high fence between the Fourniers' house and the one next-door.

He then ran back towards Pierre, who tried to grab him but was knocked sideways to the ground. That might have been the end of it had the next-door neighbour, Sione Taumalolo, not just brought his dog Buster outside at the same time for a final evening piddle. Sione is the Tongan full-back in Canberra's famous Rugby Union team, the Brumbies, and he apparently did a splendid text-book tackle of the intruder. He held him down, with Buster, his Staffordshire bull terrier, on further guard right beside the intruder's face, growling at intervals and breathing Pal breath all over him.

We heard this from Pierre's wife Claire, who rushed inside to call for an AFP team to attend – fast. The intruder was taken into custody, and is currently undergoing questioning, which I imagine is being very thorough. To put it mildly....

That was bad enough in itself, but the even more alarming aspect was what the intruder had been doing on the lawn. He had laid out three cylindrical objects with fins on the grass, together with what looked like a radio controller. The initial consensus was that they were probably guided incendiary devices, which the intruder was preparing to shoot through the front window of the house. The team carefully loaded the devices into a storage container and took them off for further examination.

* * *

Next morning as I arrived at work I found an urgent summons for a meeting with Marcus and some top brass. It turned out that a great deal had been happening during the night.

Interrogation of the intruder had been swift and determined. It quickly became clear that he was yet another rent-a-thug, as we were now sure earlier ones involved in the assaults had been. He swore that he had no idea who had contracted him to do the job on Pierre's lawn. He had been contacted and given his instructions by phone. He had been told where to pick up the incendiary devices, and he was to phone another number when he'd completed the job. Money would be then passed to him indirectly, and at no stage would there be any face-to-face contact.

The interrogator was sure that the guy hadn't had a chance to phone anybody after he'd been arrested, and the number was a pre-set one on the phone. So they set up tracking and called the number, and that produced the nastiest surprise of the night. The trilocation placed the phone as apparently being somewhere inside the AFP Barton Headquarters….

But maybe it wasn't such a surprise after all. We'd already mentioned our suspicion of some AFP involvement in the meeting with the Deputy Commissioner, and this just confirmed it. The fact was reported straight back to the top brass, and this meeting was then convened. We were told that the case was not to be discussed with anyone in the AFP except those directly involved, and some surveillance would be started on certain AFP staff who were already under some level of suspicion of involvement in right-wing activities.

* * *

It took a bit longer for the objects found on Pierre and Claire's lawn to be examined. They were indeed guided incendiary devices, but of a type that our specialists hadn't seen before. There were no maker's marks anywhere on any component, so they were possibly specially prepared for jobs where their origin needed to be concealed. They were sophisticated radio-controlled weapons, and they would have done enormous damage had they been fired into the house. The bosses discussed with Pierre and Claire what they wanted to do in relation to their own personal safety – I didn't hear what was finally decided there.

WHO IS SURVEILLING WHO?

Our surveillance of the mobile phones and the movements of the nominated persons of interest was beginning to show some results, but the attack on Pierre and Claire Fournier made us wonder if the other side also had us under surveillance. Why else would they want to attack an officer unless they knew that he was watching and spying on them? We need to assess just how much they do know about our operations, and we summoned Donovan to give us his take on what he was finding out from the surveillance people he was liaising with.

Our operations were casting up one or two puzzles. There was significant contact between Dr Rafael Paulsen of AGRICOZ and Senior Constables Ray Coombs and Allen Briggs of the Specialist Protective Command. The two charmers just down the corridor from my office who like to refer to me as Wog Boy. One wouldn't normally expect people of such different backgrounds to have much contact, and it didn't sound like having kids at the same school or anything like that.

A number of the messages had the BLANK name and design, and they spoke of raising issues at the next meeting, without specific detail of what the issues were. There was also talk of Target A having to be taken sooner rather than later, but again no further indication of who, what and where.

As we were discussing this Layla suddenly said: 'As well as Target A you know we've also been seeing references to someone just referred to as R, and we were guessing that it could be Ratko Petković, Rafael Paulsen or Ronald Varghese because they were three senior scientists who were R's. But does it have to be a scientist? If you're talking about right-wing terrorism rather than just the science, there are other senior people who could be interested too. I'd have to look at a personnel list to see who might be eligible, but one could be Remy Marchand, the Assistant Chief Administrator. He could be close enough to the clique to be part of it.'

I thought about this for a moment, and it seemed to make a lot of sense. Why hadn't I thought of that sooner?

'Good thinking, Layla. I'll get the team on to investigating Remy Marchand's background, and I'll see if there are any other senior R's in the personnel list as well.'

* * *

There weren't any other obvious R candidates when I looked down the personnel list, but what was interesting was what turned up when Remy Marchand's background was investigated. He was born to a white French family living in Réunion, and before coming to Australia he had been a fairly prominent member of a right-wing organisation there. No history of violence or any criminal investigations made against him, but he had been quite outspoken on matters around white supremacy. He's certainly a possible for the R of the messages. We decided to monitor his communications, and Donovan said he'd organise that through counter-surveillance.

Fairly quickly we picked up messages about meetings that didn't sound like work assignments, parent and teacher meetings or that sort of thing, and a detail was put on to following him from work on a day when such a meeting had been ordered. However, as luck would have it the detail lost him when two cars collided in his path between his car and Remy's. The detail said it seemed to have been a genuine accident rather than a deliberate intervention, though the doubt is always there.

After further discussion with Marcus it was decided to put tracking devices on four cars – Dr Paulsen and Remy Marchand of AGRICOZ, and Ray Coombs and Allen Briggs of the AFP – and a member of the surveillance unit was put on to recording where all four went each day.

Layla suggested that we get a bit more help for Donovan, who was going to be liaising between us and a lot of different counter-surveillance people. I thought that sounded sensible, and I said I'd talk to Marcus about it.

A WORRYING ABSENCE

I was a bit later than usual getting home this evening because Marcus had held me back for an update on progress. I knew that Ella would be home early because her Office of National Intelligence project had just finished and she was waiting for a new assignment. However, when I drove into our driveway the house was in darkness.

This was puzzling because for security reasons we always keep each other informed of our movements, and Ella would normally have texted me if she'd changed her plans. I'd checked my phone as I left work and there was nothing. I parked in the driveway and went indoors.

The house was completely empty, with no sign that Ella had ever returned to it. Now it was getting a bit alarming, given the sort of work that we both do. I got my phone and called her mobile. Absolutely nothing – it didn't even ring. I tried several times – same result. It had been working OK this morning – what the hell was going on?

I thought I'd better check that she hadn't had a prang and been injured or something like that, though that wouldn't explain the silent phone. I called Emergency Services and gave them her name and car registration details – no, the car hadn't been reported as being in a crash, and she hadn't been collected by an ambulance or anything.

I called back to the office and managed to catch Marcus still at work, and when I told him about all this he sounded as worried as I did. He said he'd put a general alert out for Ella and the car and get back to me.

It was almost an hour later when he rang back. And my whole world fell in....

SENIOR CONSTABLE
LAYLA MACKENZIE

MEETING WITH INSPECTOR WIERSMA

I was about to start cooking dinner when my phone rang. It was Inspector Wiersma, and his voice told me immediately that there was some sort of crisis.

'Layla, brace yourself for a shock. It appears that at the very least Ella Mazzini has been abducted, and possibly injured or killed. No other details available at this stage. Tony, needless to say, is totally distraught, and I'll need you to take his place in the investigations at least for the moment. I'm not sure how much more of use I can tell you at the moment, but I'll have to brief you further soon.'

The Inspector himself was sounding a bit disorganised by all of this.

'Sir, I can come in now if you want. I hadn't started cooking, and I think I've just lost my appetite after what you've told me. I could come in now if you like.'

'That would be terrific. See you as soon as you can get here.' He sounded relieved – I think he needs to share this load.

I was in his office in fifteen minutes, and he gave me the background.

'Tony got home this evening to find that his wife wasn't there, and she should have been. He tried calling her, and her mobile wasn't even ringing. The emergency services denied any knowledge of her in an accident or anything, so he called me. I put out a general alert, and a patrol passing at the back of Black Mountain saw a car awkwardly parked in one of the public areas.

'On checking the number-plate they found that it was Ella's car. No Ella, and the worrying thing was that there appeared to be some slash marks on the driver's seat, and quite a lot of blood splatter. A forensic team is collecting the car at this moment, and I'm about to go to their lab to see what they can find.

'Tony's shattered, needless to say. He's going to be out of any effective investigating for a while, and I'm going to have to ask you to take over his role. I'd like you to come with me now to look at the car, because I think you're going to need to be right across every-thing that's happening with this.'

'I'm with you all the way on this. I have a horrible feeling that we've just discovered who Target A is.'

Marcus looked at me and frowned.

'Ella's full name is Antonella...'

He looked again and groaned. 'And I've got a horrible feeling that you're right.'

He drove at speed, and we arrived at the forensic lab just as Ella's car was being unloaded.

Marcus went over and looked at it, with its slash marks and splattered blood, and just said 'Shit....'

'Good evening to you too, Marcus,' said the forensic. 'Don't jump to too many conclusions yet, mate, because there's one or two odd features about this.'

Marcus raised his eyebrows but didn't say anything.

'If you look at these slash marks on the seat, they look to me more like someone was cutting an empty seat to try to make it look like an attack. If there'd been a person in the seat, how could you get cuts like this across the back? Also there's quite a bit of blood in the driver's seat area, but it's in places that haven't come about from normal spurting from wounds. It looks more like it was just thrown around.'

Marcus said: 'Are you saying that Ella may not have been attacked after all?'

'Well, attacked in that she was maybe dragged out of the car, but if we're lucky not slashed or killed. Though God knows what might have happened afterwards anyway. I'll get straight on to this and give you an update as soon as I can. Two things I'll need as soon as you can get them are the owner's fingerprints and her blood type. DNA as well if possible. That might give us some idea of who else has been in the car recently.'

'That shouldn't be a problem. Ella works for ONI and I'm sure they'll keep a file of all employees' fingerprints, and I think I remember her husband telling me that she's a regular blood donor so they'll have blood details. I'll get on to that while you do your analysis.'

* * *

Marcus got hold of the fingerprint details and blood type and DNA data and passed them to forensics. After that it was a painful wait because there was little more we could do. There were no CCTVs anywhere near where the car was found, and the last mobile phone call recorded by her provider was earlier in the day, when she rang a friend. Marcus got me to call the friend to see if Ella had said anything particular to her, but all the call had been about was organising some golf in two days' time. So we waited.

* * *

When forensics eventually called us in, the answers weren't what we expected.

'I'll give you the good news first. The blood wasn't Mrs Mazzini's, and neither she nor anyone else bled inside the car. The slashes seem to have been for effect rather than anything, and the blood isn't human.' He gave us a long look. 'You're gonna love this one. It was pig's blood. I'll leave you guys to draw your own conclusions from that, but I'd imagine that the reference is deliberate.

'We're still working on the fingerprints side of it. There were of course plenty of Ms Mazzini's prints everywhere, but there are a number of others, some apparently recent, and we'll be recording all of those and checking them against our database of prints.'

Marcus looked somewhat relieved. 'Thanks, guys. Let's hope that it's just an abduction, not worse. Not that we've got any idea of where she may have been abducted to, but we'll get on to it.'

He then rang Tony and gave him the update, and told him to hang in there – we'd be doing our best.

The trouble was that there was little we could do in the absence of even the slightest clue as to where Ella might be….

* * *

It was early the next morning when we were saved by the wonders of modern technology. Tony called Marcus in a state of great excitement, saying that he'd just received an emergency message that came from Ella's wristwatch, which provided a locating signal. Apparently Ella had a GPS wristwatch with an emergency SOS feature. When a tiny button on the watch is pressed it sends out a pre-recorded message to a set recipient, in this case Tony's mobile phone, and it would be most unlikely that her captors would be aware that that had been sent because there's no noise from the watch itself when it transmits.

We immediately set about tracking the exact location, which

turned out to be a rural property in the small settlement of Royalla just south of Canberra. Royalla comprises a number of smallish farms and homes – rural lifestyle rather than primary production. The signal was coming from one of the more isolated of those properties.

We assembled a Tactical Response Group, who went out to the area with two SAS soldiers who happened to be training the Response Group at the time. They took up a position from which they could see the property without being obvious, and they reported that there were no overt signs of activity. However, we didn't want to go in without knowing what we were up against. Ella should be relatively safe if they didn't know we were around.

We thought about sending a drone or a helicopter up for a closer look, but decided that that might alert anyone who was inside. However, Royalla is on one of the approach routes for aircraft to Canberra Airport. The airport is only thirty or so kilometres away, so we got a small plane up quickly. It approached from the south, flying over Royalla as low and slowly as it could without sounding suspicious, as though it was approaching the airport. The observer in the plane reported one four-wheel drive vehicle parked in a yard at the back of the building, but again no obvious sign of life or activity.

The signal was still coming from the wristwatch, and it was pinpointed as within the building, so it was decided that the TRG should go in. They were equipped with stun grenades just in case, but would only use them in the last resort as we didn't want to have negative impacts on Ella if that could be avoided. Tony desperately wanted to be among the people who went in, but that was firmly vetoed – he was still in a very agitated state.

The TRG moved nearer the building, in the shade of a large tree that would conceal them. Two men then moved quietly forward to try doors and peer surreptitiously through windows. They came back to report that all doors were locked, and one person could be seen in what appeared to be a kitchen.

The information was being digested when a house door to the left of them opened and a woman came out carrying a pail. Four men rushed towards her and grabbed her, but not before she'd shouted out. She was pinned down by two of the group while the rest rushed into the building through the open door.

Those of us outside stood with very bated breath – none more so than Tony who looked panic-stricken. After what seemed a very long time two of the group came out escorting Ella. She seemed to be dazed and confused, but didn't look obviously injured. Tony rushed over to her. They embraced in total silence, and I noticed that Tony was shaking.

One of the TRG guys said: 'We found her in a bedroom, hand-cuffed to a bedframe. She seemed pretty woozy – I think they must have doped her with something. We had a quick recce through the rest of the building – no other prisoners, and nobody else in evidence. The rest of the team's doing a thorough search, and we'll be gathering all the evidence that we can. We'll go back and help with that now, but we thought that you'd want to know that Ella's safe and sound. Well, pretty much, anyway. And we'll leave you to interrogate the sheila.'

Inspector Wiersma turned to me. 'Layla, you're our interrogation expert these days. Fire away and we'll chip in as we need.'

I looked at the woman carefully. Probably around forty years old; dressed in jeans and a loose shirt, a bit scruffy overall. She was glaring at the group, me in particular, so I gave her a hard stare back and spoke to her.

'You realise you're in big trouble here. We can give you one chance to make things less bad for yourself by telling us what's been going on here.'

The woman curled her lip, then spat at me. Fortunately not accurately.

'Fuck off,' she said.

'Well, we won't be doing that any time soon. Have it your own way, then.' I noticed that she kept darting glances towards the road, which led me to think that she might be expecting some backup to arrive. I alerted Inspector Wiersma to this, and said: 'We might need one or two of our guys to come back out here in case more opposition turns up.'

He started to move, then froze as we heard a vehicle approaching from the road. We all shrank back under the trees.

A battered Toyota Land Cruiser roared up the driveway and skidded to a halt near the house. The woman that we'd apprehended tried to rush towards the car but we held her too tight, but she did get out a yell. Two men leapt out of the vehicle with guns, and dropped behind the Landcruiser, with shots exchanged from both sides. However, what the new pair hadn't realised was that we still had our other guys inside the house. They came out and crash-tackled the two with guns, disarming them and hand-cuffing them.

At my suggestion we kept all three miscreants separate so that they couldn't cobble up stories together, and Inspector Wiersma summoned more vehicles to take them away, and a larger forensic team to examine the building systematically. Then he went over to Ella and Tony, both of whom looked rather shattered.

'Ella, you're going to have to go for a proper medical checkup after all this, but do you want to tell us anything about what happened to you before you go?'

'I'm sorry, I've still got a rather thick head. I remember that I was driving home round the back of Black Mountain, on the usual route that I take to go home, and I think there was someone lying in the road. I stopped to see if they needed help, and I was grabbed by somebody. After that I don't remember anything, until I woke up in this place, shackled to the bed. I don't know how long after Black Mountain that was.

'My phone was gone, but I still had my watch which could put out a locating signal. I couldn't get to the button for a while, but eventually I wriggled round enough to reach it. They wouldn't have been able to tell that there was a signal going out, but I hoped it wouldn't occur to them that my watch might be that sort.'

'Yes, thank God they didn't or we wouldn't be here. Were there just the two guys and the woman, or did you see more people?'

'I only saw the woman that I can remember, but I did hear a male voice once or twice. But as I said, I was very groggy for much of the time.'

'Okay, thanks Ella and thank God you're still with us. Go and get that medical check. Tony, you should go along with Ella as well, and please take her home when the check's done. Assuming they don't want to keep her in, of course.'

He turned to me. 'We'll take all three in separately to interrogate them. Whatever it takes to make them talk, and they're not leaving until they've done so. We're not stuffing around on this one. It's a declaration of war.'

INTERROGATIONS

We briefed our top brass on Ella's kidnapping and the events at the Royalla property, and we were relieved that they were now taking this very seriously. We were anticipating resistance when it came to interrogation, but we weren't in any hurry to ask questions until the full forensics and searching had been done at the Royalla property. The three were in separate cells in the Canberra City Watchhouse, and we made sure with the Watchhouse staff that the three would exercise at different times from each other so they couldn't confer.

Forensics collected a large number of fingerprints from the Royalla property, and we'd collected the prints from the three when we arrested them. The woman's prints didn't appear in any fingerprint databases; the other two were in databases against several crimes, but with no names attached to the records. Rohypnol was found in one of the kitchen cupboards, and was most likely what had been given to Ella when she was captured. Apart from that the only thing that wasn't really normal were handcuffs on one bed, though that's not unheard of in some households either.

Two days after the arrests we had each in for interrogation – separately. Both guys refused to say anything until they had legal representation. We asked each if they wished to name a lawyer to represent them, and both said that they didn't know the name but they wished to call one of the numbers on their mobile phones. Which were in our custody.

We pointed out that they were not allowed to call anyone other than a lawyer, and that their phones were anyway still under examination. We offered to check whether they would like to use a court-appointed lawyer if one could be obtained, but both declined. After which stalemate the questioning ceased.

Then we had the woman in, and initially we got the same response. But it was more hesitant, and I decided to try a bit further.

'For your information, the two guys who were with you are getting nowhere at the moment. They're insisting on getting a lawyer, but they can't tell us who they want. Is that the line you'd like to take as well?'

There was a long silence while she turned that and probably other things over in her mind. I sat still and let it all mature – or ferment. Finally she said:

'Sod it. That's what I was told to say as well, but I'm sick of this whole fucken business. I'm probably stuffed whatever happens.

'It's all down to my mongrel of a husband. He started working for those thugs, and he got into debt with 'em. That place at Royalla began as our dream of a country home. We were going to have chooks, maybe horses, a few livestock – that sort of thing. But when he couldn't pay off the debt, those cunts made him turn the farm over to them.

'They've been using it as a sort of private motel for all sorts of people who they want to put up but they couldn't put in a normal motel in public view. They took me on as a sort of housekeeper for the place, as a further payment of the debt. I got my board and lodging, but bugger all else.'

'So can you give us any names, contact details, that sort of thing?'

'The main guy's called Leo – at least that's what I was told to call him. They don't give out any other details.'

'You've got a mobile number for him?'

'There's one on my phone, yeah. You guys have got the phone, anyway. I'm sure you've already had a good look.'

'It would help us, and maybe help you as well, if you could show us which number it is. And any other numbers there.' I gave her a long stare. 'And quite frankly anything else you can give us as well. You've heard of witness protection, I'm sure, and I reckon we could fix something like that up for you.'

We paused once more while the bait settled in. Then she spoke again.

'I was never told anybody's name except for Leo, which may not be his name anyway. I did hear some bits of chat while I was going about my housekeeping, and I got the impression that what they were aiming to do was get people who they reckoned were foreign out of Australia. Any coloured people of any sort. Any Muslims – that sort of thing. They used to talk about ways to frighten those people, and possibly hurt or kill them. And you're probably not going to want to hear this, but I reckoned that at least one of them was a cop. Maybe more than one. So you can see why I don't want to talk to cops. I might be talking to the enemy.'

'Well I'm not one of them – I swear on my grandmother's grave. I'm part of a task force that's trying to track them down. But I'm sorry to have to say that you're probably right about a few cops, like you said. We haven't pinned them down yet, but we're certainly working on that angle as well as others.'

'Well, good fucken luck to yer. What are you going to do with me in the meantime?'

'Well, first of all I'll ask you some questions about what sort of things went on at the Royalla property, and then I'll show you a series of photographs of people. See if you remember seeing any of them at the property. So at the property, you said they brought various people there. What sort of things were they doing there?'

'Aw jeez, just about everything. Some of them I reckon were there to hide. They had a couple of rooms where people just sat out of sight for some time. Some of 'em were there to talk and plan. I reckon plenty of suss activities got worked out there, but they didn't say much when I was close by so I can't give you much detail.

'And I reckon some of 'em were brought there to get information out of 'em. They had one room that I was never allowed in, even when it was empty, but there were times when I heard screams coming out of that room. And twice I saw something being carried out that I reckoned was a body, though it was wrapped up. They dumped it in one of the trucks and it disappeared.'

'Yeah, I think we've seen that room ourselves when we did our search. It had bloodstains and blood spatter over quite an area.'

'Shit...' Even though she'd told us that, she looked shocked to have had it confirmed.

'We found the blood, but we haven't found any bodies around the property. Do you know what they used to do with them?'

'One of the guys keeps pigs on his property. I believe that's all you need. They just lob the bodies into the pig pen and that's the end of them. Old mob trick, I believe.'

'Any other happenings that you can think of?'

'Well, they used to bring in sheilas for sex, if you want to call it that. Rape might be a better word for it. I'm not sure that most of the women wanted to do it. I used to have to clean up that room afterwards and it was disgusting. Blood too sometimes. I could have wept for the poor girls.'

'Did that ever happen to you?'

'Nah. One guy did try it on once, but Leo told him to back off. Said the boss guy wouldn't like anything happening to me. Don't reckon that was out of kindness to me, but. I think they just wanted to keep my husband owing them.'

'Anything else you'd like to tell us?'

'Can't think of anything right now, but I'll work on it. Those bastards deserve anything I can put on 'em.'

'Okay, can I show you some pictures now?'

'Yeah – I'm on.'

I got her a cup of coffee while I quickly put together a portfolio of pictures of all sorts of people who'd come up in relation to this case, and some others thrown in to see how careful she was being with her answers. Amongst others there were some general hoons for hire for any jobs, some AGRICOZ staff and a number of AFP and New South Wales policemen.

I shuffled the pack so that there was no particular order, and showed her each one in turn. After she'd looked at each I put it down on one of three piles – ones she didn't think she'd ever seen, ones she might have seen but she wasn't sure, and ones she was pretty sure she'd seen at Royalla.

The negative ones were of course the largest pile, but there were several significant ones in the "definite" pile. Two were AFP guys, and neither came as a surprise to me – Allen Briggs and Mark Zeigler. The other significant one that I'd at least half expected was Dr Rafael Paulsen of AGRICOZ.

I thanked her and told her that what she'd done was quite useful. I said we were putting her back in detention, well separate from the other two, and I'd brief my bosses on how helpful she'd been. I said I'd point out that there could be significant risk to her for doing this, and ask them to take appropriate measures.

* * *

I went to brief Inspector Wiersma on all this, but found him dealing with yet another crisis.

'Layla, you won't believe this, but as Tony was getting home with Ella he was climbing out of the car when he somehow tripped and fell. He's probably broken his right ankle, and he's on his way to Canberra Hospital at the moment. We've asked Tony's mother to go to them to cope with all of that. She lives in Canberra – she's a travel agent with Qantas, and I think we're going to persuade the airline that they can do without her for a week or two.

'So Tony's going to be out of action for a while with all of this, and you're going to have to take over an even bigger role in all this at the moment. As soon as you've written up the report from this interviewing I'd like you to get hold of Donovan Lewis, so he can brief us on what all the surveillance by counter-terrorism has been finding out.'

DONOVAN LEWIS

I hadn't seen Don for a while since he was over with counter-terrorism, and he was looking weary when he turned up.

'Hi Don. You look tired. They working you too hard over there?'

He gave me a weak smile. 'It's not that. It's just that there are four different people doing it on their side, and one of me to keep up with them.'

'Oh, bugger. Tony was going to talk to Marcus about that, but with all the business with Ella I guess he didn't get round to it. We're a bit short-staffed at this end these days with Tony out of action. Do you have any thoughts from your end?'

'Well, it keeps me off the wine if nothing else, but it would be more effective if we can get someone. I'll check at our end and get back to you.'

'So are all the spooks coming up with useful stuff?'

'Sure are. Is Inspector Wiersma going to join us? He needs to hear this as well.'

Marcus joined us, filled Don in on Tony's latest disaster, and then said: 'Fire away.'

'We've established that Dr Rafael Paulsen is a leading light in BLANK. He sends lots of messages to various sources, most through the dark web. He's involved with recruiting, policy development and various administrative matters. One of his frequent contacts is someone called Topman, but we haven't identified yet who that is. Not sure whether it's a surname Topman, or Top Man. Probably the last.

'An equally leading character is Allen Briggs of the AFP, and we've identified five other AFP personnel who have at least some involvement with BLANK. I'll give you a consolidated list at the end.

'There was a lot of traffic about the taking of the property at Royalla, and it sounds as though that was a significant setback for them. They have, however, got at least one other property that serves similar functions, and we're working on exactly where and which property at the moment. It's possibly near Bungendore or Tarago, but we're not sure at this stage.

'We've also noted messages going between here and CROWD in the United States, and there were messages from the Australian end thanking the US lot for having disposed of Dr Harrington in the south of France. So that answers what happened there, and there's some pretty direct contact and cooperation between the US and here.

'We're currently working out who to bug and where. We've put tracking on several vehicles, and if we can we'll put something close to or in the apartment of Dr Paulsen.

'One other thing that's come up is that some people in the group appear to be using the old Dickson Bowling Club as a meeting place. The Club sold out to a developer some years ago. The developer closed down the bowling greens but hasn't done anything with the site yet. The greens have gone to weeds, but the clubhouse is a solid building and it's still standing, even though there's a small tree growing right near the front door through the concrete.

'The building's locked up but somebody's got a key, and people have been going in and out on occasion. Mainly during the day because there's no power in the building. Paulsen's certainly one, and Allen Briggs, but there are others too. Our guys are currently working on some sort of surveillance that they can install inside the building – vision and sound, they hope.'

Marcus said: 'Thanks for that, Donovan – that's good progress. Keep us posted here – Layla in the first instance, and she can pass it on as necessary.'

* * *

Don and I left the meeting, and I said to Don: 'This is great stuff you're getting with surveillance, but all the more I'm thinking we need to be keeping in better touch with you day by day. Do you have any thoughts?'

Don thought for a moment, then said: 'I can suggest one possibility – Polly Jones. She's one of the people I liaise with most in surveillance, and she's good. If we could get her liaising more directly with Marcus and the rest that could work out well. I have great admiration for her.'

I raised my eyebrows a bit. 'She's not also your girl-friend, by any chance?'

Don grinned. 'Never going to happen – I'm the wrong gender!'

I raised my eyebrows a bit further. 'So tell me more about her.'

'Well, her greatest asset is that she's absolutely nondescript and unnoticeable, while at the same time she's very smart. It's brilliant for surveillance, because her targets tend to overlook her because she's a nobody. And given that I've been doing actual surveillance recently as much as liaison, she could slip into that role very well. Why don't you organise a meeting with her? She's very nice as well as smart.'

'I don't know if I can do that without going through Marcus.'

'I think you need to drive this whole thing a bit more directly. Can I suggest that you call her and say you'd like to brief her on something specific – you can think of something, I'm sure – and you need to have me there as well. With the three of us together, I'm sure we could work something out.'

* * *

I called Polly, and she sounded quite happy to be asked to come over – she said she'd be free next day.

When she turned up I could see why Don had said she was a nobody. Small in stature, plain in features, quiet in personality, nondescript hair style, dressed in a light brown top and mid-brown slacks – you wouldn't notice her unless there was a reason to do so.

Don introduced me as his boss, and I glared at him for that.

'I'm not his boss – I'm a colleague! Anyway, I don't think anyone could boss him around – I don't know if you've tried?'

'No, I've got more productive things to do with my time than try to control him…. Anyway, I do know you because I've seen you with Sergeant Mazzini a few times, and more recently with Inspector Wiersma on a couple of occasions.'

That was interesting because I don't recall ever seeing Polly anywhere – she certainly does keep a low profile.

'What Don and I were hoping to discuss with you is a possible closer liaison between your sections and us. Don – fire away.'

Don outlined the liaison role, combined with surveillance, and then said: 'But we're not sure if your mob will be happy with us nominating you just like that.'

Polly said: 'You and I have already worked together quite a bit. I think we could just suggest that it formalises that. I don't think any noses will get out of joint at our end – are you right with your bosses?'

I said: 'I haven't discussed it yet, but I reckon Marcus'll be only too happy to go with the idea. I'll put it to him this afternoon and let you know.'

She left, and I said to Don: 'Thanks for Polly Jones – she seems to be a good pick.'

'You haven't seen the half of it yet. She's great at reading people's body language – I reckon she'd have a good idea of how well or not you get on with Tony Mazzini, though she might need another go with you and Marcus. She's also a bloody good shot. She regularly competes in rifle shooting, and she can out-shoot half the males around this place. She's not quite so good with a pistol, but close.'

'Hm, the way things are going we might need those skills yet, though I hope not.'

SUMMONS FROM INSPECTOR WIERSMA

A couple of days later Inspector Wiersma called me into his office.

'Hi Layla. I've just had Tony Mazzini's wife Ella in here, at her request. Apparently Tony's going spare stuck at home, and Ella's a bit worried about it. Tony's supposed to be on medical leave for a couple of weeks yet, but Ella asked if there was any chance that he might be allowed back in some sort of sedentary role.

'I told her I'd think about it but I couldn't promise anything. What's your view on that? I wouldn't want to burden you in any way, but if there was an easy way to give Tony something to do I'd be prepared to okay it.'

I thought for a moment or two, then said: 'I think we should say yes. Tony was very kind to me when I was first moved here, and I owe him for that. He also has a very good mind and he's a good lateral thinker. I'm sure there are useful things he could do here while he sits on his backside. We're a bit light on for numbers at the moment, and there are plenty of jobs that a desk-bound officer could handle. I'm sure I can cope, and I think I'd welcome it.'

Marcus looked relieved. 'Thanks, Layla – that's good of you. Now I'm going to jump the gun slightly. Tony and I had recently been talking about putting you up for promotion to Sergeant, which we both reckon you deserve. It takes a while for that sort of thing to go through the hoops before it's substantive, but I'm proposing in the interim to make you an Acting Sergeant, and that's been approved.

'It'll have two practical advantages. One is that it'll give you more status in this whole investigation, which should strengthen you in what you're doing. The other is that it'll give you almost equal status with Tony, which might help you to keep the bastard in order. So congratulations! I've been wanting to do this for some time, and it's thoroughly well deserved.'

'Phew, thanks Marcus, if I'm allowed to call you that now. I'll try to live up to it. And I'll make sure I keep Tony in order. I'll look forward to that....'

'Good on you, Layla. I'll go and call Ella and tell her to get Tony washed, brushed and delivered to the office.'

ACTING SERGEANT
LAYLA MACKENZIE

THE OLD DICKSON BOWLING CLUB

Counter-terrorism and Don scored a major win this morning. They let themselves into the clubhouse of the former Bowling Club in Dickson and installed video and sound surveillance equipment, with a small power source since power to the building was turned off.

However, the biggest score for the day was that they found some screwed-up paper that had been caught up underneath a rubbish bin. The tops of the pages had been torn off, but the pages had lists of names which included Allen Briggs, and we were sure that it must be a list of BLANK members. There was no date, and the team couldn't determine how up-to-date it was, but it was a significant step forward.

It obviously wasn't complete, but it still had a number of significant names on it. At least two of the names in the list are current federal politicians – neither in major parties, though one of them, Stephen Hargreaves, was a Liberal until he decided that the Libs were no better than a bunch of Commies and he defected. The other one, Ollie Dahlstrom, is the member for a wild west electorate in far north Queensland, and has been notorious for a while with comments about reffos and the like. There was also a professor emeritus at Monash University, two leading figures in large businesses, and a whole lot of other names that would need to be checked out. It was clear that the total membership of the organisation was larger than we had originally anticipated, and that was going to make it impossible to run any sort of surveillance on more than a small fraction of the membership.

* * *

Over the next days the hidden camera that we'd installed in the Dickson Bowling Club gave us a whole lot of faces of members as they came in for meetings, and we compiled a large photo dossier for further investigation of names and affinities. The sound recorders didn't yield quite as much, but we picked up references to "the main storage" and "Fyshwick", this latter being a Canberra suburb of shops, businesses, brothels and – significantly – large self-hire storages. Time for some further investigation of those.

* * *

One other investment that was beginning to pay off was the installation of tracking devices on four cars – of Rafael Paulsen and Remy Marchand of AGRICOZ and Allen Briggs and Ray Coombs of the AFP. Coombs didn't show up anything much, but Allen Briggs and Rafael Paulsen went to a number of private addresses around Canberra, mostly for quite short visits. It didn't seem likely that they were all social visits, and they weren't moonlighting as Deliveroo drivers – more likely that it was visits to BLANK members, and we noted all the addresses.

Remy Marchand also went to a few private addresses, one of which was in the apartment building where Dr Harcourt Johnson lived, which he visited three times. However, given that Remy was a senior administrator in AGRICOZ which Johnson headed, that might just have been for work purposes.

AN ATTACK ON DONOVAN

A couple of days later I received a call from Bill Hansen to say that Don Lewis was currently in Canberra Hospital suffering from unspecified injuries following an attack – no other information available at this stage except that it had occurred a day ago. It was the first that we'd heard about it, and I thought I'd better check it out quickly so I shot off to the hospital.

I discovered after a lot of questioning which ward he was now located in, but still no other information. I got lost twice on the way to the ward, and when I finally tracked him down I was startled to see how he looked – pale, and quite grim-faced.

He almost seemed embarrassed to talk about what had happened, but it turned out that he'd been trying to do direct-sight observation of people loitering around the Dickson Bowling Club when he was seized from behind, cuffed and dragged away.

He was blindfolded and taken to a room, location unknown, and questioned about what he was spying on. He was told he was suspected of being part of a plot by some members of the Federal Police to spy on and discredit a legitimate political movement in Australia.

He told his interrogator that he'd only been looking to see why people were loitering around a clubhouse that was supposed to be closed, but he was told that was bullshit. He was then forcibly stripped to his underpants, and he felt extreme pain across his lower abdomen. It turned out that the word RAT had been painted across his abdomen, with what was probably concentrated acid of some sort. The pain became excruciating. He was then taken to an isolated spot near the Majura rifle range and released – minus his trousers.

Unfortunately the range was not in use at the time, though the point of release was close to a water butt and luckily Don had the foresight to sluice cold water all over the burns before he made off. That would have reduced the amount of burn damage. Then he plodded in great pain to the Majura Parkway and tried to flag down a motorist. A number must have thought that he looked like a dangerous loony because they wouldn't stop, but eventually someone who turned out to be an off-duty paramedic stopped, and she took him to Canberra Hospital. She managed to get him bumped up for rapid treatment, which was simply an attempt to wash off any residual acid and dress the burns. When I found him he'd been somewhat sedated, but he was still in a fair degree of pain.

However, even more concerning, it turned out that someone from the surveillance unit to which we'd attached him had already been to visit, and had suggested to him that he'd been careless in his approach to surveillance and it was all his fault. Donovan himself was convinced that this wasn't so. He told me he thought the whole thing was a set-up – he felt he'd been lured there, and they'd been expecting him.

I heard all this with mounting horror, and with disgust at such an attitude by the other person, and at the fact that they hadn't bothered to tell us about an attack on one of our staff. I told Don that he had my greatest sympathy and we'd do whatever we could for him, but I needed to get back first to discuss this with Marcus Wiersma. He was a bit dopy anyway, so I felt I could leave him at that stage. I promised to be back.

* * *

Back in the office, Marcus shared my views and was equally mystified at the negative actions of the other surveillance person. He said: 'The only explanation I can think of is that there's someone in surveillance who's gone over to the Evil Empire as well, and they set this up. I'd trust Donovan's statement that he wasn't been careless, and that someone had lined him up. We're going to need the paperwork that's required when someone's injured in the line of duty. Could you maybe start doing that while I phone surveillance and try to get their version of all this.'

He came back to me half an hour later and said: 'I'm even more puzzled now by all of this. I spoke to Hamish McKay who's the boss guy of surveillance – you met him the other day, I think. He hadn't heard about the attack on Donovan, and furthermore he was surprised that any of his staff would think that Donovan was careless in any way. He said that from what he'd heard Donovan was a very professional officer. I think it might be a good idea if you go back and speak further with Donovan, maybe sooner rather than later. With luck he may be a bit less groggy by now. You could try to find out more about how he assesses the people over there that he's been working with. Whether he's had any suspicions or doubts before this event.'

* * *

At least I knew where to go in the hospital this time, but as I got to the corridor that led to Don's ward I pulled up short and watched. A male figure was in the corridor ahead of me, and he was going along opening every door in turn and looking inside. He presumably didn't know where the person he was looking for was located, but the staff could have told him if he'd asked, and he mustn't have wanted to do that.

I pulled out my phone and took a couple of quick pictures, though they wouldn't have shown much from my distance. Then I took out some paper which I could be studying if he turned and saw me.

When he reached Don's door he looked in, and then quickly slipped into the room and I heard the door close. I shot along the corridor and followed him inside. The male was just passing the foot of Don's bed.

I called out: 'What exactly are you doing in here?'

'I'm looking for Mr Staines, but I don't know what he looks like.'

A load of rubbish, but I couldn't disprove it. 'Well, this isn't Mr Staines, so you can leave.'

He gave me a rather dirty look, but went. I got another not very good picture as he left.

I turned to look at Don, who was staring in amazement, but seemed to be a bit more with it than before.

I said: 'Hi Don. It was good timing that Marcus just happened to send me back to see you now. That guy was certainly suss, and we'll need to get you some sort of protection. You can't protect yourself in your present state.'

I phoned Marcus and told him what had happened, and he said he'd send some backup to keep an eye on Don until we could organise a more permanent safe house for him to stay in. Then I just waited until the backup came, which in the first instance happened to be Bill Hansen. It turned out that Marcus couldn't get anyone else at short notice, but he'd thought it would be good for Don to have someone he knew to chat to. If he could stay awake long enough, that is....

* * *

Before leaving the hospital I thought I'd check on their surveillance systems for a picture of Don's intruder. I went to the main reception, showed my ID and asked to meet with the security officers. The main one on duty was a helpful female called Rosie, and when I told her which ward Don was in, she brought up several CCTVs on her screen. Two of them showed the intruder clearly, with good facial shots. She allowed me to photograph them with my mobile, but then she asked if I'd like to have them sent to me by email. That was even better, so I gave her my email address and she fired them off.

Then back to the office, and I went straight in to Marcus again.

'I got a couple of rough shots of the intruder in Don's room, but they aren't good. However, I've also got some shots on my camera from the hospital's CCTV, and they've emailed them to me as well. I have no doubt at all that the intruder was in there to do harm – maybe lethal. Don's going to take a bit of time to recover from his burns, and we need a safe house to store him in, with the minimum number of people knowing where he is. You may have some thoughts on somewhere suitable – if not I have a suggestion.'

Marcus looked at me suspiciously, which I'd expected. I waited.

He thought for a few minutes and then said:

'Can't think of anything obvious at the moment. Shoot.'

'Please let me say this right through, and then you can object. I'm going to suggest my apartment as a safe house. I live in the C5 precinct in Campbell. I have an apartment with two bedrooms and two bathrooms. Each of those rooms is quite separate from the others, and I do not use one bedroom and one bathroom. The security at the apartments is about as good as that of Dr Hardcastle's apartment in Kingston. Access to foyers and lifts is only by fobs, and there are high-quality locks on the front doors. Only three keys exist for my front door, and I have all three of them. The only way in which my set-up differs from Dr Hardcastle's is that there are two other apartments on my floor – but I still have the only door keys to my place.

'I cook every day and I could feed Don, and we can arrange for a nurse to come daily or whenever to dress his wounds, and bath him as necessary. I'm fairly sure that you're now going to tell me that this isn't acceptable procedure, but I'm thinking of Don's security. If Don doesn't like the whole idea then we forget it, but maybe we could at least ask his views before we dismiss it?'

Marcus stared at me. 'This is nearly as bad as being interviewed by you. Yes, I'm pretty sure it isn't correct procedure, but in the absence of any other ideas I guess we could at least ask Donovan's view on the whole idea. That'll give me a bit more time to come up with an alternative, anyway.'

* * *

Marcus and I went back to the hospital and up to Don's ward, where Bill and Don were still chatting.

Marcus said: 'G'day, Donovan. Been through the wars, mate?'

'Yeah, stupid, really. I guess I wasn't careful enough.'

'From what I've heard it wasn't your fault in the slightest. Our appraisal of the situation is that you may still be at risk of another attack, and we want to find you somewhere safer to go to recuperate. I don't think we could safely send you somewhere like family because you could still be tracked down, and I can't at the moment find any safe house that would be practical for your situation.

'Layla has come up with a suggestion which I'm sure is totally against correct procedure, that you go to stay in her apartment in Campbell until you're fit and able again.'

Don looked startled, and I saw Bill absolutely goggling.

Marcus went on to list the practicalities of the suggestion, including a private bedroom and bathroom, then said: 'Layla has said she'd be happy to offer this, but only if you feel totally comfortable with the idea. What's your take on it?'

Don looked at me, but I thought I'd better stay poker-faced. Then he said: 'I guess if it's okay with Layla it's okay with me. From what you're saying it does seem that I might I need somewhere guaranteed safe until I'm fit again. I certainly don't want to be injured any further. So yes, and thanks Layla.'

Marcus said: 'I'd have to say that I'm still not happy about the protocols of this, and I'll be looking for alternatives, but it's a last resort if we have to. Layla, can you check with the medicos how soon Donovan can be moved from here to private facilities, and we can then organise his removal. I'll mention it to the staff on my way out, but they'll have to ask a doctor first. I'll keep you posted. Right now I've got to get back to the office for a meeting.'

Bill said: 'Any chance that I can come with you? I've got things I have to finish too.'

So I said: 'Leave it to me, guys. I'll stay with Don until you can organise another watching shift.'

* * *

That gave me a chance to have a more private talk to Don.

'Don, are you sure you're happy with my suggestion? It's out of left field, I know.'

'Well, I'd certainly be happy if you are. But it's a big thing to offer to someone you don't really know.'

'I think I've seen enough of you over recent weeks, including France, to work out that I should be able to keep you under control....'

'I think I ought to show you the burns before you finally agree to take me, so you know what the damage is. Don't worry – there's no indecent exposure involved. It's only on my abdomen.'

He folded down the sheet and light blanket that covered him, and then gently lifted off the large dressing pad that was just lying on his abdomen.

I'd expected it not to be nice, but it was nastier than I thought. There were three large letters spelling RAT across his abdomen, and they were still bright red and inflamed, and seeping at the edges.

He said: 'It's going to be hard to go surfing again with that all over my middle.'

'Well, you're in luck then because we don't get much surf in Canberra, do we?'

'I was thinking of when I go back and visit my family in Bondi.'

'I'm sure we can get Marcus to shout you a wet-suit…. Anyway, how often do you have to get this cleaned and dressed?'

'At the moment they're doing it three times a day – morning, midday and evening. It's not quite as bad as you'd think. A nurse comes and bathes it all very lightly and puts more of something sanitising on it – nothing more than that. And I think Marcus said that he could arrange for a nurse to call at your place.'

'Thanks, Don. Seeing this makes me all the more determined to beat these bastards. And regarding the dressing, I reckon I could keep an eye on it and do anything necessary, at least while I'm at home. I had to do something like that once for my mother, when I was still living at home. Though hers wasn't acid burns.'

At that point there was a knock on the door, and Polly Jones from surveillance came in. She cast a rather horrified look at Don and said: 'Hi Donovan. I just heard that you've been through the wars – I thought I'd come and see how you are.'

'Thanks, Polly – everyone's being very kind to me at the moment. I've been better I'd have to say, but I'm getting there.'

I chipped in and said: 'While I've got both of you here I'd like to show you something. This is a picture of the intruder who came into your room, Don, and was definitely up to no good. Do you know the face at all?'

I showed Don my mobile phone with the picture that the hospital staff had emailed to me. He said: 'I know the face – he's in surveillance, though not in my area. I think he's in the section that does surveillance of dodgy embassies. I can't give you a name at the moment, but Polly might know.' He passed the phone to her.

'No doubts about it – that's Erwin Harris. He is in embassy watching, like you said. I've always thought he seemed a rather unpleasant person, but I didn't realise it was anything like this. It really does seem that we have to be careful now – trust nobody until they prove themselves. One way or the other….'

She chatted to Don for a minute or two more, but he was fading and she obviously decided that he needed peace more than he needed company so she made her apologies and left.

I said to Don: 'Thanks yet again for Polly – she seems to be a great pick.'

* * *

When I met with Marcus later, I had a win and a loss. He was only too happy to agree to my earlier suggestion about formalising liaison with Polly Jones, and he was interested to hear that Don's "visitor" at the hospital was AFP Surveillance. He said he wasn't totally surprised because he's been worried about inside enemies as much as I am.

However, he told me that Don coming to my apartment was off. He said they'd managed to organise secure accommodation close to the hospital, and a nurse would come over daily to bathe and dress Don, so he wouldn't need to come to my apartment. I wasn't surprised because I knew he wasn't happy with my idea, but I was a bit sad because I'd been quite looking forward to the company.

A COFFEE BREAK

Half way through the next morning at work, I was in need of a cup of strong coffee so I dropped in to the staff canteen. As I walked in I noticed Marcus Wiersma and Tony Mazzini in earnest conversation at one of the tables, amongst a number of other patrons. One of the patrons was sitting two tables away, and would have been within earshot of Marcus and Tony. Nothing surprising about that, except that he wasn't paying any attention to his cup of coffee and he seemed to be jotting notes on a pad of paper.

Still nothing surprising, but I thought I'd sit at another table with my coffee instead of taking it back to the office. And it struck me that the guy was listening quite intently to Tony and Marcus, and his notes were quite likely on what the two of them were saying.

I didn't recognise the guy, but I tried to memorise his features as accurately as I could. I also pulled out my phone and tried to take a photo, but I couldn't do it too obviously and it didn't come out well.

After a while Marcus and Tony swigged the last of their coffees, took the cups back to the counter and walked out. The guy got up shortly afterwards and walked out as well. His coffee looked untouched.

I mused on this while I drank my own coffee, when suddenly a

voice at my shoulder said: 'You obviously thought he was suss too?'
I turned round and saw Polly Jones.

'Were you looking at him too?'

'Yes, I was sitting over at the table near the wall.' She pointed
behind me.

I hadn't even noticed her, though to be fair there had been a few
other patrons as well.

'Do you have any idea of who he was?

'His name is Ian Perkins, and he's in Diplomatic Protection. I've
thought for a while there was something dodgy about him, and now
I'm sure of it. I reckon he got a good transcript of what Inspector
Wiersma and Sergeant Mazzini were talking about. I hope it wasn't
anything too disastrous. They shouldn't really have been doing it in
the tea room, though I think they actually met in here by chance.'

'As soon as I get back to my room I can ask Tony what they
were talking about. I was trying to get a picture of the person, but I
couldn't do it obviously and it didn't work.'

Polly pulled out her own phone, and showed me a clear picture
of the individual. 'I'll email that you when I get back to the office.'

I'm beginning to realise that Don's praise of Polly was pretty
accurate.

We drank the last of our coffees, and I said to Polly: 'I had a great
aunt called Polly, but it's not a common name these days, is it?'

'You're right, it isn't common but it isn't my name either. I was
christened Pauline, but for some reason I got Polly from the family
from a young age and I've stayed that way. I quite like it. I reckon it
sounds sort of innocent. Nobody called Polly could be any sort of
threat, could they?'

I just smiled. I'm beginning to reckon that Polly could be quite a
threat if you were on the wrong side of her.

* * *

Back upstairs I dropped in to Tony's room and asked him what he and Marcus had been talking about in the tea room, and told him why I was asking.

'We were basically discussing what I can do to be of most use in the section while I'm half incapacitated. Luckily because I'm deskbound there weren't any direct operational things, but we did discuss some evaluations that I can do, and that might have indicated what some of the operations have been. I should have noticed that guy. I'm not back up to full speed yet, obviously.'

'He wasn't all that obvious. I didn't notice him all that quickly, though Polly did have him tagged early on. She did say, though, that she was already suspicious of him for other reasons.'

'Well, this is something else that we didn't need. I'd better at least mention to Marcus that it's happened. We all need to be even more careful in future.'

How true....

THE SPREAD OF BLANK

The interception and identification of emails, dark web messages and other communications is helping us to build a picture of the extent and distribution of BLANK membership around Australia. Slow and painstaking work, but well worth it.

The core of the membership appears to be in Canberra – the Australian Capital Territory and immediately surrounding areas. Not surprising since the central focus seems to be Topman, and he must be a Canberra resident.

The next largest number of members is in Melbourne and around various parts of Victoria. This is also not surprising since Melbourne has had a long tradition of small neo-Nazi groups, who do street parades and similar every so often. As far as we can tell, those groups are quite separate from BLANK – it's just that such activities seem to appeal to Victorians more than others.

After Victoria comes Queensland – again not surprising given the prevalence of outspoken right-wing views in various parts of the state, especially the more remote areas. Tasmania has a few members, but then it isn't a large state anyway. South Australia only has a couple that we've picked up, and none yet in the Northern Territory or Western Australia.

The surprise is New South Wales, which ought to be similar to Victoria from its overall population balance, but isn't. Maybe that's just a lapse in our surveying, but maybe not. There are certainly some members, but not as many as we'd expected.

All the names with contact details are going into an ever-expanding database, so that we'll be ready for the big round-up when the moment comes.

And then along came Marvin….

MARVIN

Marvin Smith was the living definition of boring, though some would even dispute the use of the word "living". He was short in stature, plain of face, and almost totally lacking in any social skills. He was, however, intelligent and had published a number of scientific papers on birds, mainly on the feeding and breeding habits of various birds of prey. He had published these under the name of Merlin Smith, because like everybody else he considered Marvin to be a tacky name, and he called himself after his favourite bird of prey – the merlin. Small, compact, and very adept at its job of catching other small birds. The thought of Merlin the wizard was also appealing.

Marvin's latest goal was a study of the habits of the brown goshawk in the Grampians area of Victoria. His normal practice was to find a nesting pair of his target species, and then build a hide from which he could observe the birds. The hide was a small tent frame covered with vegetation so that it looked like the brush around it, and Marvin would sit inside on a camp stool, with a powerful camera on a stand, a small video camera, binoculars and a notebook.

Marvin had located a nesting pair just outside the Grampians

National Park boundary, since hide-building was not allowed within the Park. A narrow and rather obscure track led through trees to a small open area, probably a frost-hollow, and it was an ideal spot from which to watch the birds so he built his hide there.

He was happily filming and annotating one day when an extraordinary disturbance occurred. From along the track came figure after figure dressed in military camouflage gear and carrying weapons. They spread out in the clearing and then appeared to be practising various military manoeuvres. There was also simulated combat and finally some actual firing of the weapons – presumably blank ammunition since nobody seemed to get injured.

Marvin was well concealed in his hide and he watched with increasing amazement, then with alarm at what these men might be, and anger at the fact that they had disturbed his birds. First one flew away from the nest, then the other, and Marvin doubted that they would ever return.

He studied the uniforms, each of which had a badge on the shoulder. He had a reasonable knowledge of military uniforms and badges, and this was not one that he knew – a white rectangle with a black edge and nothing else, except possibly a word written under it – he couldn't quite make it out. So these couldn't be regular troops – terrorists perhaps? He was in two minds as to whether or not he should report all this. He didn't want to cause trouble for himself, but the deciding factor was his rage at the fact that his perfect study had been totally disrupted, so he decided to photograph and film the goings-on as comprehensively as he could.

After quite some time the manoeuvres ended, and the men sat down, drank from flasks and ate some food that they dug out of backpacks; then finally they formed up and left the area via the rough footpath. Silence reigned again, but there was no sign of the goshawks returning. Still seething, Marvin decided to drive to the Police Station in Ararat and report what had happened.

* * *

Marvin wasn't an impressive person and the initial reaction in the Ararat Police Station was scepticism, but when he showed the officer some of the footage the eyes opened a bit.

'I think I might give Melbourne a call about this and get some advice. Would you mind waiting a bit while I contact them.' Then as an afterthought: 'Would you like a cup of tea or coffee or something?'

Marvin opted for black coffee and then waited. And waited and waited. He was about to call out and ask if he could go now when the officer returned from the back. Distinctly more animated than earlier.

'Looks like you've really stirred up something with this one. What you've filmed is something that's a priority target for both us and the Feds. Melbourne's sending a helicopter here right now, and they're asking you to go in the chopper to Melbourne with all the material that you've filmed. Some Feds are flying from Canberra to Melbourne at this moment to meet with you, and one of our guys from here will drive your car to Melbourne for you.'

Marvin gulped, but the thought of the helicopter decided it. He'd never been in a helicopter before, and he'd always wanted to because he thought it would probably be like his beloved birds soaring and gliding in the air. He loaded his equipment into the helicopter, handed over his car keys, and they were off.

It wasn't quite as good as he'd hoped – too noisy for a start – but he liked the way the machine could shoot straight up into the air like a bird taking off.

They were fairly soon in Melbourne, and they landed on a helipad on top of the police HQ. Another ten-minute wait and then the federal police arrived. Marvin had expected a couple of burly cops, but the main one was a relatively young female. She spoke.

'Hi, Marvin Smith? I'm Layla Mackenzie, Acting Sergeant in the Australian Federal Police, and this is my offsider Bill Hansen, who's a Senior Constable. We're very keen to have a look at this material that you've managed to record.'

Layla sounded nice, and Marvin reckoned he could cope with the two of them. He ran them both through all the still pictures on his camera, with Layla stopping him at intervals for a closer look. She gave some little squeaks of excitement, and said to Bill Hansen: 'Bill, mate – this is pure gold!' Then they ran through the film clips, which weren't so easy to see on the small screen, but there was plenty of enthusiasm for those too.

Finally Layla said: 'Marvin, Australia owes you a debt for getting this material. You won't be getting any public recognition, I'm afraid, because it's totally classified, but you'll be helping to undo a nasty terrorist group. So what's next? I'll have to get this material back to Canberra, but Bill would like to go back to your site near Ararat with you, and you can show him exactly where you were when you filmed this. There'll be an extra man from the Ararat station as well, and they can inspect the whole area carefully. There might just be some extra evidence there too.'

'Okay by me,' said Marvin. 'But are you saying you're going to take my cameras and all the film?'

'I was trying not to say it quite like that. If we can copy both the stills and the film clips that would be enough. We can get the copying witnessed so that it can be used in a court of law.'

'Well, you needn't do that with the stills – I can just take the camera card out and give it to you. I only just put a new one in for this shoot. It's got two rather crappy pictures of a brown harrier at the start, which can go, and then the rest is the soldiers or whatever they were. I've got plenty more cards back home – you're welcome to this one.'

'Thanks, Marvin – that'd be great. What about the movie part though?'

'I'm not sure about that one. I think there's some sort of hard drive or disc that records the stuff – it's not film, anyway. I suggest you take the whole camera with you and get one of your technical experts to download it. Then hopefully you can give me the camera back when you've done it.'

'You're on. I'll have to say one more thing, though. Whatever we do, there won't be any of these specific images left on either of your cameras. That's because this is classified material, but it's also for your own safety. If these people knew that you had the material, you could be at significant personal risk.'

Marvin just gulped. 'Okay….'

* * *

He enjoyed the trip back to Ararat, which they did in his car so that he could stay on afterwards and sort out what to do with his hide. Bill was quite a laid-back sort of guy, and it turned out that he knew something about Canberra birds so they were able to compare notes on various species.

Back at the hide with the extra policeman, all three of them looked around the area. Marvin couldn't see anything unusual, so he spent his time thinking about where he might move the hide to, and how to dismantle it while salvaging some of the brushwood covering. The two policemen did find some empty cartridges and other bits and pieces that they seemed quite pleased with. They also got him to show them the hide in detail, and they photographed it. Bill told him that if he ever needed another job, the AFP could use him for camouflage duties as the hide was a pretty good effort.

Finally the two policemen departed, and Marvin was left staring in silence at the empty scene. When suddenly he noticed that it wasn't quite as deserted as he had first thought – there was a bird back on the nest that he thought had been abandoned. He got out his binoculars, which the police hadn't taken, and peered at the cleft in the tree. Yes, it was one of the brown harriers, and it appeared to have settled well on to the conglomeration of sticks that was the rough nest. And then – even better – the second bird arrived back at the nest and fed something to the sitting bird. No need to move the hide anywhere else – he was back in business!

As long as the military didn't return, of course….

MARVIN'S MATERIAL

No messing around this time – Tony, Marcus and the Deputy Commissioner came to see Marvin's material, with me and Bill Hansen doing the commentary. Don was still not very mobile, but I'd show him the material later.

We'd set up the best projection system we could rustle up, and a large screen. We'd cut every face from Marvin's pictures and highlighted them as mug shots for possible identification. On some the military headwear obscured the faces a little, but it was a start.

It was no surprise that two of the faces were Allen Briggs and Ray Coombs of the AFP, but we hadn't expected Terry Moore who works in the AFP Surveillance area. That was a distinct worry since we're relying on surveillance ourselves to make progress, and this is yet another enemy in that camp. We're going to have to restrict access to our operations even further than we already do. Then there was one federal politician and one Queensland one, tying up with names in the list that we'd found in the old Dickson Bowling Club. A number of other faces seemed rather familiar but we couldn't name them at this stage. Work in progress.

The disappointing feature was that the man who led the entire operation from start to finish had his face very effectively screened by a scarf tied around it, and unfortunately it didn't slip from start to finish. My guess is that this was Topman, whose name has cropped up in various emails that we've intercepted. I've never thought that this was an actual surname. It's a brand of men's clothing but I've never heard of it as a personal name. However, we're going to have to wait a bit longer to put a name to him. The person was of average height, average build, and didn't limp, stoop or have any other distinctive features. More work in progress on that one, too.

STORAGE FACILITIES

The surveillance of email traffic had continued to pick up references to material being "taken to the storage", and we'd gone round the various self-storage facilities in Fyshwick and interviewed the managers. We didn't want to alarm them by suggesting that they might be storing guns and ammunition, but we asked what sizes and natures of storage they had. Some were mainly open cage areas and would have been too public, but two had a number of enclosed areas of different sizes. We set up surveillance of those two premises, and we saw the large storage facility called Hoarders being visited more than once by known members of BLANK.

The Hoarders website indicated that it had electronic security entry and exit gates controlled by your own PIN, 24/7 video surveillance, digital security systems, daily lock checks and individually alarmed units with back-to-base monitoring if alarms were set off. It was unlikely that we'd be able to get undetected access to the unit even if we identified which unit the group was using, so we'd have to get the manager on side.

Bill Hansen and I went round to the facility, and we found the manager in residence. We introduced ourselves, and I said: 'Sir, we've received some information that suggests that a quantity of arms, ammunition and explosives may be in storage in one of your facilities. We're very keen to ascertain whether or not that's true, and I imagine that you'd be concerned yourself if it's so.'

The manager gulped a bit, and said: 'We certainly would. We have a total ban on anything like that in our premises under any circumstances, and it would have to go.'

Time for a bit of delicacy. 'We're anxious to do this a bit quietly at first. It's part of an undercover investigation, and if we alarm the people involved too soon we may lose a lot of them – they'll go to ground. We think we've narrowed down which of your facilities is involved, and what we'd like to do is have a quiet look and see just what's there. Once we know that we can consult with you on where we go from there.'

The manager looked a bit dubious, but said: 'Which facility do you think it's in?'

'Building B2. Would you be able to gain access to it without the users being aware that you've done it?'

'That's good if it's B2, because that one's only got two large storages inside it so we won't have to poke into much. We have of course got skeleton keys that can do all the doors, and codes to open anywhere. I can let you in to B2, but there'd be hell to pay if they came along while we were doing it and we were caught. We guarantee to them that we won't do it except in a dire emergency, but I would certainly like to know if there's anything that risky in our place.'

'If you have your keys and codes ready, it wouldn't take us very long. We wouldn't be doing any sort of inventory – just seeing whether or not the goods are there. We wouldn't have to open any crates or anything. We should be able to recognise them, and they'll probably be marked to indicate what's inside. I reckon it would take us about five minutes inside each storage room, and my suggestion would be that we bring a few uniformed police along to block off the access to the building temporarily on some pretext or other –

nothing to arouse anyone's suspicions – for fifteen minutes at the most. Would that be possible?'

'Yes it would be, and I can suggest one extra thing. When people access their facilities they have to go through the electronic entry gate and they put their personal PIN into the system to do it. Our system keeps a record of entries for a long time in case there are any claims or queries. I can look at the records for the two storages to see when their owners mostly come and go. That's no guarantee that they won't come at a different time, but it might be a slight help.'

'That would be great – thank you. Could we maybe do that bit now, and then we can plan on the basis of that?'

It didn't take long. 'Well, the user of B2-1 last accessed their unit three months ago, at 7 pm one evening. We can probably say that they aren't likely to be along within the next hour or so. The user of B2-2 has been coming several times a week for the last few months, and at quite variable times. However, it's now 10 in the morning, and almost all their visits have been later in the day, most after 4 pm. I'd be prepared to say that we should be safe at the moment, but if you could set up the diversion that you suggested that would be good.'

'We can certainly do that. And on the basis of those details I'd be sure that the facility we're interested in is B2-2 – the other hasn't been accessed enough. I'll call up some more troops.'

It took about thirty minutes to get several tactical response people out here, with a couple of traffic barriers and an explosives vest. Meanwhile the manager had dug out his access keys and codes. When the response people arrived we set the barriers up in front of block B2, and one of the men put on the vest. If anyone turned up to get into B2, the story would be that a suspicious package had been found outside the block and was being removed – wait for about twenty minutes and you'll be able to get into your shed.

Meanwhile the manager, Bill and I put on gloves and went into B2. We opened B2-1 first just to be able to write it off. It was a large shed, empty apart from some miscellaneous pieces of furniture – chairs, a table, a chest of drawers, a sideboard and a few other small pieces. Nothing in the drawers or the cupboard – on to the next shed.

And we hit pay dirt in B2-2, as I knew we would. There were stacks of boxes that would undoubtedly contain firearms. There were further stacks that were definitely ammunition boxes as they were clearly marked, and there were others that were labelled "Danger: Explosives". And in case we had any further doubts there was a pile of exposed weapons that were probably those that had recently been used the operation that Marvin saw.

We took care not to disturb anything, but Bill and I took cameras that I'd brought, and we photographed everything that we could see – overall shots, close-ups of markings on boxes and so on. I also made a rough count of the numbers of boxes of each.

Then I nodded to the manager. 'That's all we need. Thank you, sir – let's go.'

He closed up B2-2 carefully, then the main door of B2 and we went back to his office. Time for some careful diplomacy.

'We owe you quite a debt for this, and we won't forget it. You're probably horrified at what we've found and you'd like to get rid of it straight away, but I'd like to ask for your patience for a bit longer. This is confirmation of something that we've been suspecting for a while, and we're getting close to being able to close the whole thing down and arrest the key people. However, if we close this store down now we'll lose them all, so we'd like to ask for your patience for a little while more. That stuff has been in your store for quite a time now, and I can assure you that it's actually very safe as it's packed. The risk isn't going to change.'

He stared at me for some moments, then said: 'I guess we'll have to settle for that. Good luck in getting it closed down as soon as you can.'

'Thanks, sir. And please don't breathe a word of this to anyone else. There are eyes and ears around everywhere with this one, and we don't want to lose it.'

* * *

Back in the office and it was time for another urgent conference. Bill and I were joined by Marcus Wiersma, Tony Mazzini and an Assistant Commissioner, and the AC took the chair.

'I'd have to say that I'm not happy with having a large cache of guns and ammo just sitting around in Fyshwick like this. But the trouble is – correct me if I'm wrong – that you haven't yet identified the ringleader or ringleaders?'

It appeared that I was the one expected to speak. 'I'm afraid you're right, sir. We've got quite a few names so far, but by no means all, and we still haven't been able to identify the person that they've all been referring to as Topman, who does appear to be the overall leader.'

'Okay. It seems to me then that we might use this to try to flush out some more of the people, including your Topman. You've told me that at least some of your messages are being intercepted by the other side. Why don't you start dropping some hints that you might be getting near identifying a cache of weapons somewhere in Fyshwick, and see what happens. I'm guessing that they might just be prompted to move them somewhere else in the circumstances. Comments?'

'Fully agreed, sir. Watch this space. We'll keep you posted on what we do and what reactions we get as a result.'

I did get a faint nod from the Assistant Commissioner for that....

PROFESSOR YEVA THOMPSON

I'm not the only one whose reputation and career's on the line with all this, but I've become the most conspicuous one. Time for some very deep thought.

I have a nagging feeling that we're still missing something with the senior scientists of AGRICOZ. Tony had told me more than once how useful he'd found Professor Thompson from the Australian National University for background on scientists, so I thought I'd see if she might be able to help me too.

I phoned the number that we had for her and told her about what had happened to Tony and his wife. There hadn't been any media stories about it, and she was quite shocked. She said I was welcome to come round to talk to her, though she warned me that she felt she'd already told Tony all that she knew. She said I was welcome to come round straight away, but otherwise not for another fortnight as she was going away. I couldn't afford to wait that long so I went straight round.

When she answered the door I could see immediately why Tony found her such an impressive figure – tall, slightly stooping, and with a most penetrating gaze.

'Acting Sergeant Mackenzie? I'm pleased finally to be meeting you. Sergeant Mazzini has told me a lot about you.' She must have seen me gulp a bit because she added, with a faint smile: 'All good, I would have to say.'

She sat me down and said: 'I was horrified to hear what had happened to Sergeant Mazzini and his wife. I have both respect and affection for him, and I liked his wife when I met her once. If you think I may know anything that might help to solve the crime, please do ask.'

I told her that we were now sure that at least one person in AGRICOZ was involved, and probably more, but we were having trouble pinning down individual names. I didn't mention anyone because I didn't want to prime her in any way.

'I'd like to run through our possible names. Sergeant Mazzini has told me that you've probably been involved at one time or another with a number of them on committees, and I'd very much welcome your own personal thoughts on all of them. You'd probably have a different and shrewder view of them than many would. May I ask you about them?'

'You flatter me and judge me too kindly, but you're right that different people see others in various ways, so fire away.'

'The first one is Dr Rafael Paulsen, the Chief of Pest Management.'

'I have met him once. He's not a Fellow of our Academy, but he came once to one of our discussion panels on modern approaches to pest management. He was rather quiet, and didn't participate as much as we'd hoped. He'd spent some time at a private research facility in the States, and I don't know whether he regarded some of us as inferior or what, but he wasn't very forthcoming. Especially to people of different backgrounds, by which I mean ethnic origins. That may be unfair, but I had that feeling.'

'That's very helpful – just the sort of thing I'm after, thank you. The next candidate is Dr Ronald Varghese, the Chief of Molecular Science.'

'Ah well, he is one of our Fellows, so I know him better. I think he has an excellent brain. You may or may not know that he trained originally as a physical scientist, and then when he went to Berkeley University he switched to molecular science and genetic engineering. However, he sees things very much as a physical scientist would, not as a biologist. Everything is process-driven by physical rules, and the living world is not always like that. So there's something slightly inhuman about him, but he's a very bright man.'

'Thank you again for that. The next is Dr Helena Sweetman, the Chief of Environmental Science. She's originally American and trained at Harvard, but she has been over here for some time.'

'She's also not a Fellow of the Academy, but as with Dr Paulsen she's been a resource person in two of our discussion panels, I think. She's a very clever and able scientist, and in my view also a very nice and ethical person. And just in case you start thinking that I may judge female scientists differently from male ones, I can swear to you that I don't consider gender at all. I look at their scientific abilities and their personal qualities regardless, and Helena comes out high up the scale.'

'Okay, thank you. What about Dr Ratko Petković, the Deputy Director General?'

'Ah well, I know Ko quite well because his wife's Armenian, and he and she both come to quite a few Armenian events in Canberra. I think he's a very nice man. I have no direct knowledge of his scientific background, but as a person I think he is absolutely ethical and delightful company. He's good with other people, which he has to be for his work because he seems to be the person who sorts things out when personalities go wrong. And in somewhere like AGRICOZ there are always plenty of difficult personalities.'

'It's interesting that that's the same assessment of Dr Petković that various of the AGRICOZ staff have given us. My next is Dr Barbara Plumley, who's a fruit fly expert.'

'She's also not a Fellow of the Academy, and I've only met her once when we had a meeting on fruit flies. I couldn't really judge her, but she didn't seem the sort to be an extremist.'

'Dr John Newman, the animal physiologist?'

'One of our Fellows. A straightforward man, and I would think decent. Not an extremist.'

'This is very helpful. Dr Claudia Thomson, the crop breeder?'

'She's not a Fellow, but I do know her as a friend. She's an absolutely honourable and decent person, who also does quite a bit of good work in the community outside her AGRICOZ work.'

'Thank you again for all of that. And finally the last person that I wanted to ask you about – the Director General Dr Harcourt Johnson.'

There was a longish silence while Professor Thompson looked at me, with her formidable hooded eyes.

'I can't say I know him at all well. We have overlapped rather occasionally over a number of years, but never in a way that gave me a chance to appraise him. My first impression was that he seemed pleasant and approachable, but then after that terrible affair with his sister he was never the same again. Remote and cold, though one can understand that.'

For a moment I was stunned. What happened with his sister? Tony hadn't ever mentioned anything.

'I haven't had any information about other members of his family. His sister, you said?'

'It was truly awful. She was a member of a United Nations team that went to Afghanistan some years ago to investigate women's education, which is of course a very delicate subject in that country. The team went to a remote area in the northwest of the country, and they were captured and killed. It's believed that they were tortured before they were killed, but the bodies were never found so nobody was sure. However, what did happen was that they were beheaded and the heads were displayed on stakes at the edge of the village concerned. Pictures got into the international press and there was a brief international outcry at the time, but then some other event quickly overtook that news and nothing more was heard.'

'That does ring a faint bell because I worked for a time in counter-intelligence before my present position, but I don't recall anyone called Johnson being involved.'

'Ah well, you wouldn't because she was known by her married name. Let me just look it up. I keep a file of events involving women that I might need to refer to again.'

She rummaged for a few minutes in a folder and pulled out a newspaper cutting. 'It was a five-person UN team – three men and two women. One of the women was named as Harriet Bukowski. Her husband was Polish, but her maiden name was Harriet Johnson, and she was Harcourt Johnson's sister. All five were killed and had their heads displayed. Truly horrible.'

I felt instant sympathy for the Director General – an appalling thing to have happen to someone you know and love. It would be impossible to forget or forgive, and it would be understandable if he had turned to extremist activity himself as a result. The only trouble with that, of course, is that you're then making yourself as evil as the perpetrators of the original crimes.

'Thank you so much for this information. I can't understand why we hadn't already picked that one up, but we can now take that into account in our investigations. And you may just have given us the breakthrough that we've been waiting for. We'd been focusing on scientists of AGRICOZ, and not on other senior people in the organisation.

'As you've been so helpful to Sergeant Mazzini, I'm sure he wouldn't mind me telling you that our enquiries are pointing us more and more towards right-wing terrorism in Australia, and that Dr Hardcastle was somehow mixed up with these people, though he wasn't necessarily right-wing himself. But please don't pass that on to anyone else yet – it might prejudice our investigations if it got out. Thank you so much for seeing me at this short notice, and I wish you good and safe travels.'

I think we may have just found Topman....

* * *

Back in the office I met with Tony, and Don who was back and fully in action again after his injury. I briefed them on this latest information. Don agreed that he and the rest of the surveillance team should give top priority to Harcourt Johnson – personal movements and activities, communications to and from – everything.

The movements and activities didn't reveal a great deal at first, but the communications did. He was regularly posting messages via the dark web – instructions on how to become more combat-ready, names of people to be targeted and threatened, orders about movements of stores and items to be stockpiled, names of AFP officers suspected of being part of the surveillance against BLANK (a bit too close to home with some of those). Although it never said it specifically, it was clear that he was Topman. We prepared a detailed briefing on all of this for the Assistant Commissioner, who then summoned Marcus and me to a meeting.

The AC said: 'I had heard a few comments previously that Harcourt Johnson might be involved with this terrorist mob in some way, but I never thought it would be on anything like this scale. It shocks me that someone of his position and status should be like that, but I guess the history of his sister explains it. He does appear to be the kingpin, or one of them, and we have to take action.

'I think the best would be if the three of us could have a private interview with him, preferably out of his office but not in AFP premises, and see what he has to say. I suggest that I ask the initial questions, which would be appropriate to his seniority, and either of you could come in later with specifics. I would propose to start by saying we'd like to find out more about activities of some of his staff at AGRICOZ. That would inevitably lead into his own activities too.

Any comments on all that?'

We both indicated we were in agreement, so he said: 'I'll get my office to ask if we could make an official call on him at his apartment, as soon as possible to ask about AGRICOZ staff. I'll let you know when and where.'

INVESTIGATIONS AROUND TARAGO

One of our outstanding tasks was still to locate the second property like the one at Royalla where Ella Mazzini had been taken. Communications from BLANK had indicated that there was a second property somewhere, but with few clues as to where it was located – just a possible hint of Bungendore near Canberra, or Tarago which was a bit further away.

We did an aerial survey of Bungendore, but no real possibilities stood out. It is quite a populated township, and there didn't seem to be many clusters of buildings that were likely. However, when we flew over Tarago there did seem to be a possible site. There was a rural property a little way out of the township that had a large old homestead, with outbuildings including a shearing shed, but what was interesting was that two new wooden buildings had recently been erected near the homestead – one of which might have been a dormitory and the other a workshop. The property didn't seem to be one where the level of agriculture required so much extra construction, so we thought we'd do some closer monitoring.

One of our surveillance officers, Bob Powell, put on moleskins and a bush shirt, and then drove up to the homestead and pounded on the door. It was opened by a male who looked at him suspiciously.

'G'day, mate,' said Bob. 'You wouldn't 'ave 'ad a blue heeler cross wanderin' round 'ere lately, would yer? "E's gorn missin', and 'e's one o' me best dogs. Answers to Bruce.'

'No, mate. We keep a close eye on who and what's around here, and we haven't seen a stray dog.' The "who" as well as the "what" sounded like a distinct warning to Bob.

'Okay, no worries mate. If you do happen to see 'im, this is me number.' He passed a handwritten scrap of paper with a mobile phone number to the man. Not a number that could be traced back to Bob's name. Then he got back in his Land Cruiser and drove off.

He went back to his colleagues who'd set up a small base in Tarago, and said: 'I got a fairly hostile reception. Don't think they like people coming in from outside. There are certainly two new buildings that have gone up recently, quite large. Didn't see anybody around while I was there except for the guy who answered the door, and when he did he stepped outside and shut the door, so I couldn't see anything or anyone inside. What I did notice was a hill not all that far from the property, but outside the back boundary fence. It could be a good surveillance point if we want to keep an eye on the place. I reckon we could station someone up there with good binos and recording equipment, and we might get something useful out of it.'

Interestingly, a little while after Bob's visit the mobile number was rung – no doubt to find out who he really was. But the only answer the caller would have got was: 'Sorry, I'm not here at the moment. Please leave a message or call again.' No message was left.

* * *

At the same time we needed to get on with the AC's instructions regarding the ammo store. We've been fairly sure which messages of ours are being picked up by the other side, so we started sending some out. At first they indicated that we had a vague idea that there might be dangerous stuff in storage somewhere, with Fyshwick one possibility.

Then they started sounding a bit more positive, and indicated that there could be three possible sites. Hoarders was one of the three that we named, but with an indication that it was thought to be less likely than the other two. We set a watch on Hoarders, and waited to see what would happen.

A MEETING WITH
HARCOURT JOHNSON

The AC's secretary had contacted Dr Johnson, and he indicated that 1030 on the morning after the call would suit him, at his Canberra apartment. That gave us a little time to discuss a strategy for the approach.

The apartment was in the prestigious suburb of Forrest, and as with Dr Hardcastle's apartment there was a concierge. The concierge called up to Johnson, then said: 'Fifth floor in the lift, then turn right and it's at the end of the corridor. The doors will open for you.'

Dr Johnson was dressed relatively informally, and he greeted us cordially. 'Come in and be seated, please. My secretary told me that you wanted to ask about some of the senior staff of AGRICOZ, but may I first offer you some coffee?'

The AC declined on all our behalves, which was a pity because I'd have loved some. However, Johnson said: 'I'm actually dying for some coffee, so if you wouldn't mind I'll just put the jug on. And feel free to change your minds if you'd like.'

He turned on an electric jug on the sideboard in the room, then said: 'I'll just go and get my papers on the various staff members.'

He went out, and we sat and listened to the noise of the jug coming to the boil. It was quite full so it took a while. Then the jug turned off and there was silence.

Rather too much silence, and Johnson had not reappeared. Marcus looked at the AC and said: 'I think I'll just go and see what's happening.'

He went out, and a few moments later rushed in saying: 'He's done a bunk. No sign of him anywhere, and the lift's showing at the basement level, so he's probably driven off.'

The AC and Marcus seemed surprised, but I can't say I was. I fished in my bag and came out with a sheet of paper which I handed to the AC. 'Sir, that's the rego number for Johnson's car, assuming he's using his own, but the other details on there may be even more important – they're the details of Johnson's private plane. He has one, and he keeps it in a hangar at Canberra Airport. You might like to alert the authorities there to stop it taking off anywhere.'

'Jesus. Thanks, Mackenzie – I'm glad someone's on the ball with this. This is a direct admission of guilt by Johnson, and I never expected that he'd react this quickly.'

He phoned his office and gave them instructions to put out an alert for the car, and have the airport put a hold on the plane. Top priority...

* * *

The office probably acted as fast as they could, but I was worried because it doesn't take long to drive from Forrest to Canberra Airport. He'd had a bit of leeway before we started to act, and I was wondering if we'd been fast enough.

However, he didn't turn up at Canberra Airport, and there were no reports of his car being seen anywhere.

He'd vanished into thin air.

* * *

While we were there we felt we should look at the other rooms of the apartment, and it quickly became clear that Johnson had planned his departure – or escape might be a better word – carefully. The lounge room in which we had sat was untouched – all furniture and fittings there, the electric jug carefully placed and so on. However, in the main bedroom the furniture was there but all of Johnson's clothing had gone. The study was similar – books present in all the bookshelves, but any personal papers, finance documents and so on were missing.

The AC ruled that the property would need to be searched from top to toe. He phoned the Commissioner to advise him of what had happened, and asked him to have the Minister told of the events. Then he ordered us to get someone in to guard the property while a search detail was organised. After that he left the property, fuming….

Downstairs, recalling that at Hardcastle's apartment the concierge had been able to tell us who'd used Hardcastle's electronic keys at any time, we stopped at Johnson's concierge's desk to ask the same question. He checked his system, and said the lift fob had been used 35 minutes earlier, and nine times during the day before. Johnson must have been moving all his important belongings out then, into his car or some other transport. Definitely a well-planned departure.

* * *

Following the AC's orders we got a team together to make a thorough search of Johnson's apartment, and they found nothing of use at all. There were absolutely no papers of any sort, and nothing that might indicate whether he had another bolt-hole available anywhere – or that he had the remotest connection with BLANK.

And he himself had simply vanished.

* * *

Back in the office I thought hard about what Johnson might do next. His escape from the interview with the Assistant Commissioner proved beyond doubt that he's involved with BLANK, and is probably Topman. He's now wanted for criminal activities, and he's completely finished as far as any role in government – or anywhere else – is concerned. When that happens to a very senior person, and one probably with a big ego, it's hard to know how they'll react. Some who think they are finished may decide to go out with a bang – might Johnson be one such?

It occurred to me that Johnson is a proficient pilot, and he has a plane. Yes, Canberra Airport has been told to impound his plane, but there would be nothing to stop him hiring another plane from somewhere. And if he wanted to go out with a bang, why not a major bang by crashing the plane directly into the Afghanistan Embassy in Canberra. He hates Afghanistan bitterly because of what happened to his sister – this might be the ultimate – and for him very final – revenge.

I looked on the map to see where the Embassy of Afghanistan is located, and found it is in West Deakin just down from the Royal Australian Mint. I was horrified to see that it was in close proximity to several other diplomatic missions. Very close were the missions of Timor Leste and Mauritius, and not much further away were Brunei Darussalam, Bosnia and Herzegovina, the Solomon Islands and Hungary. Cyprus and Botswana were not much further either. An aerial attack on Afghanistan would probably affect them all, and it would be catastrophic – for Australia's reputation as well as for the people killed. We need to locate and neutralise Harcourt Johnson as quickly as possible.

I wondered if I was being paranoid with all of this, but the more I looked at it the more I thought that it was something we should take seriously. I decided to go to Marcus Wiersma and share my thoughts with him.

OBSERVATIONS AT TARAGO

As Bob Powell had suggested, Mount Woolowolar which lay behind the Tarago property had some convenient places on which to set up an observation post. We'd picked one that shouldn't be too obvious from the property, and we'd set up a watching point inside a bit of natural cover, with good binos and a camera. The observation point was on the slope of the hill, and the property was between it and the Goulburn to Braidwood road. We were able to see and record vehicles that came into the property from the road, and also movements in the back areas of the property away from the road.

There was reasonably steady traffic in and out most of the day – probably a bit more than one might expect for a place that was just for primary production – and there were occasional trucks delivering some sort of goods, mostly boxed and the observers couldn't see what it was. At one stage a car drove out of a garage and was away for a short time, possibly just into Tarago and back, and the observers thought that it might have been Harcourt Johnson's car but they couldn't see the number plate clearly enough.

* * *

And then the messages had their effect. There were emails going out from BLANK to selected members telling them to report to Hoarders in Fyshwick at 10 pm that night for the first of several removals of goods from the storage. The exercise was described as "relocation", and the destination was not mentioned – the message said that would be advised on the evening.

We told the manager of Hoarders that he was about to have his storage area emptied of explosives, and he was only too happy to let us in for one last operation. This was the placement of inconspicuous tracking devices on a number of the boxes, so that we could follow where they were taken without needing to follow them on the roads. We didn't want to alert them with a road pursuit. From a static vehicle nearby in Fyshwick we saw a number of trucks leave Hoarders, and the tracking devices then saw them drive towards Tarago and turn in to the property that we were watching. At least we'd got that one right.

We estimated that with the truck space available they could have moved a third to a half of their store. The next day they sent out instructions for another removal operation, and the trucks again went to Tarago. The morning after that we got the manager to let us in again, and we found that most of the boxes had gone. However, there was no summons for a third night of moving, so we thought we'd better now work out a plan of action. Quickly....

TWIN RISKS

Marcus wasted no time. He summoned me, Tony Mazzini and Don Lewis to his office for an urgent evaluation of the situation.

'Layla, you're on top of all this as much as anyone is. Give us your analysis of where we're at, please.'

Talk about being put straight on the spot. Luckily I'd been awake for half the night thinking of all of that, so I dived in.

'In my view we've got two separate issues that have to be addressed very quickly. The first is the stash of weapons and explosives that's now on the Tarago property, and the second is what Harcourt Johnson's next actions might be.

'First Tarago. They now have a large quantity of arms and ammunition on the property, presumably just dumped into their storage sheds at this stage. Our watchers up the hill should have a bit more information on the exact location within the property. At the moment it won't be very organised, but I'm guessing that they'll soon get it all sorted and they may then think about laying out some sort of protection.

'This might possibly be surveillance devices to warn of people approaching, but also it could be some sort of booby-trapping in case people do get inside. At the worst they might rig the shed to blow up totally if it was attacked, and I think we should act urgently to prevent that possibility – it could be catastrophic for us if we did have to go in, and dangerous also for the general community.

'Now Harcourt Johnson. He worries me greatly because he's an intelligent and resourceful man, and I suspect he is now completely unpredictable. When we went to his apartment with the AC the other day he seemed calm and relaxed, and he acted as though things were perfectly normal. It was a total front, because he would have known perfectly well that he was totally ruined. He's been exposed as the leader of a terrorist organisation that has already been responsible for many serious criminal actions, and he's potentially facing prosecution and lengthy jail time.

'I can't see a man like him accepting that humiliation, or the prospect of a long term in the Alexander Maconochie Centre, and he could do absolutely anything to prevent it. My greatest worry is that because he's lost everything he might even be prepared to lose his life as well, in a final and spectacular suicidal act. He has a plane and he can fly. I know we've had his plane impounded at Canberra Airport, but he could still hire another. What if he were to fly over central Canberra and dive the plane straight into the Afghanistan Embassy or something like that? That would be in revenge for what Afghans did to his sister, of course. Or it could be another major building – anything to cause a sensational splash.

'An additional complication of the idea of the Embassy attack is that a number of other diplomatic missions are in close proximity to Afghanistan's. I looked on a map just before we came here, and I could see Brunei Darussalam, Timor-Leste and Mauritius very close by, and Bosnia and Herzegovina, Hungary and Solomon Islands not much further away. The diplomatic fallout from collateral damage in such an attack would be huge.

'So what responses can we make to that risk? I can only say that we have to locate Johnson as a matter of the utmost urgency, so that we can neutralise any threat that he poses. But that's easier said than done. He might be at the Tarago property, but we have no confirmation of that, or he could be almost anywhere, and planning almost anything.

'Over to you, gentlemen.'

'Many thanks for all that, Layla. A good assessment, pretty threatening, and I don't think I can add anything to that. Tony or Don?'

They both shook their heads, so Marcus said: 'We're going to have to go into Tarago as soon as we can. That'll neutralise the weapons and ammo part of it, and if we're really lucky we might find Johnson there too. This'll have to be set up and controlled from the top. I'll go to the AC right now.'

A NIGHT OPERATION

The powers higher than us put together a strike force, as quietly as possible so that Tarago was not warned by any of the renegades in the AFP who were sympathetic to them. At quarter past midnight they made a ring around the main building, with outliers around the three storage areas as well, called with a loud-hailer for people to come out, and almost simultaneously started battering on the doors to force an entry. We were not part of the force, but we were allowed nearby in protective gear to watch and advise as necessary.

Nothing happened for a few moments, then we heard a small amount of gunfire, and then members of our force reappeared escorting people who'd obviously been inside the building.

But Harcourt Johnson was not one of them.

* * *

The next activities were something of an anti-climax. The various people who'd been inside the buildings were arrested for being in possession of an illegal hoard of weapons and ammunition; their names were taken and they were transported to the AFP Headquarters for further interrogation.

After that there was a very thorough search of all the buildings on the property, including all barns and outhouses. Large quantities of paper were recovered, which should give valuable details about BLANK and its operations, and various other bits and pieces for further analysis and investigation. But still no sign of Harcourt Johnson, nor was his car on the site.

All possible hiding places such as lofts, other roof spaces, cellars and so on were investigated, but they were empty. Interestingly, one new subterranean room was in process of being excavated – probably intended as a future hidey-hole, but it wasn't finished yet. If Johnson had been here, he was gone now. We would make sure that that was one of the most urgent questions that were asked of all those who'd been arrested.

* * *

Given the scale that the operation against BLANK had now reached, control was taken over higher up in the AFP. A Commander was appointed to organise and lead the operation, and a larger force was assembled under him. However, our team led by Inspector Wiersma was given the specific and top priority task of chasing down and arresting Harcourt Johnson, who was still a potential high security concern.

But where was he....?

THE SEARCH FOR
HARCOURT JOHNSON

Photographs of Harcourt Johnson were circulated throughout Australia and through Interpol, but no sightings were reported. There seemed to be two other possible ways to track him down. One way was through his car, which was quite distinctive. The registration was HJ 333, though that probably wouldn't be of much use because he'd almost certainly change the plates. However, one thing still in our favour was that the car itself was unusual. It was an expensive sporty Mercedes – a model of which there were few in Australia, and it was white with a black stripe on either side. That might stand out somewhat, and alerts were sent out to all police around Australia to watch for this car.

The other way to locate Johnson might be through his mobile phone usage, if we could locate which phone or phones he's using and then locate where the signals were coming from.

And it was the mobiles that provided the information. We'd taken all the people at the Tarago property into custody, but there were still others in the community (doubtless including some AFP) who were still corresponding with Topman. After some difficulty we pinned him down in or near Orange in the New South Wales Central Tablelands, and we then narrowed it down to Lucknow, an old gold mining town 10 kilometres SE of Orange. Gold hasn't been mined there for more than half a century, but it has some historic old buildings and is a popular stop for tourists.

The town only has a population of around three hundred, so you'd think that a new arrival would stand out. However, there are many old buildings around the area, some rather derelict, and Johnson could easily settle in one of those without being very obvious.

We were debating how we could go and look around a small place like Lucknow without being too obvious, when Polly Jones piped up.

'My partner Belle Hobson comes from Orange, and I'm pretty sure she's got an auntie who lives in Lucknow. That's the only reason that I've heard of the place. Belle's on leave at the moment, and she and I could go up and poke around without being obvious. We'd be locals, sort of. Any thoughts?'

I was the first to respond. 'I think it's a great idea, as long as Belle doesn't get exposed to any danger, but I wouldn't think that's a high risk if you're just wandering round. I don't think Johnson knows you by sight. And there's one extra thing you could do while you're in the area. Orange has a commercial airport and planes for hire, and we would want to make absolutely sure that Johnson can't hire one from there for any suicide missions or the like. You could take his photo to the airport management and stress that under no circumstances should anyone looking like that be allowed to hire a plane or fly one out of there.'

* * *

In the end Marcus decreed that I should accompany Polly and Belle to Orange and Lucknow. He said it was because I had more knowledge of Johnson's activities which might be useful, but I think given the importance of this part of the mission, he wanted me there for him too. I'd have to keep a low profile, though, because Johnson would recognise me, whereas he doesn't know Polly or Belle. Polly would drive herself and Belle up there, and I'd go in my car to give us more flexibility up there.

I was interested to meet Belle, who couldn't have been a greater opposite to Polly. While Polly is petite and talkative, Belle is tall, built like a weight-lifter, and says very little. A classic case of opposites attracting. If they do bump into Johnson they'll have to be a bit careful. While Polly never stands out in a crowd, Belle does catch the eye because of her build and size. There'd be no reason for Johnson to suspect her of surveillance, though.

We didn't alert the New South Wales Police to our mission at this stage, because we're still worried about BLANK members in law enforcement agencies around the country. We booked a couple of rooms in a central but inconspicuous motel in Orange, and drove up there in our two cars.

Belle contacted her auntie in Lucknow that evening, and said she was up here with a couple of friends and could we all come over some time to see her? Her aunt agreed on the next day for a mid-morning cup of tea. After breakfast we went in Belle's car to have a preliminary look at Lucknow before we met her aunt. We drove out of Orange along the road to Bathurst, and not very far along we came to a tall triangular metal structure which Belle told us was the headframe or poppet head over an abandoned mineshaft. She said gold was discovered here and at nearby Ophir in 1851, and it used to be a bustling community. Now there are a few rather desultory tourist sites, other mining remains, and a scattering of houses, not all occupied by the look of them. Where might Harcourt Johnson be amongst all this?

We met Belle's Auntie Maisie at her house at half past ten, and she brewed a pot of tea. We all sat down to chat, which was mostly Belle updating Auntie on various family members. Belle introduced us as friends from Canberra who work for the government. Which was true, and more neutral than saying police.

As the family news was in progress, there was a knock on the door and a woman came in carrying a box of groceries which she dumped on the kitchen counter.

Auntie Maisie grinned and said: 'Thanks, Allie! You're just in time for a cuppa. I'm sure you need a break from all your efforts.'

It turned out that Allie worked as an independent deliverer of groceries from various Orange supermarkets, taking them to outlying communities like Lucknow.

Auntie Maisie paid for the groceries and the delivery fee, then said: 'You seem to be out in Lucknow quite a bit these days. Are we such good customers now?'

'Oh, you're all great customers here, but there's a couple of new people who seem to be stocking up on all sorts of supplies at the moment. One's the lady who's moved in four houses further on down your street, and then there's the posh guy in the old farm just along the Emu Swamp Road.'

Auntie Maisie said: 'I've met the woman who's just down the street. A bit quiet, but she seems very nice. I haven't met the man yet. Posh, you say?'

'Well, he's got a real flash car. I saw it in his garage before he shut it when I took the first delivery last week. It looks like it would have cost money, and it had a very fancy stripe down its side.'

Polly gave me a quick glance, and we were both trying not to look too interested. Polly said: 'Doesn't sound quite like someone who's living in an old farm. On Emu Swamp Road, you said?'

'Yeah, it's the one just past the first bend right in the road. Old Mr Wilson used to live there, but he's in a home now. He hadn't done much to it in the last few years so it's a bit run down, but I think it's sound. I don't reckon that guy'd have taken it if it wasn't okay.'

We all chatted for a bit longer, and then Allie said she had to get back to Orange to pick up her next shipments. We also took our leave of Auntie Maisie, and got back into the car. We agreed that it would look obvious if we headed off along the Emu Swamp Road straight away, so we drove back to the main bit of Lucknow and looked at a map of the area.

Then Belle drove with Polly in the front passenger seat, and me as inconspicuous as possible in the back seat, and went slowly along Emu Swamp Road. I felt the car swinging round a sharp right bend, and Polly said: 'You can look safely, Layla. I reckon that might be the farm on the left, but there's no-one obvious at the moment.'

Belle stopped the car, and Polly put her window down and took a series of photos with her mobile phone. I said: 'The house itself is quite big, and it doesn't look in too bad a condition, at least from outside. There are also a number of sheds and outhouses. I could see Harcourt Johnson setting himself up with a new base in somewhere like this.'

We drove on further down the road, but there didn't seem to be any other likely houses to which Allie would have been referring, so we turned round and drove back to Orange.

* * *

My next most urgent job was to alert Orange Airport to Harcourt Johnson. We left Belle to catch up with another relative in Orange, and Polly and I drove to the airport, which was a bit of a way out of town. We requested an interview with the chief controller of traffic at the airport, and after a bit of a wait we got in to see him.

He did at least take our concerns very seriously. He said there are two plane hire companies in Orange, and he would pass our information and photos of Johnson on to both. He said that if Johnson got a friend to bring a plane in for him it was possible that it would slip through the net, but they'd be as alert as they could be. He also noted that there were several other airports in the overall area, any of which would also have planes for hire. These were at Bathurst,

Rylstone, Mudgee and Dubbo, and we might have to contact them too.

Polly and I drove back to our motel in Orange, and I had a long phone call to Marcus in Canberra as we discussed what should be the next step with Johnson. We decided that before any sort of raid we should try to get some firm evidence that he was actually there.

Marcus asked me if there were any obvious places where we could install surreptitious surveillance of the Emu Swamp Road property, but I told him that the place was quite isolated. It stood in flat open land – no trees or anything else around for a hidden camera – so we decided on the old dodge of a broken-down truck at the edge of the road near the farm. The truck is parked and hazard markers are placed around it as though it's a breakdown, but the truck has a hidden camera mounted on it. The camera's pre-fitted, and the trick is to park the truck so that the camera points at the house – we don't need pictures of the cattle in the adjoining paddock.

We got our pictures over two days, and during that time nobody at all came to the house. What now?

Marcus suggested that we assemble a small armed force and go in quietly to the house to see if we can raise anyone, being prepared to fight if necessary. We could force our way into the house if needed, but I pointed out to Marcus that the place might have been booby-trapped if BLANK had got wind of our interest in the place. Marcus groaned and said that he'd come up with the armed force to direct operations and take responsibility.

If only we'd managed to apprehend Johnson in Canberra before he got away….

We organised the raid as quietly as possible, being aware that our own communications might be being intercepted. We went into the property and up to the house. No signs of anyone around from outside; no response when we knocked on the door. We forced our way into the house, using precautions against possible booby-traps. No booby traps, but no people either.

The only item of any significance that we found was Harcourt Johnson's fancy Mercedes with its side stripes in one of the sheds. He'd obviously dumped it and got himself a new car. We were back almost to square one.

* * *

Our one remaining hope was that we could repeat the way that we had found Johnson in Lucknow, using location of signals being sent to him to find where he is now. It took several days, and Belle eventually had to return to Canberra so she took Polly's car. We eventually pinned Johnson down to another town further west of Orange, namely Dubbo. Home of the well-known Western Plains Zoo, and also another regional airport. Contacting the airport had been on our "to do" list while we were in Orange, but we hadn't got round to it yet.

We upped and left Orange, found ourselves a motel in Dubbo, and then went to the airport control office with our photos of Johnson.

When we showed them to the main controller, he said: 'I think there was a guy who looked a bit like that in here yesterday asking about plane hire. He was dressed a bit smarter than we normally get around here, so I don't think he was a local.'

'Sounds a bit like the guy we're after. He didn't give you an address, did he?'

'No, he just said he'd be back again soon. I gave him the details of who hires planes here, and he went off again.'

'Could you give us the names as well, please, and we might just do the rounds of them to make sure they don't hire him a plane.'

He gave us the names of three aviation companies and their managers, and we went to each in turn. At the last one, Plains Aero Hire, the manager said: 'This looks like the guy who's just hired a small Cessna from us.'

I said: 'What name did he give you?'

He looked through the paperwork in the tray on his desk. 'Here it is – John Harcourt.'

'He gave you ID with that name on it?'

'What do you think we are here? We may be in the bush but we know perfectly well what's required. He had a driver's licence – here's the photocopy.'

He showed me, and it was certainly Harcourt Johnson. He'd been able to get a licence issued through somebody under this new name.

'Thanks, mate. I didn't mean to imply you were doing anything dodgy – it's just that I know this person and that isn't his real name. What name was on the credit card that he gave you to cover the plane hire?'

The manager dug in the tray on his desk and pulled out a docket. 'It was a company card, like many that we get here. Unity Corporation. It went through with no problem.'

'Okay. Could you give me details of the plane's model and numbers, and I'll get out an urgent call to intercept it. We're very worried about what he may be going to do. With your plane….'

The manager looked suitably concerned, and gave us all the details. I told him we'd be back in touch as soon as we'd had an urgent consultation with our higher-ups, and we left the manager looking even more worried.

INTERCEPTION OF
THE PLANE – WE HOPED

Polly and I went back to the motel and made an urgent call to Marcus in Canberra. We explained that Johnson now had a plane – destination unknown, but I was worried that it might be the Embassy of Afghanistan in Canberra, as I'd previously suggested. Marcus said he didn't know what happened in the case of a need to intercept a plane on a possible suicide mission, but he'd take it to the top level immediately. He told us to stay where we are, pending further instructions.

Nothing happened for about an hour; then Marcus called back.

'I don't know what the hell's going on, but the bugger seems to have done a vanishing act yet again. We got all the aviation surveillance in a wide area around Canberra looking for a plane with the details that you gave me. Nothing. Nada. Not a trace.'

There was a slight pause, then he said: 'Hang on a sec. There's something more coming through now.'

Another longer pause, then: 'Well, no wonder we didn't find him in Canberra airspace. He's just filled up with fuel at the Gold Coast airport and flown off. We hadn't sent out details of the plane that widely, so they weren't alert for him.'

I thought for a second or two, then said: 'I can only think he's got some entirely different destination in mind. North Queensland, perhaps? Overseas? Leave it with me for a short while to do some thinking and calculations, and I'll get back to you.'

The plane that he hired is a Cessna Skylane, a small four-seater. I doubted that it would have a large enough fuel capacity to go huge distances, but I need to find out just how far.

I looked on my laptop for the relevant statistics, and it said that the plane had a range on average of 1,695 kilometres on one fill. Dubbo to the Gold Coast airport was 909 km, so filling up there was fair enough, but where might he go after that? Further north in Queensland was a possibility, but would that really be much help to him? We could quickly alert the authorities all over Australia, and he'd be found sooner rather than later.

And then a thought struck me. New Caledonia was not all that far out in the Pacific Ocean from Brisbane, and he'd probably be safer there than in Australia. New Caledonia also has an element of far-right wing activity among French settlers, and it's not impossible that he might already have sympathetic contacts over there.

I checked on the computer again, and found that from the Gold Coast to Noumea is 1,463 km – within the flight capacity of his plane. I don't know whether an Australian plane can just bowl up unannounced at an overseas destination like Noumea, but maybe he'd planned this in advance anyway and got clearance.

I called Marcus back immediately. He told me to hang on pending further investigations at his end, so I sat down to wait again.

* * *

I was beginning to wonder if anything was happening, when Marcus rang back again.

'We've just established from the New Caledonian authorities

that Johnson's plane recently landed in Noumea. We advised them that he's a wanted man in Australia, possibly dangerous, and we requested that he be held in custody pending someone arriving from Australia to interview him.

'Given the potential diplomatic consequences of all this, the higher-ups decided that a top-level policeman had to go, and the Assistant Commissioner who came with us to Johnson's house will be the one. I think he wants to get his own back after Johnson outwitted us in Canberra. He's getting ready at the moment, and he's asked that you go along as well, given your involvement in the case to date. Can you get across to Noumea as fast as possible? Charter a plane to fly you to Noumea from where you are now. Here's an authority number to quote to the charter company to cover the plane.'

I wrote down the number, explained the situation to Polly, who would have to drive the car back to Canberra, grabbed my bag and got Polly to drop me at Dubbo Airport.

* * *

I was lucky that a plane and pilot were available at the airport from another charter that had just finished, and he was happy to take me. When we arrived in Noumea I explained to the authorities who I was, and it turned out that the AC had already arrived and briefed them. He'd got a faster RAAF plane to take him over.

The AC seemed a bit tense when I met him.

'G'day Mackenzie – thanks for getting here so quickly. I'd like to get this done straight away. Johnson's been taken to the central police station under arrest, and I'd like to interview him as soon as I can. Sorry, as soon as we can.... When we get him, I'd like to do the questioning and you take notes. I'd rather you didn't say anything because it might spoil the flow. If you'd like to make a comment – and please feel free – just write it on paper and pass it to me.'

'Understood, sir.'

'Okay, we'll get a taxi to the cop shop.'

On arrival there he spoke to a New Caledonian police inspector and said he'd like to interview Harcourt Johnson as soon as he could be made ready. He addressed the inspector in fluent French, which impressed me.

The authorities took us to an interview room, and brought Johnson in shortly afterwards. Johnson stared at us deadpan, and said nothing.

The AC said: 'Good afternoon, Mr Johnson. We would like to interview you about your sudden disappearance from our interview with you in Manuka the other day, and your sudden departure from Australia.'

Johnson said: 'I would like a glass of water, please. I'm too dry to speak at the moment.'

A jug of water and a glass appeared. Johnson filled the glass, drank a lot of it, then refilled it and stared at us in silence.

The AC said: 'When we came to interview you in your apartment in Manuka recently, we specifically said that we wished to ask you questions about some of your staff. You then left the room and did not return. Please explain why you did that.'

Johnson said: 'If you're to question me I need to have my hearing aids in so that I can hear your questions fully. They're in a little clip-locked box in my bag.' He nodded towards a little satchel that the attendant policeman was nursing. Something niggled me as he said all that, but I couldn't think what.

The AC asked the policeman to oblige, and he got the box out and passed it to the AC who opened it, saw two hearing aids and passed them to Johnson.

Johnson fitted them to his ears, then said: 'Bugger, the batteries are dead. There are some new ones also in the bag.'

The policeman dug them out and passed them on. Johnson removed two batteries from the pack and peeled off the tiny paper covers. He then took the hearing aids out of his ears, opened them and shook out the old batteries, put the batteries straight into his mouth and swallowed them with more of the water, and then sat and looked at us.

It had all happened in a flash, and it was a moment before we twigged that he'd pulled a big swiftie on us, and the old batteries had not been batteries at all.

The AC shouted out: 'Spit them out immediately!'

Johnson forced a half-smile, and said: 'Too late. Much too late.' He began to look strained, and then started to sway. A few moments more and he slipped sideways and fell to the floor, and began to look blue in the face.

The AC shouted out: '*Au secours, s'il vous plaît – toute de suite!*'

A medical orderly rushed in and attempted to revive Johnson, but after a few minutes looked up and shook his head. '*Il est mort, monsieur.*'

The AC said: 'Christ, what a disaster.' He held his head in his hands for a moment, then said to me: 'We'll have to get the body back to Canberra as soon as possible, and apologise to the authorities here for the trouble we've caused them.'

The New Caledonian Inspector had come back into the room, and the AC began an elaborate apology in French, but the guy just waved him aside.

'It is not your fault,' he said in excellent English. 'These things can happen, and we cannot foresee them.'

I wondered if this sort of thing happened a lot in New Caledonia, but probably not. I think they were just trying to make it easy for us – and get rid of us.

The AC and the Inspector agreed that they would keep the body in their morgue overnight, and we would take it back to Australia in the morning in the RAAF plane that had brought the AC over. That would give time for the paperwork to cover the whole incident to be done, and Canberra to be advised of this turn of events.

The AC said to me: 'I'd like to talk this whole affair over with you, please, but not in public. I'll get the people here to book us two motel rooms for overnight, and once we've finished here we can go to the motel. You could then come round to my room and we can talk.'

'Fine by me, sir.'

'Thanks, Mackenzie. And in the present circumstances you can drop the "sir". I don't think we need any formality after all this.'

* * *

We got to the motel about five o'clock, had thirty minutes to freshen up and get organised, and then I went round to the AC's room. He sat me down and said: 'With a name like Mackenzie, are you an authentic Scot?'

'I consider that I am. It was three generations back, but my ancestors came out from the highlands and I'm proud of it.'

'Good. So may I then offer you a tiny dram – I think we need it after today.' He pulled a bottle out of his bag and said: 'I think this is one of many great things the Scots have given the world. You're not teetotal, are you?'

'No, I'm not. And I would love a wee drop.'

'It'll have to be in the wine glasses – the tumblers here are a bit gross.' He poured a couple of shots, and passed one to me. We clinked glasses, said "Cheers" and drank. And my palate began to glow, magnificently.

'Wow, this is something really special. I've never had anything like it before. May I ask what it is?'

'It's a Scotch whisky from Ardbeg on Islay in the Inner Hebrides, but it's not their basic one. It's a special one called Uigeadail. I think it's the nectar of the gods.'

We sipped for a moment, and then he said: 'So today. I'm sorry that you had to be exposed to that.'

I said: 'I've had worse,' thinking of having to identify my husband's horribly mutilated body.

He simply raised his eyebrows. 'Should we have seen this coming?'

'I don't know that we could have foreseen that specifically, but I feel I should have been more alert. When he started speaking about needing hearing aids, I began to think that something wasn't right but I couldn't think what. I reckon now it was that when we'd seen him and spoken to him before, I don't think he had any hearing aids. I know that with some sorts they aren't very obvious, but I don't think he had any at all.

'The other thing is that he put them straight into his ears. My father had similar hearing aids, and he always took the batteries out when they weren't in his ears. They go flat if you don't. I should have been suspicious when Johnson's aids came out of his bag and straight into his ears.

'So I should have been more alert, though I don't think I could have stopped him swallowing the tablets – he was too quick. It was a neat and unexpected way for them to be hidden, too. He was an intelligent and organised opponent. What a pity that he couldn't have used all of that for good purposes.'

'I'd agree, but I'd have to say also that I can understand why he reacted the way he did. Did you know about the awful fate of his sister?'

'I heard about it from Professor Thomson at ANU. It was certainly horrible.'

'It was actually far worse than you would have been told. Only the basic facts got into the press, but I was in the AFP and posted to our embassy in Afghanistan at the time, and I was sent to the remote village where it all happened. The press said that the five hostages were killed, beheaded, and then the heads were put on stakes at the edge of the village, but I saw the bodies and it was far worse. They must all have been horribly tortured, and the two women were raped and mutilated on top of everything else. If any of that had been done to a relative of mine I think I might well have reacted the same way as Johnson did. Not an excuse, but I can at least understand the reaction.

'Anyway, what next? I think we should try to eat something after all this. There's the motel restaurant, or a nice-looking little bistro almost next door. I'd be happy if you'd like to join me for that?'

'It would be nice to have some company, and I'd vote for the bistro if that suits you. Though either would be fine,' I added quickly.

'The bistro it is – 7.30 if that suits you. And after all this, tomorrow we can get them to deliver Johnson's body to the RAAF plane, and we'll all go back to Canberra in it. I've sent a quick report on all this to Canberra, and they'll take the body straight off for the post mortem. After that we'll have to front the Commissioner, and I'll take the running on that. I can't see how any blame could attach to us for any of this, but I'll make sure that I'm at the front.'

* * *

The meal afterwards was light and delicious – Pacific with French overtones. I hadn't felt very hungry after all the day's events, but when it came my appetite came back with it.

And I discovered that Assistant Commissioners could be quite human, too. It turned out that this one had grown up on a sheep station in inland Queensland, and comparing experiences took our minds off the day's events quite well. I even managed to get some sleep that night.

* * *

Back in Canberra I discovered that the whole affair was being given a very low profile. Harcourt Johnson had no close relatives living who needed to be informed of his death. AGRICOZ had to be informed, but they were told that the circumstances of his death were such that it would be inappropriate to have any memorial service. The news of his death would spread around BLANK sooner or later, but they wouldn't be in a position to do any trumpeting anyway.

Now seemed to be a good time to go hard after BLANK, when they had just lost their Topman and were probably a bit disoriented, and a large AFP task force was put together to achieve this. Marcus Wiersma and Tony Mazzini would continue to be involved, but not as the bosses. I was wondering what if any role Don and I might have in the new team, when the AC summoned me once again.

* * *

I went into his office with some degree of trepidation – the more so when I found that I was the only person summoned. I suspected I was about to be hauled over the coals for my performance with Harcourt Johnson, because I realised that I'd made quite a few slips and lapses along the way.

The AC nodded at the chair in front of his desk.

'Sit down, Mackenzie. Can I offer you a coffee or anything? Except maybe not an Uigeadail on this occasion.'

It was suddenly sounding a bit less like a reprimand. 'I'd love a long black coffee if that's an option, sir.' I thought that back in the office the "sir" was still necessary at his level.

He phoned through to his secretary, then said: 'I wanted to have you in privately to sound you out about something. But first I'll say why it was you that I've picked.

'I've been very much impressed by your skills as an interviewer. You may wonder how I can say that when I've never heard you directly. However, I've heard the tape from your interview of Dr Harrington of AGRICOZ in France – also the tape of your interview of Dr Paulsen of AGRICOZ here in Canberra. The balance of tones is formidable. I haven't of course seen any visuals, but I understand from both Inspector Wiersma and Sergeant Mazzini that your body language is full on, and applies considerable pressure on the interviewee.

'In that regard I'll mention that I've also heard the tape of your test interview of Inspector Wiersma before you went to France. That totally artificial situation tested your ability to interview under any circumstances, and you managed it well. And I heard from Inspector Wiersma that he felt quite pressured while it was on.

'I've also spoken to some of the people you worked with while you were in Anti-Terrorism, and they speak very highly of you. I don't think you had to do much interviewing there – it was more analysis of information, but that's another skill that I'm after. I know why you had to be moved out of Counter-Terrorism and that it doesn't reflect on you in any way. It was unfortunate, except that if it hadn't happened I probably wouldn't have come across you and we wouldn't be having this talk now.

'So why are we here and doing this? The AFP and ASIO have been talking together about improving our detection of terrorist and related threats to Australia's security – ASIO looking particularly at overseas agents working within our country and the AFP looking at home-grown threats. There's plenty of overlap between the two, and we're discussing a joint task force to address the problems. We'll be keeping publicity about this unit to a minimum, because at least some of the threat comes from subversives within our own organisations, as you well know from BLANK and its activities.

'I will play a key role in this for the AFP, and I'm looking for some staff with particular capabilities that are relevant, and one of these is someone who is good at combative interviewing, if I can call it that. Firm and targeted interviewing, anyway. I'm offering you a position in that role if you'd be interested, and I'm aware at the same time that you have good expertise in wider counter-terrorism that would also be relevant. Any thoughts on this offer?'

He gave me a searching look, and I thought that "no" probably wasn't an option, at least if I wanted any sort of future in the AFP. But it did actually sound interesting. I have a strong personal wish to see the threatening people neutralised, and I like challenges.

'I would be very interested to take this further, sir. Eliminating these sorts of problems is a strong personal goal for me, and I enjoy the sort of challenges that this would offer. And if I might be allowed to add a personal note, I've very much enjoyed working with you over recent days and I would be happy if that could continue.' Then I gave him a very straight look, and said: 'Anyone who likes Uigeadail whisky can't be all bad. Sir....'

I got a chuckle back, and then he said: 'I'd also like to congratulate you on being confirmed in the rank of Sergeant – that's just come through. I'm sorry that I haven't got any Uigeadail here at the moment or we could drink to that – Sergeant Mackenzie. Another day, perhaps!'

Life was definitely looking up....

TONY MAZZINI

It was celebration time! Layla Mackenzie had invited a few colleagues to her place to celebrate her new position and promotion.
Ella and I were joined by Marcus Wiersma and his wife Barbara.
Polly Jones was there with her partner Belle – Polly as animated as
ever, and Belle very quiet. Bill Hansen had come with his wife, but
Jenny McIlroy was away so we were spared more hockey reminis-
cences. Donovan Lewis was busily serving drinks, and the festive
atmosphere was increased by a background of church bells. Layla's
apartment was just the other side of Anzac Parade from St John's
Church, the oldest church in Canberra and blessed with a fine set
of bells.

It was a bittersweet occasion for me because we were celebrating
the fact that Layla would be leaving us, and I'd grown quite fond of
her. She was a bit like a daughter that we never had, and I'll never
forget the way she looked after both of us when Ella was kidnapped
and I broke my ankle. Well beyond the call of duty. But I consoled
myself with the thought that in her new role our paths might well
cross every now and then.

Donovan came up and offered a plate of sandwiches to Ella and
then to me. I said to Ella: 'It's kind of Donovan to come and help

Layla out like this.'

She gave me a long stare, as though I was mentally deficient. 'You aren't very much of a detective, are you? I think you'll find that Donovan is now the co-resident of this apartment....'

Then when I looked at them happily working together for their guests, I realised that Ella was right – and ahead of me as usual. And I thought how once again Layla's determination had won through. When Donovan was in hospital after the attack, Layla had tried hard for him to be allowed to come to her apartment so that she could look after him, but Marcus had vetoed it at the time.

And I'm happy. All things come to those who wait....

AUTHOR'S NOTES

Policing in Australia

Each Australian state (New South Wales, South Australia, Tasmania, Victoria and Western Australia) has its own Police Force, responsible for all policing within its state, and so too does the Northern Territory.

Policing of matters that extend across more than one state or territory, or have a wider national significance, are the responsibility of the Australian Federal Police, headquartered in Canberra. One branch of the AFP is ACT Policing, which provides all policing services to the Australian Capital Territory, including Canberra.

The various security agencies mentioned in the story are located in Canberra. The Australian Security Intelligence Organisation, ASIO, is in the Ben Chifley Building in Constitution Avenue, Parkes. The Australian Secret Intelligence Service (ASIS) is in the RG Casey Building in Barton. The Australian Signals Directorate (ASD) has its headquarters in the Russell Defence complex, and the Australian Cybersecurity Centre (part of the ASD) is in Brindabella Business Park within the Canberra Airport land. The Office of National Intelligence (ONI) is in the Robert Marsden Hope Building in National

Circuit, Barton.

Those agencies and other features of Canberra mentioned in the story are almost entirely true to life. The large C5 development in Campbell is as described, as is the St Germain set of apartments in which Layla lived. The view down the fairway at the Federal Golf Club is as good as Tony Mazzini found it. And Chuck Doherty was right about the good coffee in Kiitos, too....

The only agency that is a complete fiction, as mentioned at the start of the book, is AGRICOZ. Some people may think it is intended to be the Commonwealth Scientific and Industrial Research Organisation, CSIRO, but it is entirely different. CSIRO undertakes research into a wide field of science and technology, including some biological sciences relevant to agriculture, but also many physical sciences and entirely technological subjects. AGRICOZ has no interests other than agricultural research.

That said, I have "borrowed" one genuine project from CSIRO's former Division of Entomology, namely its dung beetle project, simply because it suited the theme of this story. I had the honour to work within that project for ten years, and I hasten to assure readers that no events like those in this story ever happened there. Thank goodness....

The other fictitious aspect of the book is the characters. None relates to any real person – they are entirely figments of my imagination.

ACKNOWLEDGMENTS
AND THANKS

As ever, I'm enormously grateful to my wife Pam, who was first reader of the book, and pointed out all the bits that didn't work and what could be done about them. Sincere thanks also to Hugh Smith, who pointed out some inaccuracies and made many useful suggestions for tightening up the text. Any remaining imperfections are entirely my responsibility.

Finally, thanks again to Vivid Publishing and Fontaine Press for doing their usual great job in the publication and production of this book. It is always a true pleasure to work with them.